Photo Finished

Lori Roberts Herbst

Editor: Lisa Mathews, Kill Your Darlings Editing Services

Cover Designer: Molly Burton, Cozy Cover Designs

ISBN-13: 978-1-7362593-7-5

For my beautiful sister, Kristy, who always brings me such joy and laughter.

The Callie Cassidy Mystery series

Subscribe at **www.lorirobertsherbst.com** for fun stuff
(including FREE Callie Cassidy Sequel stories).

Acknowledgements

When I sit down to write acknowledgements, I always find myself filled with gratitude. My journey to the place of "official author" has certainly not been solitary. So many wonderful people have encouraged, pushed, prodded, and even carried me along the way.

As always, I'm thankful for my editor, Lisa Q. Mathews of Kill Your Darlings Editing Services. Having a top-notch editor is necessary, of course, but when you come to consider her a friend, too—there's nothing better. Lisa, thank you for taking me under your wing.

Thanks to Molly Burton at Cozy Cover Designs. I love my covers so much, and I think each one is better than the last. Her talent and professionalism make her a pleasure to work with.

My fabulous group of beta readers: Jenny Campbell, Jane Gorman, Syrl Kazlo, Ambre Leffler, Lisa Nelson, Jonna Rathbun, Mary Rosewood, Sharon Roth, Sarah Rubin, Jonna Turner, and my daughter, Katie Shapiro. Your comments and suggestions were so appreciated.

My Sisters in Crime! I tell everyone who'll listen: joining the Sisters, and especially the Guppies, made all the difference. I hope I can give back a smidgen of what I've received from them.

I'm also grateful for what I consider to be the best, most supportive group of readers any writer could hope for. Honestly, your emails, Facebook comments, and kind reviews make this labor of love so worthwhile.

Finally, to my husband, Paul: I don't tell you often enough, but without you, realizing this dream might never have happened. Now, if we can just stay married through the bathroom renovation…

1

The sight of yet another pine tree looming ahead on the trail made me grimace. Tightening my grip on the reins, I tugged to the left. No luck. Spirit, whom I secretly believed should have been named Stubborn, plodded toward the low-hanging branches, determined to scratch his perpetually itchy flank. I'd been in the branches of more trees today than the average squirrel.

This wasn't what I'd had in mind when I'd come up with the idea of a week-long girls' retreat-slash-bridal shower to celebrate my best friend Tonya's upcoming nuptials. I'd actually been picturing a lovely hotel in New York City, or maybe a beach house on a remote island. But when our friend Summer suggested a spa retreat at Moonglow Ranch—her aunt and uncle's new dude ranch in Mustang, Colorado—everyone had gone gaga, including Tonya. How could I say no?

So here I was, held captive by the whims of a horse. With a long-suffering sigh, I braced myself as Spirit thrust himself into the heart of a ponderosa pine. My cute cowboy hat, purchased for the week's festivities, dangled down my back on its braided chinstrap. Pine needles grabbed strands of my hair and yanked them from my ponytail.

Spirit pawed the dirt and let out a whinny as he wriggled his back end against a branch.

"Seriously?" I asked him.

At the beginning of the trail ride, Audra, our guide, had

promised stunning vistas and the heady aroma of wildflowers. A peaceful, relaxing experience. But mostly, what I'd viewed was the back end of Tonya's gray mare. Her horse, Serenity, was quite the multitasker, adept at excreting her weight in manure and urine without ever breaking pace.

And it wasn't a floral fragrance that greeted me.

I decided it was time to take charge. I rolled the reins around my hands and pulled upward as I gave the horse's flank a gentle kick. "Giddyup!" I commanded.

Spirit twisted his head and looked at me as if he'd forgotten I was there. Then he spotted a patch of grass and lowered his head to munch. Ugh. I had about as much control over this horse as I did over Carl, my headstrong tabby cat.

While Spirit indulged in his afternoon snack, I gazed up the trail in the direction of the corral. My friends were thirty yards ahead, their horses trotting behind Audra's like perfect show ponies.

"Hey," I yelled. "How about some help?"

At the rear of the group, Tonya turned in her saddle. She studied my situation for a moment and then responded just as I'd expected—she threw back her head and roared with laughter. Hopefully a story about my escapades wouldn't end up in *The Rock Creek Gazette*, which she owned and operated as editor-in-chief.

When the rest of our friends turned to gawk, she motioned for them to continue ahead to the stable. Then she gave her reins a swift jerk and deftly maneuvered her mare toward me. The two horses made eye contact, and I knew in my gut they were subtly mocking me.

Tonya didn't even bother with subtlety. "This is a beginner's ride. For heaven's sake, Callie. You were an award-winning photojournalist, and now you own a successful gallery. You can't steer a trail horse?"

"I can't help it if he suffers from an itchy tush," I muttered.

Tonya jiggled her reins again and made a clucking sound with her tongue. Serenity turned and loped down the path. To my surprise, Spirit followed along compliantly.

As I bounced in the saddle, I studied the woman who'd been my best friend since…well, for as long as I remembered. She appeared completely at ease on her horse. She even looked the cowgirl part in her dark blue denim jeans—designer, of course—and a red plaid shirt with shiny pearl snaps. A wide-brimmed cow-print hat rested atop her tight braids, which hung down her back like black silken ropes. A sleek pair of black cowboy boots completed the image. The woman appeared fresh off the pages of *Cowgirl Vogue*.

On the other hand, I thought, hazarding a quick glance down at myself, I was more suited to *Rodeo Clown* magazine. Like Tonya, I wore the requisite jeans and boots and even a plaid shirt fit for a dude ranch. But whereas Tonya's dark skin gleamed with a dewy glow, I probably looked as if I'd been caught downwind of a dust storm. Grime clung to every inch of me, congealing in the creases of my skin and even beneath my eyelids. I imagined the scraggly brown frizz on my head, like an abandoned bird's nest. Running my tongue across my dry lips, I tasted dirt and salt. At least, I hoped that's what I tasted…

I gestured to our horses, who traipsed along dutifully. "How did you do that? I nudged and cajoled and scolded but couldn't get this guy to do anything that wasn't on his own agenda. Are you a horse whisperer?"

"No. I just listened when Audra went over the instructions. These trail horses are well-trained and pretty easy to handle—if you just follow directions."

Our fit young trail guide had provided plenty of suggestions for riding "as one" with our horses. I'd apparently missed the summary of the owner's manual, though.

3

"I got distracted when she said we might see snakes on the trail. After that, all I heard was *blah blah blah*."

Tonya smiled. "Then I guess you didn't catch the part where she told us ninety-nine percent of those snakes are non-venomous."

"Humph," I said. "If I spotted a snake on the trail, I doubt I'd be concerned with analyzing its venom status. Nor would Spirit, I suspect. He'd rear up at the sight of a snake, and there I'd be, on the ground nursing another broken wrist."

I lifted my left hand to remind my friend of the trauma I'd suffered a few months earlier when a falling body landed on me and fractured my distal radius.

"Oh, Callie." Tonya reached over and patted the now-healed bone. "You worry too much, sugarplum. Lighten up. This trip was your idea, remember?"

Well, sort of, I thought. If it were up to me, I'd be lying on a beach with a mai tai in my hand.

"It's beautiful here," Tonya murmured. "A different kind of beautiful than home in Rock Creek Village. Hard to believe it's only an hour's drive. It's perfect, Callie. Thank you."

I followed her gaze across the sea of sagebrush and tall grasses stretching toward the distant mountain range. I'd become so accustomed to living at the foot of a giant mountain that these peaks looked more like toys in a child's play set, but that didn't diminish their majesty. Nearby, a freshwater lake sparkled beneath the sun's rays. A soft breeze rustled the branches of the pines flanking the meadow, with the sound of a stream gurgling in their midst. And now that I wasn't in the line of fire of Serenity's expulsions, I even detected that promised scent of wildflowers.

The tension melted from my shoulders.

"I see you relaxing," Tonya said with a satisfied nod. "Moonglow Ranch is working its magic on you."

She smiled and clucked again, and the horses trotted

toward the stable.

Our friends had already dismounted, and they stood in a cluster chatting as they waited for us. Summer Simmons, who owned Rock Creek Village's Yoga Delight studio, lifted her face to the sun. Jessica, a journalism teacher at the local high school, tapped her foot in pent-up energy. Renata, a hockey coach and the female doppelgänger of her brother, Raul, wiped a bead of sweat off her glistening olive skin. And Lynn, the newest addition to our squad, scanned her surroundings with the inquisitive eyes of the first-rate detective she had proven to be.

As two young ranch hands guided our friends' horses into the corral, a third man jogged out of the stable to help. When we caught sight of him, Tonya and I both sucked in our breath.

"Are you seeing what I'm seeing?" she asked through closed teeth.

"It's…it's…" We looked at each other. "Thor," we said in unison.

The man was the spitting image of the Norse god, as portrayed by Chris Hemsworth in the Avenger movies. That is, if Thor had been clad in tight stonewashed jeans, a long-sleeved denim shirt, and dusty boots. From the confines of his Stetson, the thirty-something's thick, caramel blond hair fell past his collar, sideburns merging into a scruffy beard across his perfectly tanned jaw.

Tonya and I were in our mid-forties. She was engaged, and I was in a committed relationship, but jeez. A girl could look, right?

He flashed us a gleaming smile and touched the brim of his hat. "Afternoon, ladies. Need a hand?"

Tonya giggled like a schoolgirl and shifted in her saddle as Cowboy Thor reached up to grasp her waist. She rested her hands on his broad shoulders, and he swung her to the ground in a move that might have been choreographed in a steamy ballet.

As Thor turned toward me, I cautioned myself to be cool. But just as he placed his fingers on my waist, a shout came from the stable. Summer's aunt appeared at the door wearing a frantic expression on her face.

"Colby, come quick!" she yelled. "Another horse is sick."

Without so much as an adios, the cowboy took off running toward the stable. Quickly, a pimply-faced teenage ranch hand jogged over and held out a hand to me.

I considered staying put and waiting for Colby's return, even if it took all night. But no. A sick horse was more important than my superhero fantasy. I grasped the boy's fingers and swung my leg over the horse's back, trying to mimic Tonya's graceful dismount. But my foot caught in the stirrup, and I felt myself free falling. To his credit, the boy made a gallant effort to catch me, but inevitably we both ended up in a heap on the dusty ground. After a moment's pause, we disentangled ourselves and scrambled to our feet. The boy reached out and began brushing the dirt off my shirt.

When he realized the places his hands were touching, he shot backward and blushed furiously. "Sorry, ma'am," he said, his voice squeaking. "I was only trying—"

"No worries." I felt the heat rise in my own face. Spirit emitted a neigh that sounded suspiciously like laughter.

Without looking at me, the ranch hand took the horse's reins and skedaddled off to the corral. My friends rushed over and circled around me. They faked concern, but I could tell they were on the cusp of raucous laughter.

I narrowed my eyes. "It's not funny."

"Of course it's not." Tonya's eyes danced. "Are you hurt?"

"Just my dignity."

The laughter broke free then, and I couldn't keep myself from grinning. "Glad I provided the afternoon's entertainment."

"You always do, sugarplum," Tonya said.

Arms linked, we headed across the yard to the lodge, a huge log-and-stone dwelling where my mother, Maggie, sat on the deck in a wooden rocker, reading a book. Woody, my golden retriever, raced down the stairs toward us, tail wagging and tongue lolling. Carl, his adopted feline brother, licked a paw and studiously ignored our arrival.

"Are the creatures behaving themselves?" I asked.

"Indeed they are. They seem to enjoy watching the horses and observing all the activity. It's as if they were born for ranch life."

"What they enjoy is everyone here pampering them and bending to their every whim," I said.

Carl jumped into Mom's lap and purred as she stroked his back. "Did you all have a pleasant ride?"

"Delightful," Renata said, and the others nodded their agreement.

Mom looked at me. "And you, darling?"

"It was…an adventure."

Before I could elaborate, we heard the crunch of tires on gravel and turned to see a black Lincoln Town Car pulling under the ranch's entry arch.

"Hmm," Jessica said. "That car seems a little hoity-toity for this neck of the woods."

The car braked to a halt in the adjacent parking area, and the driver jumped out and dashed to the back passenger door. When he opened it, a red, zebra-striped high heel appeared.

Beside me, Tonya stiffened.

As the rest of the figure emerged from the car, I understood why.

Our caller was Tonya's mother, Lydia Fredericks.

My friend swiveled toward me, hands on hips and eyes blazing. "Callahan Cassidy, how could you?"

2

Tonya, I swear I didn't…"

"Oh, TeeTee," Lydia crooned, waggling her fingers.

She wore a satiny red knee-length dress, flared at the hem, with a wide leather belt. Her jet black hair swept across her forehead. She attempted to glide toward us, but the red zebra heels kept sinking into the grass.

I looked at Tonya. "TeeTee?" I mouthed.

"Don't ask," Tonya whispered, her lips tight.

Once Lydia reached the deck stairs where we had all gathered, she raised her red-tipped fingers and cupped Tonya's cheeks. "Surprise," she said gaily.

"Lydia, what are you doing here?" Tonya asked.

"TeeTee, you really must call me Mother." She stepped back and studied her daughter with a frown. "Tsk tsk, darling. Jeans and boots? I thought I'd trained you better."

"Lydia…Mother…it's a dude ranch. Heels and satin are not the proper attire."

"Sweetheart, heels are always proper. Except in bed, of course…"

The driver had lugged over a fake alligator suitcase the size of my Honda Civic, which he dropped on the ground with an unceremonious thud. When Lydia ignored him, he cleared his throat. "You gonna pay me, lady?"

"Oh, dear me." Lydia turned to Tonya. "I don't have any cash. Darling, please take care of this young man. He was kind enough to transport me from the airport."

Tonya scowled. "That's an hour's drive. It must have cost a fortune. I don't have that kind of cash."

Lydia glanced at me, and I shrugged. "Nope."

Jessica wrestled her phone from her back pocket and stepped toward the man. "Do you take Venmo?" He nodded, and the two of them completed the transaction. The driver hopped into his sedan and sped away, churning gravel in his wake.

Tonya exhaled. "Thank you, Jess. Mother will reimburse you promptly."

"Oh, of course," Lydia trilled. "As soon as I'm able to dig my checkbook out of my suitcase, dear."

At that point, we noticed Summer's aunt trudging toward the lodge. Even from across the yard, I could see worry in her eyes. The horse was sicker than we'd realized.

When she reached us, she tried to rally, giving Lydia a smile. "Hello. I'm Amaryllis Bauer—Ryll for short. My husband, Fritz, and I are the proprietors here at Moonglow Ranch."

"And I'm Lydia Fredericks, the mother of the bride. I wish to secure your most luxurious suite." She eyed the lodge as if it were a shanty.

"You are most welcome," Ryll said. "But I'm afraid we weren't expecting any additional guests."

Lydia wrinkled her nose. "Yes, my invitation must have gotten lost in the mail. Luckily, TeeTee's charming fiancé called to inform me about the event, and I purchased the last first-class seat out of Las Vegas." She patted Tonya's cheek. "Anything for my girl."

Tonya shook her head. "You weren't listening, Mother. Ryll and Fritz weren't planning for more visitors. They might not have a room available."

Lydia looked up at Ryll. "Now, Amaryllis, I heard you say I was most welcome. I assume that means you have a lovely suite I can occupy."

"We have three vacant guest rooms, but I'm afraid

they're still being painted—drop cloths over the furniture and such. They won't be ready for guests until later in the week. We aren't officially open for business yet, you see." She tapped a finger against her bottom lip. "We do have a small employee apartment that isn't being used. I suppose we could put you up there."

Lydia's downturned lips indicated her lack of enthusiasm at the thought of moving into employee quarters. My mother noticed, too, and came down from the deck. Her thick silver hair framed the soft porcelain skin of her face. She wore a short-sleeved navy blue sweater and gray slacks. Even casually dressed, she looked more elegant than Tonya's mom in her finery.

"You're welcome to room with me for the week, Lydia," she said. "There's plenty of space. It…well, it could be fun."

I could see my mother wasn't crazy about the idea. The two women had never gotten along well, even when Lydia lived in Rock Creek Village. Though she'd never voiced her opinion aloud, I knew Mom disapproved of Lydia's parenting style, which was essentially non-existent. For her part, Lydia had always been jealous of my mother's bond with Tonya. The tension between the women made Mom's offer even more generous. The woman bowled me over.

"Hello, Maggie," Lydia said. "I didn't realize you'd been invited to my daughter's bridal shower."

Mom waved breezily. "Oh, I'm just here to look after Woody and Carl while the girls do their thing. So, what do you say? My room has two beds."

Lydia eyed Mom and weighed her options. After a moment, she turned back to Ryll. "Kind as Maggie's offer is, I'll choose the apartment. I do value my privacy."

"Certainly," Ryll said. "I'll take you right up." She moved toward the stairs. Lydia gazed pointedly at her suitcase. "Oh, yes, let me get that for you."

Ryll hefted the heavy bag, tugging it with effort up the

first step. Fritz, who was working on the landscaping at the side of the lodge near the pool, dropped his shovel and ran over to relieve his wife of the burden. She murmured a few instructions, then watched as he grabbed the suitcase and hauled it into the lodge. Lydia swayed along behind him.

Before she went through the door, she turned back to her daughter. "We'll chat in a bit, TeeTee. Just wait until you see the expensive shower gift I've brought."

Once Lydia disappeared through the door, Tonya held up her hands as if she were choking someone. "Wait until I see David. I'm going to wring his neck."

"Now, Tonya," Mom said, "I'm certain David's intentions were pure. He's clearly trying to broker a treaty between you and your mother."

"That would be the best thing," Summer agreed. "A reconciliation would offer you a sense of peace."

"Humph," Tonya said. "My relationship with Lydia has been on the skids for as long as I can remember. Her being here for the shower won't transform us into the perfect mother-daughter duo."

Summer smiled serenely. "Progress rather than perfection, my friend."

Jessica pointed to herself. "All I know is that I'm going to need a ton of progress before I'm presentable for dinner. I'm dirty and grimy and gross, and no offense, but you're all the same. I suggest we go clean up."

Ryll looked at her watch. "Good idea. You have an hour before we serve the appetizers and drinks. We'll meet back here then."

We followed our hostess into the lodge and headed upstairs to our rooms. I figured it would take at least an hour to put out the fire roaring in Tonya's eyes.

3

Promptly at six, our group sat in comfy, cushioned Adirondack chairs around a crackling firepit in the yard—minus Lydia, who'd sent word she was fighting a headache and needed to lie down. We chatted as we sipped mojitos from tall, sweating glasses. The sun hung low on the horizon, coating the meadow like a glaze of honey. A gentle breeze softened the evening heat.

Ryll and Fritz emerged from the lodge and set covered platters beside stacks of blue stoneware plates and utensils on a long serving table. Our hosts were accompanied by an attractive middle-aged woman wearing a beret and an apron displaying the Moonglow Ranch logo, along with a similarly attired younger woman. The two looked so much alike I realized they must be mother and daughter.

Fritz hustled back into the lodge as Ryll called for our attention. "Welcome again. I wanted to take this moment to give you an overview of the rest of your week at Moonglow Ranch. We'll start with the food. As you know, Fritz and I created this ranch as a retreat designed to cater to the mind, body, and soul. In keeping with that theme, our meals will include only natural, healthy food and beverages."

Jessica raised her glass. "Even the mojitos?"

Everyone chuckled, and Ryll grinned. "Of course. You're drinking skinny mojitos, without sugar or carbs."

"Huh," I said, taking another sip. "I would never have guessed."

"That's the point," Ryll said. "You can eat and drink well without feeling deprived. That said, let me turn this over to our lead chef, Valerie Foster. She'll tell you more about the food she's prepared."

The chef stepped forward. Tall and lean, with dark hair pulled into a knot at the back of her neck, she made a good advertisement for healthy eating.

"Good evening," she said. "As Ryll mentioned, I'm Valerie. Not only am I the lead chef, I'll usually be the only chef. For the summer, though, I'm lucky enough to be working with my daughter, Haley. She's studying for her hospitality degree, and Ryll and Fritz have been kind enough to take her on as an intern."

We exchanged waves and hellos as Haley blushed and fiddled with a leather bracelet on her wrist. Then Valerie began lifting the covers off the platters, pointing as she spoke. "For tonight's appetizers, we have prepared a spinach artichoke dip served with crunchy baked sweet potato strips, keto stuffed mushrooms, and seasoned cauliflower bites."

I tried not to wince. Healthy eating wasn't my preference. Give me a greasy burger and fries over kale and tofu any day. But unless I wanted to starve this week, I'd have to suck it up.

"Sounds delicious," I said, hoping I sounded sincere.

Valerie beamed. "Later, we'll be serving dinner at the outdoor dining table." She pointed to the pergola a few yards away. "Tonight, we are presenting an Asian theme. We'll begin with a light noodle and vegetable salad, along with spinach and tofu dumplings. For the main course, chicken and shrimp stir fry with brown rice. And for dessert, a lovely Chinese custard tart."

Everyone clapped, and I forced myself to join them. I hadn't heard kale in the mix, but had I heard the word spinach twice? Still, my stomach growled. Perhaps I could just pick out the offensive green bits, then close my eyes and inhale the rest.

The chef and her daughter headed inside to finish the preparations, and Ryll trailed after them. The rest of us filled our plates from the buffet and began nibbling. After one tentative bite, I took another, finding myself pleasantly surprised.

Then a burst of male laughter rang out from the yard near the ranch manager's cabin. A trail of smoke rose from a nearby grill, followed by the aroma of sizzling red meat. Suddenly, seasoned cauliflower bites didn't seem so tasty.

"Maybe I'll join the boys for dinner," I said, only half joking.

"If that good-looking cowboy is there, I'll come too…for dessert," Tonya quipped.

"Hey, you'd better behave," Renata said. "You're about to become a married woman."

"Even married women can appreciate a work of art," Mom chimed in. "I noticed that ranch manager myself, and I must say, he is a specimen."

"Mother!" I said, appalled, as my friends laughed.

Ready to change the subject, I turned to Summer. "What's going on with the horses? Sounded like a few of them have been sick."

Summer dabbed at her lips with a napkin. "Three horses have taken ill so far. It's particularly distressing to Aunt Ryll because those beasts are her babies. She rescued each of them, you know—mostly former racehorses who could no longer make the cut." She smiled at me. "The horse you rode today, for example. Just two years ago, Spirit was a top contender on the circuit. Then he came in second in the biggest race of the state. It was a photo finish, and the owner lost a great deal of money. The poor horse was destined for an unpleasant ending."

"Photo finished," Jessica quipped.

"That's terrible," Lynn said. "The horse's situation, as well as the pun."

I nodded, feeling a little guilty over my earlier irritation at the horse's penchant for pine trees. Sounded like he'd earned the right to a leisurely scratch.

"Aunt Ryll heard about it and talked the owner into selling Spirit to her," Summer continued. "That's how she got all her horses—other people's discards. She trains them and loves on them and gives them a new purpose."

"So what's making the poor things so sick?" I asked.

Summer shook her head. "It's a mystery. They're experiencing stomach issues, though I won't go into more detail while we're eating."

Jessica nudged Summer's foot with her own. "Tell them the other part."

Summer finished her last sweet potato crisp and returned her plate to the table. Then she shot a glance at the lodge, folded her legs into a yoga pretzel, and leaned forward. "Ryll wouldn't want me sharing this—she's determined to make this week a fun and upbeat experience—but they've had a rough go of it since they decided to turn the property into a guest ranch. The business plan has met with local resistance, especially from their neighbors on the adjacent property. The couple wields a great deal of wealth and power and managed to convince the Town Council to drag their heels on the licensing process. Every time Aunt Ryll and Uncle Fritz jump through one hoop, the council sets up another. First it was zoning, then health department regulations. Now animal control issues. The sick horses won't help."

"Why do the neighbors object?" Lynn asked.

"They believe if the ranch opens to visitors, it'll disturb their peace and lower their property values." Summer looked around the circle. "That's why I'm so pleased you agreed to hold Tonya's bridal shower week here. Even though it's a private affair, Aunt Ryll and Uncle Fritz hope it will help persuade the council—and the neighbors—that ranch guests won't disrupt their lives."

"So we're guinea pigs," I said.

"Yes. Aunt Ryll and Uncle Fritz couldn't charge us, of course, since they aren't yet licensed. That's why we're here as family and friends. It gives them the opportunity to run their program and show the council that everything will be fine. It might force the council's hand. If they still won't budge after a successful week, my aunt and uncle may have to take the matter to court."

Mom cocked her head. "So you girls need to behave. Go easy on the mojitos. No wild drunken bedlam that might cause the neighbors to object."

"Bummer," Tonya said. "Wild drunken bedlam was number one on my bucket list for the week."

***

Lydia had joined us just as dinner was served. She'd changed into linen trousers and a silk blouse—more suitable than her earlier attire, but not by much. The rest of us wore shorts and casual shirts—except Tonya, who was dressed in a knee-length sleeveless dress and strappy sandals. In some ways, she was very much her mother's daughter. I'd never dare say that to her, though.

Despite my concerns, the meal was delicious, and I felt self-righteously indulgent when I asked for a second dessert. It wasn't overeating if the food was healthy, right? By the time we'd polished off the last spoonful of Chinese custard, dusk had fallen. Stars glittered in the growing darkness, a prelude to what purported to be a magnificent light show later in the night.

As Valerie and Haley cleared our dishes, Ryll stood beside the table, hands folded in a pose I'd seen Summer use a hundred times. "Thank you again for choosing Moonglow Ranch as the venue for this wonderful event. As you know, you're our trial run, and you'll be testing many of the activities we plan to offer guests. In addition to today's horseback riding, we'll host daily meditation and yoga sessions, guided serenity hikes, and a spa day, complete with facial mud masks, massages, and pedicures. There will also be lasso lessons, and even target shooting on the last day."

"Target shooting?" Summer said. "I didn't know you offered that. You know how I feel about guns…"

"It's just an entertaining activity, dear," Ryll said. "We added it because we have Haley with us for the summer, and she was champion of her high school league. You don't need to take part if you have a moral objection, of course, but as your pacifist aunt, I will tell you that I've tried target shooting and found it to be quite a rush."

Summer didn't look convinced, but Mom clapped her hands. "Butch took me a few times, and I enjoyed it. Wagering on the outcome can add to the thrill."

"Watch out, ladies," I warned. "I fear we're being hustled. But Ryll, everything sounds fantastic. I, for one, can't wait to experience it all."

"I'm glad," Ryll said. "Because the fun continues tonight. We have arranged a special event—something you won't soon forget. So if you'll please follow me, we'll get this party started."

Ryll led us inside and into the large living room. Beneath the dimmed lights of an antler chandelier sat an overstuffed couch and loveseat, matching double-wide armchairs, and several cushioned wingback chairs. On a long, low oak coffee table, tapered candles flickered, their wax dripping down brass candlesticks. A red satin pillow rested on the table next to a crescent-shaped ceramic dish holding a burning stick of incense—sandalwood, if my nose was correct. An oversized deck of black cards, embossed with gold, fanned out across the table. And was that…a crystal ball?

I leaned toward Tonya. "Do you think we're participating in a seance?"

"A psychic reading, I'm thinking." Her eyes gleamed with intrigue.

As soon as we took our seats, Ryll exited, closing the door behind her. A moment later, a soft gust of air swirled across the room, causing the candle flames to shudder. We all went still, sensing something mysterious about to happen.

Through the doorway, a tiny woman appeared. Her back was to us. From somewhere in the distance, chimes tinkled.

Slowly, the woman turned to face us. "Good evening, my friends. I am Carmen. People refer to me as a psychic, but I prefer the term *healer*. Prepare to open your mind and your souls."

Despite the positive nature of her words, a shiver ran up my spine.

4

My forehead creased. I'd known Ryll and Fritz planned to advertise Moonglow Ranch as a destination for spiritual healing, but a psychic? Oh, well. I'd always enjoyed a good magic show, and I supposed this would be no different.

Still, as I studied the woman, I could tell she had a powerful presence. She seemed both ancient and ageless. Steel gray hair flowed to her waist. Her copper-colored face was lined and weathered, and her eyes shone like dark pools of tar. When the candles flickered just right, her hollowed cheeks gave her a skeletal cast. She wore an oversized beaded blouse tied at the waist and a flowing patterned skirt that ended at her ankles. Her feet were bare and slightly misshapen.

Silently, Carmen turned her gaze on each of us. When those ebony eyes fell on me, I experienced an almost magnetic pull.

Wow. This woman was good.

Finally, Carmen's eyes rested on Tonya. "The bride," she said. "Will you be the first to join me?"

Tonya giggled nervously as she rose. "All right. I'm game."

Carmen settled herself onto a cushion behind the table and motioned to another across from her. Tonya sank onto it, crossing her legs. Carmen reached a gnarled hand across the table and took hold of Tonya's. The…what, psychic? Healer?…closed her eyes and dropped her head back. Her lips moved in a low, unintelligible chant. Tonya wriggled, then relaxed. In a matter of moments, her eyes drooped closed.

Was the woman hypnotizing her? I glanced around the room, hoping to spot a kindred spirit to share my cynicism, but my friends appeared riveted.

After a full minute, Carmen squeezed Tonya's fingers. Both women opened their eyes and stared at each other. When the psychic spoke, her tone was soothing, otherworldly. "You've met your soulmate, Tonya."

Big revelation, I thought. *Carmen had already referred to Tonya as the bride, so this wasn't an earth-shattering declaration.*

"Yet tonight you are experiencing tension," Carmen continued. "Frustration, even. He's done something that displeased you."

Carmen's eyes flicked to Lydia. Was she referring to David telling Tonya's mother about the bridal shower? How could she know that?

"Let me put your mind at ease," Carmen said. "Your loved one meant no harm. Your happiness is his heart's greatest wish."

Tonya dropped her head. I'd known she was mad at David, but I hadn't realized how deeply her mother's arrival had affected her. Yet Carmen had somehow known…

The little parlor trick could be explained. Perhaps Ryll had witnessed Tonya's distress over Lydia's arrival and clued Carmen in before the performance. Or Carmen was a skilled people watcher and had noticed the friction herself. For heaven's sake, the woman might have been hiding around a corner, spying on us throughout the day.

Now I was getting paranoid.

Carmen turned Tonya's palm up and began tracing a line with her fingertip. "Your upcoming marriage will result in a long and happy union. The two of you will grow old together…and I see a child…no, two children…"

I nearly snorted. Like me, Tonya was in her mid-forties. I supposed our biological clocks might still be emitting the occasional soft tick, but time was draining away fast.

Tonya, though, didn't flinch. She simply stared at Carmen.

"Ah, now I comprehend the full picture," Carmen murmured. "You're considering adoption."

"Yes," Tonya whispered. "David and I have been discussing it."

A gasp circled the room. Lydia squealed. "Oh, TeeTee. How wonderful! But let me warn you—I will permit no one to call me Grandma."

My heart fluttered. Tonya—my best friend, the sister I never had, the confidante with whom I shared my secrets—was contemplating becoming a mother and hadn't said one word to me? I guess she had a new confidante now.

"You'll have those children," Carmen predicted. "And later, grandchildren. You and your soulmate will create a loving family. There will be some sadness and pain along the way, of course—normal products of a well-lived life together. But I glimpse a path bordered by joy and love—with you and your partner walking together at the center."

As Carmen released Tonya's fingers, my friend sighed. "How are you feeling?" the older woman asked. Her voice floated like a flower petal on the breeze.

I saw a spatter of tears on Tonya's cheeks, but her lips wore a wistful smile. "Warm," she said. "Light. Happy. Just...right."

Carmen nodded, and Tonya rose from her cushion and resumed her seat on the couch. She wrapped her arms around me and squeezed tight. "Oh, Callie. I think I've stumbled onto my destiny."

I returned her hug, but my mind reeled. This was too much for me to comprehend. Was it some elaborate prank everyone was playing on me? Payback for when I'd gone snooping into David's past a few months ago? Because there was no conceivable way this tiny sorceress on the floor could truly peer into the future.

Right?

When Tonya released me, I stared at Carmen. Somehow, I'd figure out how she'd managed this trickery.

The old woman rose nimbly and glided around the table. She stopped in front of me and held out both hands, inhaling once, then twice. My eyes darted around the room and landed on Lynn. Surely a detective would share my disbelief. But she, too, watched transfixed. A wave of resolve swept through me. If this woman was trying to hypnotize me, she'd have her work cut out for her. I crossed my arms.

Carmen's eyes twinkled and her lips parted, revealing a set of yellow but otherwise perfect teeth. Lacing her fingers at her waist, Carmen said, "My friends, here we have a skeptic."

"Humph," Jessica said with a snort. "Doesn't take a psychic to figure that out."

Mom smiled. "In many ways, that trait has served my daughter well."

"No doubt," Carmen said to my mother. "You've raised her to question, to search, to inspect. Worthy pursuits." She turned back to me. "But now, perhaps, it would behoove you to suspend your disbelief from time to time. Let spirit and light filter into your being."

I opened my mouth and closed it. How was I supposed to respond to that? I felt a tug, as if part of me wanted to reach out for whatever Carmen was offering. Another part fought it off.

She observed my resistance. "You're not ready to give yourself over," she whispered. "But perhaps you'll come to the table anyway? Even a skeptic can join the fun."

Summer grinned at me. "Try it, Callie."

"Yes, darling," my mother said. "You might even enjoy it."

"Nothing to lose," Renata said.

Tonya swiped a tear from her cheek. "You never know until you try."

I allowed Carmen to lead me toward the flickering candles and the trail of incense smoke. My hindquarters, still sore from the horseback ride, rebelled as I sat crosslegged on the floor. I placed my hands on the table for Carmen's perusal.

As she'd done with Tonya, Carmen took my hands in hers and closed her eyes. I started to smirk, but I couldn't help but notice the same magnetic charge between us. Had the woman weaseled herself into my psyche?

She opened her eyes and turned up my palms. With one fingertip, she stroked my left wrist. "An injury here, and not too long ago."

That was an easy one. If she hadn't heard about my broken wrist from Ryll, she could have noticed the way I favored it, or the scar. "Very observant," I said.

She ignored my comment and traced the lines on my palm. "I see a genuine strength of character, an intense desire to protect those you care for, and a determination to seek justice."

"Now you're just buttering me up," I said, but my nerves fluttered.

"Your life line is deep and long," she continued. "Your future is grounded in peace and contentment. But there will be a few…hiccups along the way. Would you like me to tell you about them?" She stared into my eyes and lifted her chin toward the crystal ball. I stared back, unblinking. The black pools carried a sense of infinity. Involuntarily, I sighed. Maybe I was being hypnotized after all.

In her grip, my hand turned clammy. Suppose she actually did possess some supernatural gift and could predict my future—did I want to know?

It was like the temptation of reading the end of a book before you've earned it. I almost wanted to hear the *Cliff's*

Notes version, but knowing the plot points ahead of time would spoil the story.

Before I could respond, Carmen stiffened. The door to the den burst open, a switch flicked, and the room filled with bright light.

An attractive, dark-haired woman about my mother's age entered the room, tugging the sleeve of a portly man with a serious comb-over behind her. A matronly woman in a tan suit followed them.

The dark-haired woman pointed a French-tipped fingernail at us. "Aha! I was right! I told you, Mayor Finkle. These people are breaking the law."

5

As the rest of us jumped to our feet, our hosts rushed into the living room. Fritz positioned himself in front of the trio. "You're trespassing," he said. "You need to leave right now."

The dark-haired woman waved him off. "Pish. Your housekeeper invited us in, as I'm sure the mayor here will attest."

The mayor stared at his shoes. The woman folded her arms. "Martin, these people are operating a guest ranch without a license. You must shut them down. Polly agrees. Don't you, Polly?"

The other woman tightened her lips. Her silver hair was styled in a slick, layered bob, and for a quick moment, I visualized an armadillo napping on her head. She shot a nervous look at the dark-haired woman, then touched the man's sleeve. "Eleanor is right, Martin. This ranch must be closed at once."

The man fidgeted with his collar, nervously glancing at Fritz. "Well, honeybun, I don't know…"

The dynamics became obvious. The henpecked mayor was being driven by his wife, Polly, whose primary aim seemed to involve sucking up to Eleanor. At the mayor's reluctance, Polly smacked him on the arm. "Martin, you are the most powerful person in Mustang. You have a responsibility to your constituents."

"Yes, Martin," Eleanor said. "Grow a spine. You must initiate sanctions against the Bauers for their purposeful and blatant disregard of the law."

Throughout her little speech, I studied this Eleanor. She looked regal in her tailored, peach-colored linen dress. A strand of pearls encircled her neck, and two more pearls dangled from her earlobes. Her makeup had been flawlessly applied. Though her brow was creased in anger, the skin around her mouth barely moved when she talked. The woman was clearly rich, elegant, and heavily Botoxed.

Ryll found her voice. "Eleanor, what you're saying isn't true. Fritz and I are not currently operating as a business. Though we would be by now, if you weren't doing everything in your power to slow the process." I could see from Ryll's pinched lips that she was struggling to keep her temper. Summer sensed it, too, and moved to her aunt's side.

Botox lady tried to frown. "I see six people here, not counting that old fortune teller."

Carmen's eyes, already black, seemed to darken further, but she remained silent.

"You've misinterpreted the situation," Fritz said. "These are not paying customers. They are family and friends. No one can keep us from hosting guests in our home."

Now the mayor's wife, Polly, chimed in. "Guests, are they? You're telling us these people haven't paid to be here?"

"That's exactly what we're telling you." Ryll put an arm around Summer's waist. "This is my niece, and these are her friends." She gestured toward Tonya. "We invited them here to celebrate this lovely young woman's upcoming wedding. This week is our gift to the bride."

"I don't believe it for a minute," Eleanor said. She pointed a finger an inch from the mayor's nose. "I want these people removed and the ranch closed."

Carmen began mumbling. Another chant, I thought. She fixed her eyes on the three intruders. Martin squirmed beneath her gaze, and Polly wrung her hands.

Only Eleanor appeared unfazed. She turned her frosty glare toward the psychic. "You're next, you old bag. The last thing this town needs is a charlatan peddling crystal balls and sorcery. We'll have you and your wretched snakes run out of town before the end of the month."

Carmen stopped chanting and reached out to stroke the crystal ball. "I could read your future, Eleanor, but I suspect your past is more interesting." She closed her eyes. "Yes, dirt poor as a child. Ridiculed for your hand-me-down clothes. Determined never to feel that way again. You're on husband number…three, isn't it? Allen Simonson, the richest of them all."

My eyes widened. Was this the wife of oil magnate Allen Simonson—one of the most powerful men in the state? Make that, the country. I'd read an article about him in *Forbes* not a week earlier. In addition to summarizing his massive holdings, including a home in Colorado, the article had characterized him as ruthless beneath a veneer of civility.

My thoughts were interrupted when Carmen opened her eyes and settled her gaze on Eleanor. "I'd feel compassion for you, if only you didn't choose to hurt others to get what you want."

"How dare you!" Eleanor growled. She lunged forward, hand raised, a slap imminent. Carmen didn't budge. I could swear a physical energy flowed from the psychic's eyes. Silly idea, maybe, but something stopped Eleanor in her tracks.

"Fine," she said. "But I hope you realize this little stunt has sealed your fate. You'd best pack up those repulsive snakes, because you'll be heading out of town on the Bauers' heels."

Then Eleanor turned to Martin. "You'll do what's right, Martin, or I guarantee you won't be mayor much longer. Allen will see to that."

Polly began fanning herself with her hand. The mayor wiped his fingers across his sweating brow. "Well, I'll need to consult with the town's attorney, and I can't do that until tomorrow. Until then—"

Fritz smacked a fist into his palm. "Martin, what are you thinking, man? You know Ryll and me. We're friends. You and I play golf together. We have beers at Stony's Saloon. My wife and I aren't doing anything wrong here. Eleanor has been after us from the moment we bought this place. She's a vindictive snob. You can't give in to her threats!"

Eleanor laughed. "If wanting to keep my home unsullied by riff raff tourists makes me a snob, so be it. I'll win this battle. My husband will see to it. If this so-called mayor doesn't have the backbone to do what needs to be done, you'll be hearing from our lawyer."

Pivoting on her heel, Eleanor marched from the room, with Polly close behind. Martin shot an embarrassed glance at Fritz and shuffled after them. The rest of us trailed behind.

Outside, we stood in a cluster on the deck. Valerie and Haley had heard the ruckus and watched from the doorway. Eleanor drew back her shoulders and gave Ryll and Fritz a wintry smile. "Nothing personal. I'm sure you're both nice people. But I won't allow you to upend our way of life here in Mustang."

Then she marched down the wooden stairs. On the last step, her heel caught between two boards, and she sprawled onto the dirt. Jessica's hand rose to her mouth, and I realized she was covering a grin. Carmen observed the scene from the window, her gaze expressionless.

Cowboy Colby, who had been working at the stable entrance, jogged over and helped a sputtering Eleanor to her feet, his hand lingering on her hip. He grinned as Eleanor slapped his hand away.

Interesting. If I wasn't mistaken, Colby's hand had been encroaching on familiar territory. *Something is going on between these two*, I speculated. *Something Eleanor's husband probably wouldn't be pleased about.*

Colby stepped back and touched the brim of his cowboy hat. "Evening, Mizz Simonson. All your parts in working order?"

A crimson blush rose from the neckline of Eleanor's dress and spread to her cheeks. Her eyes darted around the group of observers. After a moment, she composed herself and turned back to Ryll and Fritz.

"This place is a menace. I might've broken my ankle on your pathetic steps. One more incident for my lawyer. By the time I'm through with you, this place will belong to me."

She stormed off to her car, shooting a quick glance at Colby on her way. Polly trotted off after her. The mayor looked at Fritz with an apologetic gaze, but he plodded after his wife like an obedient puppy. The three got into a black Lexus SUV with Eleanor behind the wheel, and peeled through the ranch gate, leaving behind a plume of dust.

None of us spoke for a few seconds. Then Lydia placed a hand on the banister and strutted down the steps, stopping in front of Colby. She reached out and engaged in the most seductive rendition of a handshake I'd ever seen. "I don't believe we've met," she purred. "I'm Lydia Fredericks."

The corner of Colby's mouth twitched. "Well, I'm not sure how I missed out on that. I'm Colby Trent, ma'am, ranch manager. At your service."

She lifted an eyebrow. "I'll be sure to call on you when I need…something."

I glanced at Tonya, who appeared apoplectic. "Mother," she said, her voice tight. "Let's go back in the lodge. People your age should get to bed at this hour."

Oh, my. I feared the fur was about to fly. Lydia gave Tonya a death glare before turning back to Colby. "My daughter thinks she's so amusing. Thank you for your kind offer, Colby dear. I'm sure I'll be seeing you tomorrow."

She swept up the stairs like a queen and positioned herself near the deck railing, resting her chin on her hand. Colby's eyes twinkled. Then he turned to Ryll and Fritz, and his expression turned serious.

"I was coming over to tell you Doc Farrell just left. He gave Belle a thorough examination and said he expects her to be right as roses in a day or two."

Ryll's stiff posture relaxed. "That's good news. But did he say what's wrong? She's the third horse that's taken ill in the past three days."

"He can't say for sure," he said, looking troubled, "but he thinks it might be a mild virus. Wouldn't be surprised if it affects more of them before it's done. He left us with meds for the others just in case."

"Well, that's a relief," Fritz said. "Thanks for letting us know."

"All part of a day's work," Colby said. "And now, off to my quarters."

"Hold on," Valerie called out. She whispered something to Haley, who hurried back inside. "We have fresh-baked oatmeal cookies. Haley's going to wrap up a few for you and the boys."

Colby touched his hat again and smiled broadly. "Very kind. The boys have gone home for the night, but I'll try to save a few for them. A cookie will be a nice treat while I'm watching the idiot box by myself tonight."

"Sounds lonely," Lydia said from her perch on the deck. "If you need company, just give me a wave. That's my window right there." She pointed up toward the second-story.

"Please excuse my mother," Tonya said through gritted teeth. "She's having hot flashes."

Colby chuckled, unruffled by the tension. The screen door opened and Haley emerged, carrying a plate covered in a plaid cloth napkin. She came down the stairs and held it out to him.

"Thank you, Mizz Haley, Mizz Valerie," Colby said.

He took the daughter's hand and lifted it to his lips, then gave the mother a wink. I sighed. The man was a tomcat. No offense to my feline companion Carl.

As Colby headed back to his bunk, Carmen came outside, carrying a duffel bag I assumed held her crystal ball and other gear.

"Carmen, I hope you can forgive us," Ryll said. "We had no idea Eleanor and her mob would show up."

Carmen patted her hand. "Never mind, dear. The woman will get what she deserves. Karma will prevail. Mark my words."

I couldn't help but observe how closely the words Carmen and karma aligned.

6

I grabbed my pillow and shoved it across my face to block out Tonya's snoring, but even that couldn't mute the buzz saw noise. Then I looked at the clock on the nightstand. The malevolent red glow of the numbers mocked me. Heaving a sigh, I tucked the pillow back beneath my head and stared at the ceiling. Beside me, Woody snored in harmony with Tonya. From the windowsill, Carl's green eyes gleamed. At least I wasn't the only one unable to sleep.

I rolled onto my side and watched my best friend's face as she slumbered. She looked so peaceful while emitting such a barbaric noise. It was likely due to the bottle of wine we'd shared as Tonya vented her frustrations over Lydia's arrival, flirtations, and lack of maternal instinct for the past four decades. Clearly, the alcohol and tirade combo had plunged her into a deep, undisturbed sleep.

Wish I could say the same for myself.

But no, my busy brain wouldn't succumb to the lure of dreamland. Instead, it kept replaying the evening's events. The malicious Eleanor Simonson and her threats against the ranch. The wimpy mayor and his groveling wife. The mysterious psychic who'd claimed to read my future and made a chilling prediction that Eleanor would get "exactly what she deserved."

Who knew what that meant? But it didn't sound like sunshine and roses. I didn't believe the old woman could truly see the future, but the sense of doom her words carried made them difficult to forget.

Then I spent a half hour mulling over the revelation about Tonya and David possibly adopting children. I could envision Tonya as a mother, of course. She loved children and was always good with them. It wasn't the idea itself so much as the surprise of it—the fact that I'd found out from a stranger that my best friend was considering this major life decision. I hadn't broached the topic with her yet. She'd been too mad at her mother, and I needed to sort out my feelings first.

Every time I lured my brain out of its spin cycle enough to drift off, ranch noises snatched me back to consciousness. The howl of a coyote. Pipes rattling as a toilet flushed. Around two in the morning, I heard footsteps on the wooden stairs. Someone else in the lodge was battling insomnia, too.

So much for a carefree, fun-filled celebration of Tonya's upcoming marriage.

Well, I'd just have to do everything in my power to make the rest of our time here light and relaxed.

By five forty-five, I gave up on any hope of significant shuteye and got out of bed. Even at this ungodly hour, I doubted I'd be the first one downstairs. It was a working ranch, after all. Besides, the sunrise might make for stunning—and profitable—photos. I pulled on a loose pair of shorts and an oversized t-shirt. As I laced up my hiking boots, Woody sat up, eager for the day. Carl arched his back and shook himself before pouncing onto the floor. I lifted my phone from the nightstand and smiled at a message from my boyfriend, Sam—a picture of the sun rising over the beach. He and his daughter Elyse had traveled to Florida to visit his parents, and at two hours ahead of my time zone, he'd already seen the day begin. I tapped out a brief response, slung my camera strap around my neck, and tiptoed out of the room, closing the door as another snore ripped through the air.

As the creatures and I made our way downstairs, the sound of pans rattling assured me I'd been right: we weren't the only ones awake. When we pushed through the swinging door, we found four women bustling around the kitchen: Valerie, Haley, Ryll, and Mom.

"Morning, Ms. Cassidy." Haley gave me a quick smile before returning her attention to the peaches she was slicing.

"Callie," I said groggily. "You say Ms. Cassidy, and I figure you're referring to my mother. I'm just Callie."

While my mother filled Woody and Carl's bowls with kibble and water in the adjacent mudroom, I scanned the kitchen—a chef's dream by any standard. A huge prep space stood in the middle, part granite and part butcher block. Top-of-the-line stainless steel appliances glinted in the overhead light, including an industrial-sized, refrigerator-freezer combination, a double oven, and a six-burner gas stove top, where Valerie stirred a concoction that smelled of cinnamon and vanilla. Clearly, they'd spared no expense. The ranch needed to be operational soon, I figured, if they were going to pay for all this.

After she'd supplied Woody and Carl with their morning meals, Mom returned and kissed me on the cheek. "Darling, I don't remember the last time I saw you before sunrise."

"Don't they say the early bird gets the worm? I figured that would be especially true on a ranch."

Ryll held up a glass carafe. "No worms here. Would you settle for coffee?"

I nodded. "I'd love a jolt of caffeine after a night of Tonya's snoring. But it's her celebration week, so far be it for me to complain."

Ryll poured, and I wrapped my hands around the mug and sipped the pleasantly bitter brew. Then I sniffed the air. "It smells great in here."

Valerie brushed her fingers on her apron. "Fresh blueberry muffins in the oven. Vegan and gluten-free, in case you're wondering."

I snorted. "I'm not one to worry about gluten—or vegan, for that matter. But if breakfast is as spectacular as dinner, you might make a convert out of me."

Valerie grinned. "You sound surprised."

"When I heard the words 'healthy food,' my stomach clenched. But last night's meal tasted nothing like cardboard."

Haley, filling ceramic bowls with sliced fruit, laughed. "I know what you mean. Initially, I didn't like the idea, either. Who wants to go on vacation and eat the right stuff?" She cupped a hand to her mouth, as if passing along a secret. "Turns out, my mother is an artist in the kitchen. Don't tell her I said so. I'd hate for her to get a big head."

My mother nudged Valerie with her elbow. "The older our daughters get, the smarter we become. Callie speaks the truth. The meal was sumptuous. Maybe we need to consider a similar menu for the Knotty Pine Resort."

"I'll be glad to sit down with you and make a few suggestions. When Amaryllis and I first conferred on the menu, we knew we wanted guests to feel indulged, not medicated. It's been fun to experiment with different offerings."

Ryll's face clouded. "Let's just hope our work hasn't been in vain. After last night's fiasco, I'm not even sure we'll be able to secure our license."

7

I opened my mouth to offer words of encouragement, but Ryll waved me off and forced a smile. "Don't let my silly worries darken what promises to be a gorgeous day. I see you have your camera. Shall we take our coffee to the deck and prepare to worship the sunrise? I bet Haley will supply us with muffins as soon as they're out of the oven."

Haley nodded, and Mom, Ryll, and I left the kitchen and carried our coffee mugs through the dining room and out the front door. Woody headed to a patch of grass on the side of the lodge. Carl, having taken care of his own business in the litterbox upstairs, arched his spine in a greeting to the morning.

Mom and Ryll settled into wooden rockers and began to chat. I set my mug on the table and ambled down the stairs, walking halfway across the basketball court-sized yard before turning to face the east. The first fingers of pink and orange spread across the smoky blue sky. The air, still cool from the night, carried the scent of pine and sage—along with the faintest whiff of manure. Birds twittered their welcome to the barely concealed sun.

I snapped a few pictures of the pastel canvas and waited for the ball of fire to appear above the horizon. Inhaling the clean air, I smiled, enjoying such a peaceful, gentle start to the day. It gave me hope that we could move past last night's unpleasantness and get back on track for a successful bridal shower week.

A loud neighing from the stable broke the morning

quiet. Nothing unusual, but Carl's response evoked a niggle of alarm in me. He folded his ears back, let out a shrill yowl, and flew across the yard toward the stable. Woody threw out three quick barks and raced after the cat.

Ryll stood, alert. "What's wrong?"

"Oh, I'm sure it's nothing," I said, trying to soothe her and quell my own sense of unease. "They have terrible manners. You'd think they'd been raised in a barn. I'll go round them up and put them in timeout."

As I jogged toward the stable, my camera bounced against my chest, and I reached up to hold it steady. "Come here, you wretched heathens," I whisper-shouted to Woody and Carl. "You're going to wake the whole ranch."

They skidded to a halt at the stable door. Carl leaped toward the spot where the door met the jamb and squirmed through the narrow opening. Woody whined and tried to nudge the door wider with his nose, but his large frame was too big to fit.

Another neigh rang out, sounding urgent. I hoped Carl hadn't wriggled into a stall and spooked one of the horses.

I shoved the barn door, opening it on its rollers. Woody darted inside ahead of me and took off toward the nearest stall. I stepped in more cautiously. Dim light glowed from overhead fixtures, giving off a shadowy, mysterious aura. The smell of manure was stronger here, and beneath it was the scent of freshly baled hay. Down the row of stalls, horses peered over their gates, curious about what was causing the ruckus.

After a few seconds, my eyes adjusted to the low light, and I spotted my furry creatures just outside the first stall on the left. Carl dashed back to me, twisting around my ankles, as if urging me to hurry.

I took my time moving across the hay-strewn floor, aware of the possibility my foot might squish into a pile of poop. It wasn't the way I wanted to start my day. Carl meowed impatiently, and Woody pawed at the stall's wooden gate. Inside, the horse whinnied.

When I was a foot from the stall, Carl hissed and launched himself at Woody, knocking the surprised pup backward.

"Carl, what are you doing?" I asked.

The cat crept backward, his eyes fixed on the ground. Woody followed Carl's gaze and froze.

Then I caught sight of the object of their attention. From beneath the wooden board at the bottom of the stall, a yellow-brown snake slithered across the hay.

I yelped, even though the serpent, probably four feet long, was headed away from us. I couldn't help myself. Snakes were my kryptonite.

Once it was clear the snake wasn't plotting to double back and attack us with his forked tongue and sharp fangs, I bent and lifted Carl into my arms. One of us quivered, but I couldn't be sure which.

"Crisis averted," I said, giving Woody a pat on the head. "You two have done your good deed for the day, protecting the horse and scaring that slimy thing out of the stall."

Woody whined again. Carl writhed in my grasp, swiping my hand and wresting himself from my arms. As soon as his feet contacted the ground, he crept toward the stall. Then he looked inside and yowled.

My heart, not yet recovered from the sight of the snake, hitched up another notch, beating like a metronome on warp speed. I took a hesitant step forward. Then another. At last, I reached the stall door.

The wooden gate rose to the height of my chest. Beyond it, I saw Spirit, my horse from yesterday's trail ride, cowering in the corner, grunting and stomping a hoof. His eyes were wide with terror.

"What's wrong, fella?" I asked. He whinnied and pushed himself even farther into the corner, as if trying to make himself smaller. Carl scrambled up the gate, perching on the top slat and staring toward the stall's far wall.

The shadows loomed deeper there, and it took me a few seconds to recognize what I was seeing.

Or rather, who I was seeing.

First, I made out a high-heeled shoe. Then a leg. Next, a swatch of peach-colored cloth. A length of dark hair fanned out across the hay.

Finally, I focused on the face. Eleanor Simonson. Her eyes were closed, arms splayed at her sides. I'd have thought she'd settled in for a nap, if not for the gray cast to her skin—and the bloody purple crevice above her right eye.

8

I n the corner, Spirit swayed and snorted, his brown eyes wide and nostrils flared. When I turned back to Eleanor, what had happened became clear. Something had spooked the horse, and he'd reared up and struck the woman in the head with his hoof. I remembered the snake slithering out of the stall—had that been what agitated him?

Poor horse. He'd already been through so much.

I didn't stop to analyze the fact that I was feeling more sympathy for the horse than the human.

But why was Eleanor in the stall in the first place? I didn't want to blame the victim, but seriously…what had she been doing here?

I heard the click of a switch, and the overhead lights changed from dim to bright. In response, the rest of the horses neighed and shuffled in their stalls.

"Callie, what's going on?" Ryll called out. She walked briskly toward me with my mother close behind her.

I caught Mom's sleeve. "Call 9-1-1. Right away. We need police and an emergency medical team."

Without a word, Mom hurried back toward the lodge. As a former police chief's wife, she knew when to ask questions and when to act.

As she ran out, Colby ran in, his shirt unbuttoned and his belt unbuckled, though he'd put on his boots and hat. He stopped next to Ryll, and I caught the scent of blueberry muffins.

"What's going on?" he asked. "Is Spirit sick?"

"It's...worse than that." I took a deep breath and plunged ahead. "It's Eleanor Simonson. She's dead. I think Spirit may have trampled her."

Ryll's hand flew to her mouth, but Colby's expression didn't change. I tilted my head, curious at his reaction— or lack thereof. He didn't seem especially surprised or upset. Then again, maybe he was simply a stoic cowboy type who didn't cotton to public displays of emotion.

Ryll moved past me toward the stall door. She steeled herself before peering inside. When she spotted the body, she gasped. "What was Eleanor doing in Spirit's stall?"

"I wondered that myself," I said.

Her eyes roamed the space. When they settled on the gate in front of us, she frowned at Colby. "This door is bolted from the outside," she said, pointing at the slide latch. "Why would she lock herself in there?"

Colby stepped forward and examined the latch. He shrugged, and I chided myself for noticing his pec muscles rippling beneath the tanned skin. A girl could look, as my mother had noted, but now wasn't exactly the time. "Not sure," he said.

Spirit's ears were pinned back. The horse was stressed, and no wonder. A body lay in his bedroom.

"We need to make sure she's dead," Ryll said.

I scrunched up my face. "It seems obvious."

"Just the same, we have to check. We can't leave her lying there if there's any chance she's still alive." Ryll looked at Colby. "When I open the gate, you get Spirit and take him to the corral."

"I'm not sure that's a good idea," I said. "These are suspicious circumstances. You could be disturbing a crime scene."

Ryll lifted her chin. "I don't care. Eleanor might need our help."

I nodded, contrite. She was right, of course. I'd been hardwired as the daughter of a former police chief and by my own career as an investigative photojournalist to

41

always consider the evidence. But if a woman's life was on the line, preserving the crime scene came second.

Stepping back, I positioned myself where I could be out of the way while maintaining a line of vision. Woody and Carl sat beside me, watching as Ryll slid the latch open and tugged at the slatted wooden door. Colby stepped inside tentatively, shooting a quick glance at Eleanor's body before stroking the horse's nose.

Spirit snorted but allowed Colby to slip a halter over his head. "Let's get you out of here, big guy," he said.

With the tenderness of a mother caring for her newborn, he led Spirit out of the stall, down the wide aisle, and into the corral as the other horses watched.

Ryll tiptoed in, as if reluctant to disturb Eleanor's slumber. She crouched, pushed the unmoving woman's silk scarf aside an inch, and pressed two fingers against Eleanor's neck. After a few seconds, she turned to me, her face ashen, and shook her head. "She's gone."

They were the words I'd expected, but I still felt a ripple of disbelief. I dropped my eyes, offering a moment of quiet respect. The little I'd known of Eleanor I hadn't liked, but everyone deserved that consideration.

Then I heard voices. I turned to see Mom standing at the stable door, accompanied by the entire crew: Valerie and Haley, the two young ranch hands, and the whole bridal shower group—except Lydia. The ranch hands looked pale and frightened. This was probably their first brush with death. Human death, anyway.

"The police are on their way," Mom said. "Five minutes."

Lynn broke from the group and stepped toward us. "What's happened?" she asked, in detective mode. "Maggie didn't tell us much."

"Eleanor Simonson is dead," I said. I filled them in on what few details I had.

By that time, Colby had returned, and Lynn's eyes darted from him to Ryll. "You entered the stall?"

"We had to see if she needed help," Ryll said. "And Spirit was scared. He's had a rough time the past few days. I don't think he can tolerate much more trauma."

Her voice broke, and she buried her face in her hands. Summer rushed over and put an arm around her. "Where's Uncle Fritz?"

"He left a couple of hours ago to drive into Durango. There's a horse there that needs rescuing. Of all days…"

Lynn's expression briefly turned sympathetic, then reassembled into her professional countenance. She faced the group standing at the door. "Okay, everyone out. Wait in the yard for the emergency responders." She turned to Colby and Ryll, whose head now rested on Summer's shoulder. "You three, too. Callie, you stay here with me. If you wouldn't mind, that is."

Behind us, the horses whinnied and huffed. Ryll squared her shoulders. "Lynn, these horses are frightened. Some of them have been sick. We need to get them away from this madness. The stalls have outer exits leading to the corral. Is it okay to remove them?"

Lynn considered the request and nodded. "I don't see what it would hurt."

Ryll gave her a grateful look and said a few words to Colby. He gestured to the ranch hands, and they hurried off. I heard doors squeak on their hinges and the sound of horses being moved.

I waved to Renata and then motioned to Woody and Carl. She crouched and whistled, and Woody trotted over to her. Carl tossed me a defiant glance before sprinting behind a bale of hay. His eyes shone from his hiding place, and I shook my head. "No sense trying to round him up. He'll come out when he's good and ready."

Lynn stood at the stall door, examining the gate. I mentioned that it had been bolted when we arrived, and she bent to examine the latch. "This lock is pretty low," she mused. "It would have required a bit of a stretch to reach over from the inside and slide it shut. Why would

Eleanor do that?"

It was a rhetorical question, and I knew Lynn didn't expect a response. She surveyed the stable, finally spotting a metal step stool leaning against a wall. She grabbed it, setting it up next to the gate and climbing the three steps. After a quick look around, she took out her cell phone, flipped on the flashlight, and swept it across the hay, pausing at a spot a few inches from Eleanor's hand. Next, she focused on Eleanor herself, slowly moving the light the length of the body. When she reached the left knee, she studied it for a moment.

"Huh," she muttered.

"Care to be more specific?" I asked.

Lynn jumped off the stool and twirled a strand of ash blond hair around her finger as she thought. Though she looked younger than her thirty-two years, her intelligent gray eyes lent her an air of authority. I thought, not for the first time, how lucky Rock Creek Village had been to lure her into our two-person detective squad.

"I can't be sure what killed her," Lynn said at last.

"What about that hoof shaped indentation in her forehead? Seems like an obvious cause of death to me. I figure Spirit reared up and trampled her. Doesn't that make the most sense?"

She shrugged. "Could be. But lots of people survive a kick from a horse. Besides, the wound doesn't appear that deep, and there's not a lot of blood."

"True. But brain damage can be sneaky."

She paused, weighing her next words. "Listen, Callie, this isn't my jurisdiction, of course, but since I was the first detective on the scene…"

"You want to investigate."

"Just a preliminary look before the police arrive." She gestured at the camera around my neck. "Feel up to taking a few photos?"

A ripple of adrenaline flowed through me. "Always," I said. "Tell me what you need."

9

I took Lynn's place atop the stool and lifted my camera. "Where shall I start?"

"How close an image can you get from here?"

I estimated the body lay less than ten feet away, and I currently had a decent zoom lens on my Nikon. "If you aim the light at it, I can shoot anything you need."

Lynn carefully climbed onto one of the gate's lower beams and directed her flashlight to the spot near Eleanor's calf. I held the camera to my eye and focused. "Puncture wounds?" I asked, snapping the shutter.

Lynn nodded. "I'm thinking snakebite."

I told her about the yellow-brown snake I'd seen slithering from the stall. "That might be what spooked Spirit. Maybe Eleanor was bitten even before his hoof struck her."

"Could be, I suppose. I'm not an expert on snakebites. Yesterday, our guide said most of them around here are non-venomous, but I guess that means some aren't. But a bite probably wouldn't cause immediate death."

"So she should have been able to go for help."

She shrugged. "We'll have to wait for the coroner to answer that question."

"Anything else?" I asked.

Lynn directed her flashlight to the place in the hay I'd noticed her examining. "See that?"

As I turned the camera toward the spot, her beam reflected off an object. A twist of the camera's focus ring revealed a syringe.

"A needle in the haystack," I murmured. "What on earth is that doing here?"

Lynn didn't respond. I took a picture of the syringe, then zoomed out for a wider angle to document its position relative to the body.

I looked at Eleanor, then at the needle. If the scenario taking shape in my mind was correct, Eleanor would have a lot of explaining to do. If only she were able.

"Do you think she brought the syringe into the stall with her?" I asked. "And she was holding it, preparing to commit a dastardly deed, when the horse reared? The needle could have flown from her hand…"

"That's one explanation," Lynn said. "Or—"

She was interrupted by a commotion at the stable entrance—raised voices, a door banging, footsteps approaching. I stepped off the stool just as Polly Finkle appeared, her expression frantic. Her husband followed a step behind her.

Polly looked disheveled, as if she'd gotten dressed in a hurry. Her wrinkled button-up shirt didn't match her slacks. If yesterday her hair had looked like a plated armadillo, today it appeared the armadillo had met a porcupine and produced a baby with it. She hurried toward us, her eyes darting around the stall. Lynn moved to block Polly's view of the body, but she wasn't fast enough. Polly put her hands to her face and screamed. Martin followed her gaze and pulled his wife to him as she shook with sobs.

After a few ragged breaths, Polly composed herself and broke from her husband's embrace. Her expression went from distress to fury as she pointed a shaky finger toward the stable door.

"This was all her doing," Polly shrieked.

We turned toward the object of her fury. Sunlight streaming inside rendered the woman in the doorway a semi-silhouette, but her flowing skirt and long, silver hair made her instantly identifiable. Carmen, the psychic

46

who'd read my palm last night.

The same woman who had cursed Eleanor and predicted her doom.

***

The wail of an approaching siren drew closer. While Lynn guided Polly and Martin outside, I hurried ahead and to pull Carmen in a different direction, hoping to avoid an angry confrontation.

Carl streaked out of the stable and wound his furry body around my ankles. I scooped him into my arms. His eyes glinted as he stared at Carmen. She stared back.

When the two of them broke their kinetic connection, I noticed that Carmen appeared unperturbed. "What are you doing here?" I asked her.

"I was called."

"Who called you?"

"The universe."

"The universe filled you in on Eleanor's murder? That's a handy news source. Better than cable TV, even."

One side of her mouth quirked up. "The universe alerted me. Then I walked over and saw the commotion. I rent Ryll and Fritz's cabin on the back of the property near the stream."

That bit of information gave me pause, but Carmen didn't give me time to think about it. "We were interrupted last night, Callie, but it seems we have a moment now. I'm happy to finish your reading. Do you want to hear what I've glimpsed in your future?"

A shudder ran through me. For a moment, I almost believed this tiny woman before me might contain such power. But I shook off the thought and replaced it with another. Carmen was a fine performer. Could she also be a killer? Perhaps the universe hadn't informed her of Eleanor's death. Perhaps she'd known because she'd perpetrated the act herself.

A blue Ford Explorer, its side emblazoned with the word POLICE, roared beneath the Moonglow Ranch entrance arch, spewing dirt and gravel in its wake. When it ground to a halt, the passenger door swung open, and a hefty man in a cowboy hat stepped out and hitched up his khaki pants. A bronze star that signaled he was the head honcho hung on a bolo tie in front of a brave set of buttons that strained to keep his shirt closed.

He lifted a Styrofoam cup to his lips and spat a stream of brown liquid into it. Chewing tobacco, I realized. Ugh.

As he ran meaty fingers through his bushy gray mustache, Polly waved frantically. "Chester! It's Eleanor. She's been murdered!"

The police chief spat again. The driver door opened then, and a skinny young man merged. He wore a similar uniform to the chief's, but his badge was smaller.

Chester spat into the cup yet again. "Stay by the car, Jake. I'll call ya when I need ya."

The young officer looked disappointed, but he obediently leaned a hip against the car and crossed his arms. Meanwhile, the chief sauntered toward Polly and Martin, addressing Martin as if Polly wasn't even there. "How'd you get here so fast?"

Polly stepped in front of her husband, inserting herself into the chief's line of vision. "It's Eleanor," she said. "Didn't you hear me? She's in there, in a stall like an animal. Oh, no…Oh, Eleanor…"

She wailed, and her husband patted her shoulder. "There, there, honeybun. It'll be all right." He turned to the police chief. "Polly had the police scanner on and heard the call. We live so close, you know, and my wife insisted we hustle over here."

Polly took a handkerchief from her purse and wiped her nose. On closer inspection, I noticed that she had expelled no tears.

"Chester, I don't know how, but this was Carmen's doing. She's the killer! You should arrest her at once!"

I had a quick flash of a Puritan accusing a woman of witchcraft in early Salem, Massachusetts. Though I'd suspected the psychic myself minutes ago, now I felt a surge of protectiveness and moved closer to her, as if I could shield her from the allegation.

The police chief stared at Carmen for a moment, his face expressionless.

Polly wrung her hands. "Are you going to arrest her?"

Before he could respond, Lynn stepped forward and held out a hand. "Good morning. I'm Lynn Clarke."

The man moved his spit cup to his left hand and grasped hers. I grimaced. My friend would need a bar of heavy-duty soap following this encounter.

"Chief Chester Ward. What is your stake in this, little lady?"

Lynn's forehead creased, but she maintained her diplomacy. "Detective Lynn Clarke, Chief. I'm with the Rock Creek Village department. Prior to your arrival, I examined the scene, and—"

"You what?" he bellowed. "I don't know how they do things in your creek town, little lady, but here in Mustang, we know better than to trample all over someone else's business."

Reflexively, Lynn took a step back. She spoke in a cool, professional voice. "I can assure you, Chief, I did not break protocol. I didn't trample all over, as you put it. I simply took a look—from outside the stall. I'm happy to share my observations."

She shot a look at my camera and gave her head a small shake. I nodded and shifted it to the side. Best not to mention the photos she'd had me shoot.

The man puffed out his chest, and I was convinced a button or two would pop, but they held. "Little lady, if I want your observations, I'll be sure to find you."

"Detective Clarke," she growled through clenched teeth.

"What's that?"

49

"My name is Detective Clarke, not Little Lady. I'd appreciate being addressed as such."

The police chief grunted. "I'll surely keep that in mind. In the meantime, I'm ordering you out of here."

Lynn and I looked at each other.

"Get out of here," he repeated. "Vamoose. I don't want to see anyone near this crime scene until I release it." He pointed at Ryll and Colby. "You two stay put."

"What about us?" Polly asked.

Again, he ignored her and addressed Martin. "Mayor, your wife's been through an ordeal, I expect. Run her on home. I'll stop by when I'm through here and let you know what's happening."

Polly clutched her husband's arm. "Someone needs to tell Eleanor's family what's happened. Allen is out of town on a business trip, but Martin and I can inform Gordon and then get in touch with Allen."

I looked at Ryll and mouthed, *Gordon?* She mouthed back, *Eleanor's stepson.*

The chief's lips turned down, but he nodded. "Yeah, okay. Just hang tight at the Simonson house. Tell 'em I'll be by with more information."

Dragging a bewildered Martin behind, Polly hurried off toward the car, waiting as her husband opened the passenger door. She paused long enough to glare at Carmen one more time. Then she and Martin got in the car and drove away. I breathed a sigh of relief, and Carmen and I walked over to join the others.

Chief Ward whistled to Officer Jake, as if summoning a dog. "Come on, boy, let's see what we got."

Jake jogged over to him, glancing at Lynn as he passed.

Once the lawmen were out of sight, Ryll headed over to Colby and the ranch hands. She spoke to them, gesturing toward the corral. Colby nodded, and the three men headed toward the horses.

Next, Ryll pulled Valerie and Haley aside and gave them a few quick instructions. They hurried up the wooden stairs and into the lodge.

Finally, she approached our little group. She took Tonya's hands in hers. "Tonya, I'm so very sorry about all this. It's certainly not how I wanted your bridal shower week to play out."

Tonya smiled at her sympathetically. "Nothing to apologize for. It's not as if you…" She dropped her eyes. "Anyway, I'm wondering if it might be better if we…well, reschedule. With everything you have to deal with, you surely don't need us under foot."

Ryll squeezed Tonya's fingers. Her eyes, glistening with tears, flitted around the group. "I'll understand if you want to leave, but I hope you won't. Selfishly, I, um…I could use the companionship."

Lynn rubbed her chin. "It wouldn't be a good idea for us to leave, anyway. They'll need to question us as part of the investigation, I expect."

"Investigation. It sounds so…" Ryll choked back a sob, and Summer hugged her aunt tight. Then Jessica moved in, wrapping her arms around the woman too. Suddenly, we were all surrounding Ryll in a group hug.

Ryll wiped her cheeks. "Thank you. Your support…it means the world to me. Now, let's see if we can get put these thoughts aside, as best we can, at least. We'll serve breakfast inside this morning. Afterward, we'll try to maintain a semblance of normalcy and continue with the scheduled activities as planned. Guided hike today. Tomorrow is the luncheon in town. Tuesday, we'll have Colby's lasso demonstration and instruction. What do you think so far?"

We responded with enthusiasm. Ryll started toward the lodge, and I trotted up to her. "I heard the police chief tell you and Colby to stay put. You won't get in trouble, will you?"

"I'm only going inside the lodge. If Chester is any kind of investigator—which between the two of us I'm not convinced of—he'll be able to find me."

10

Ryll went to the kitchen to see about breakfast, and Summer, Jessica, and Renata followed to help. I took Woody and Carl upstairs and shut them into my room, much to Carl's chagrin. When I returned, Mom had settled herself into an armchair, and Lynn stood by the front window, alternating between staring at the stable and tapping on her phone. I found Tonya and pulled her aside.

"I can't believe this happened," I said. "I realize a woman is dead, and I don't mean to sound insensitive, but this is ruining your celebration. Are you sure you're okay staying?"

Tonya flashed her megawatt smile. Her makeup was subtle this morning, except for her signature red lipstick. Her beaded braids hung around her shoulders, and she was dressed in fashionable jeans and a tailored t-shirt. How did she look this good so early in the morning?

As she leaned in, the citrusy fragrance of her perfume enveloped me. "Ryll and Fritz are the best, aren't they? I'm happy to stay. Besides, from one insensitive broad to another, this'll make a great story, won't it, sugarplum? Anyway, the dead woman seemed vile. It's not as if the world lost a saint."

I suppressed a smile and smacked her arm. "Hush. You should know better than to speak ill of the dead."

Tonya pouted. "And I thought we were sisters in insensitivity. Come on, let's go find out what our detective thinks."

Jessica marched out of the kitchen and joined us as we headed toward Lynn. "The kitchen is no place for me," she announced.

I knew the feeling. As far as I was concerned, someone else could always do the cooking—even if it meant I'd be stuck with healthy food.

Once we'd positioned ourselves in front of the window with Lynn, Jessica crossed her arms and gazed at the stable. "Betcha a hundred dollars that fat man calls it an accident."

"Well, it's not," Lynn said. "I'm ninety-five percent sure. And if Chief Wade's investigation isn't thorough enough to suit me, I'm happy to go over his head."

"Over his head?" I asked. "What do you mean?"

"An inept small-town police chief shouldn't be handling a murder. The county sheriff needs to be notified."

I felt a twinge of unease. The idea of trodding on any police chief's authority bothered me. After all, most law enforcement people I knew were professional, thorough, and intelligent. Frank Laramie, Rock Creek Village's Chief of Police and Lynn's boss, was one such example—as was her partner, Raul Sanchez. My father, the former chief, epitomized the role.

"You work for a small-town police chief," I pointed out. "You guys investigated a murder a few months ago. No county sheriff involved."

She bristled. "I said inept. Our department is perfectly...ept."

I snickered, but I understood what she was saying. As with every profession, though, there were a few bad apples—people who were either incapable of logical thought, too lazy to pursue every possibility, or in the pocket of someone powerful who pulled the strings. From what I'd observed, I suspected this Chief Wade fit into all three categories. If so, I supposed Lynn would be right to call in the cavalry.

"We should bring Raul into the loop, too," I said. "Don't tell him I said this, but your partner occasionally supplies a decent insight."

"I've already been in contact with him," Lynn said. Did I notice a slight flush in her cheeks? Tonya and I shared a quick look. We'd engaged in a bit of speculation about whether there was more to Lynn and Raul's partnership than just professional. When Lynn and her two young daughters had moved to Rock Creek Village, we'd sensed there might have been a spark between the two partners. If a personal relationship was developing, Tonya and I would be on the sidelines cheering for it.

Ryll summoned us to the dining table. Valerie and Haley had arranged platters of spinach and egg white omelets, turkey bacon, biscuits (gluten-free, I was assured), and fresh fruit salad, along with carafes of sparkling juices and skim milk. I relished every bite. In fact, everyone ate with gusto and chattered during the meal. I marveled at the normalcy of the scene, given that someone lay dead just a few hundred yards from us.

Ryll looked around the room. "Where's Carmen? Did she go back to her cabin?"

I frowned, realizing I hadn't even thought about the woman since we'd come inside. It was as if she'd wiped our minds of her image, then disappeared.

"Oh, well," Ryll said. "I just hope she's as far away from Polly Finkle as possible."

Haley brought baskets of blueberry muffins to the table, and we dug in. Then the front door banged open, and Chief Wade lumbered into the room. Jake slunk in behind him, looking uncomfortable.

"Amaryllis Bauer, I told you to wait for me outside," the police chief grumbled, as if scolding a child.

"Well, you've found me," Ryll's face was grim.

"Who said you could take them horses outta their stalls? That's obstruction of justice, that's what it is."

Lynn jumped up, nearly toppling her chair, and stood

toe to toe with the big man. "Don't be ridiculous. It was a kindness to the poor beasts. If you need to point a finger, point it at me. I told her it was okay to move the horses to the corral, and in my professional opinion, no damage was done."

The chief's face bloomed red. "Let me remind you, little lady, that you are not the law here in Mustang." He touched his badge. "That responsibility belongs to me. What I oughta do is kick you outta here. Declare this place a crime scene and be done with you."

Ryll stiffened. She opened her mouth to speak, but the chief held up a hand. "No need to get your knickers in a twist, sweetheart. Since I may need to question these girls anyway, they can stay. For now."

We *girls* could stay? This pompous jerk was granting his permission? I was seething, and I could see I wasn't alone. Mom pursed her lips, and Tonya clenched her jaw. The only thing keeping Jessica from launching herself at the man was Summer stepping in front of her.

"Where's your husband?" the chief asked our hostess. "I got a question for him."

Ryll explained that Fritz had gone to check on a new horse, and the chief shrugged. "Well, maybe you'll know, then. This place got any security cameras?"

"Not yet," she said. "We keep meaning to install them but haven't gotten around to it."

The chief lifted his Styrofoam cup and spat another stream of brown liquid into it. "No matter. Doubt it's a crime scene, anyhow. I'll wait to hear from the coroner, but I figure I'll be ruling this an accident."

"I was afraid of this," Lynn muttered. She twisted to face him. "Did you see the syringe near the body? Did you hear me tell you the stall door was latched from the outside? An accident seems unlikely."

He waved dismissively. "That can be explained, but I'm not gonna spend my time schooling outsiders. It's none of your business. Like I said, you can stay, but only if you keep clear of my investigation." He leaned toward Lynn, and she pulled back. "Don't even think of sticking your nose into this. I can make trouble for you if you do."

At a buzzing noise on his hip, he unsnapped a leather pouch and pulled out his phone, squinting as he read the screen. "Coroner's heading up the drive. You girls enjoy your breakfast."

Brushing past the officer, Chief Ward barreled out the door. The younger man moved to follow, but Lynn called, "Hold on, Officer…I'm afraid I didn't catch your last name."

His eyes darted to the door, then to Lynn. "It's Williams, but you can call me Jake," he said, his voice barely above a whisper. Here was a young man who didn't want to cross his boss, but who also must have been raised to treat others with respect.

Lynn smiled at him. "Jake. As fellow law enforcement agents, we both want the same thing—to make sure this case is handled properly and that the victim gets justice."

Jake nodded.

"Given everything you saw in there," Lynn continued, "do you agree with Chief Wade that this was an accidental death?"

He scuffed the toe of his boot on the floor. "Well, no, I can't say as I do."

A thump came at the door, followed by the chief's bellowing voice. "Jake, get your scrawny behind out here."

Jake jumped and looked around guiltily before scampering out the door.

No one moved for a moment. We heard footsteps coming downstairs and turned to see Lydia, dressed in a pale blue silk robe and feathered slippers with heels. Her hair was sleek and styled, her makeup freshly applied.

"What's everyone doing up so early? I thought we were supposed to be on vacation. And are those muffins I smell?"

11

Our guide Audra was due in a half hour to lead our nature walk, so Ryll suggested we take the time to get ready. The confrontation with the police chief, along with the coroner's arrival, had left us frazzled. We could use the break. Besides, Ryll wanted— no, needed—this day to proceed as normally as possible. I felt it was important for Tonya, too. Her bridal shower was being overshadowed by murder and mayhem. Time to have some fun in her honor.

Besides, we could talk on the walk.

While Tonya stayed to keep her mother company at a late breakfast, I headed upstairs, thinking I might touch base with Sam. He'd want to hear about the drama at the ranch.

When I opened the door to my room, Carl gave me the stink eye, and Woody's tail drooped at my betrayal. I deduced that Woody's concern revolved around missing out on scraps from our breakfast. Carl, on the other hand, likely felt annoyed at being left out of the drama.

I sighed. Having the creatures around was the universe's way of reminding me I'd never be able to make everyone happy all the time.

First, I dealt with my golden retriever. I pulled a napkin out of my pocket and unwrapped a piece of turkey bacon. The dog perked up, sat at attention, and lifted a paw. Once he was happily ingesting the morsel, I turned my attention to the cat, taking a moment to fill him in on the police chief's antics. He pretended to be disinterested, but I could see from his twitching whiskers he was listening intently.

When I got to the part where Chief Wade said he'd rule Eleanor's death an accident, Carl let out a screech.

"My thoughts exactly," I said. "It's a ridiculous theory. Lynn went ballistic."

My phone beeped with an incoming text. Another picture from Sam—this one of the ocean waves lapping at the beach. I smiled and stretched out on the bed. Carl jumped onto the windowsill and curled his tail around his flank, staring out the window as he no doubt solved the crime in his kitty head. Woody leapt over me and curled up in a ball at my side.

I tapped the FaceTime icon and grinned when Sam appeared on the screen.

He'd only been in Florida for two days, but he already looked tanned and rested. His blond hair ruffled in the breeze, and his blue eyes glinted in the sun.

"Hey, beautiful," he said.

"Hello there, handsome. You look chill."

"I have sand in every crevice of my body, but other than that, it's the bomb. How about you? Staying out of trouble?"

I winced. "Not exactly. There's been—"

Before I could finish my sentence, someone wrenched Sam's phone from his hand. A woman's voice came through the line. "Is this your girlfriend? Hand her to me. I need to meet the woman who's stolen your heart."

After a little nauseating jostling, the screen focused on a female figure. I sucked in my breath. She was stunning, with cascades of long, black hair, smooth dark skin, and full lips.

"Hola," she said. Even her voice was alluring. "I am Isabella. You must be the famous photographer I've been hearing so much about."

"I…uh…hi. I'm Callie." Self-consciously, I ran a hand through my hair. I'd rolled out of bed before dawn and hadn't bothered with personal grooming, not realizing I'd be face-to-face with a woman worthy of a cover spot on the *Sports Illustrated* swimsuit edition. How had this woman acquainted herself with my boyfriend?

"Nice to meet you, Callie. We're all quite smitten with your Sam. But I'm sure we'll let you have him back." She giggled. "When we're done with him."

From the distance, Elyse's voice rang out. "Come on, Isabella. Get in the water with us."

Isabella wriggled her fingers at me. "Talk to you soon, Callie." She handed the phone back to Sam. He fumbled the handoff, and I caught sight of Isabella skipping off toward the water—in a bikini that barely covered her well-toned backside.

When Sam's face was back on the screen, I saw a blush beneath his tan. "That was Isabella," he said.

"So I heard."

"She's my parents' new next-door neighbor. Her daughter, Ana, is Elyse's age, and the girls have become fast friends. Elyse invited them to the beach with us."

Sam was prattling on as if someone had pressed his fast-forward button—a nervous habit he'd had since we were kids. I experienced a pang of petulant jealousy and told myself I was much too mature for such feelings.

Still, maybe I should find Colby and take a selfie with him. Maybe he'd even take off his shirt for the event.

I took a breath and gave Sam my sweetest smile. "Hey, it's great that you and Elyse are making new friends. That's just peachy."

He graced me with a sexy smile. "I wish you were here," he said in a husky voice. "The sun, the sand, the waves—the only thing that's missing is you."

The frost in my attitude thawed. "I miss you, too. This trip has been—"

"Dad, Grandma and Grandpa are here!" Elyse called. "They want you to help them carry the cooler."

He looked at me apologetically. "Call you later?"

"Sure. Enjoy the beach. And the neighbors."

He ignored the jab. "Love you, beautiful. Can't wait to have you in my arms again."

He disconnected, and I sighed. Woody licked my cheek. Carl meowed from his perch, then jumped on the dog's back. I laughed. How did the creatures always know what I needed? "You guys are the best," I said.

Just then, I heard a car outside. I scrambled to my knees and looked out the window in time to see it pull into a parking spot. Three people got out and started walking across the yard. I recognized Polly and Martin, but not the person who accompanied them. He was a broad-shouldered man in a tan suit and polished loafers, and from my second-story window, I made out a bald spot on the crown of his scalp. Polly and Martin had said they'd inform Eleanor's husband of her death, but this man seemed too young to be Allen Simonson, despite the thinning hair.

Then it occurred to me—this must be Eleanor's stepson. Gordon, wasn't it?

The three of them stopped halfway to the stable just as Chief Wade waddled out, tugging at the waistband of his pants. The stepson stood ramrod straight and didn't budge. His body language didn't say grief to me. No, he looked furious. I'd bet money that a confrontation loomed. And I wanted to be there for it.

12

I tucked Carl into his backpack carrier and draped my camera around my neck. That way, I could profess to be heading outside for the hike rather than positioning myself to snoop. With Woody at my heels, I stepped into the alcove as Lynn and Renata came out of their room. Lynn held her phone, and Renata was pulling her hair into a ponytail.

"The mayor and his wife are back," I said. "And there's a man with them."

Lynn nodded. "We saw. It's got to be the stepson. I don't know why they'd bring him here, but from the look of him, things could get chippy."

We hurried down the stairs and onto the front deck. Mom and Tonya stood near the rocking chairs, and Valerie, Haley, and Georgia, the head housekeeper we'd met on our arrival, gathered to the side. At the foot of the deck's stairs, Summer and Jessica huddled next to Ryll. Carmen had reappeared, no doubt summoned by the spirits, and she stood on Ryll's other side. Colby and the two young ranch hands pretended to busy themselves across the yard. Guess I didn't need to worry about being perceived as a snoop. Everyone wanted in on this action.

The three new arrivals waited about ten yards from the stable. Polly and Martin kept their eyes on the door, refusing to look at any of us. Gordon Simonson rocked back on his heels, his hands tucked into the pockets of his expensive-looking tailored suit. Though he'd appeared angry earlier, now he projected a calm and collected demeanor. Chief Wade approached, with Jake a step behind him, and spoke to Gordon in a voice so low we couldn't make out the words. The chief gestured toward Ryll and Carmen, and Gordon glared at the two women.

Then three men emerged from the stable, rolling a stretcher with a black body bag toward a van marked CORONER. Suddenly, Gordon threw back his head and wailed. He stumbled toward the stretcher and threw himself across it. "Oh, Mother!" he cried. "Mother. Mother."

The skepticism on Mom's and Tonya's faces echoed mine: this was a piece of theater we were observing. So far, Gordon had run the gamut of emotions: from anger to calm to exaggerated grief. I'd seen soap opera actors with less range.

Polly hurried to Gordon and pulled him off the body, wrapping her arms around him as he buried his face in his hands. Chief Wade averted his gaze, embarrassed by the display.

After a brief pause, the two coroner's assistants continued the trek to the van, while the third man—the coroner, I figured—approached the chief and spoke to him. Gordon pulled away from Polly and dropped his hands to his sides as he listened. The chief nodded and spat tobacco juice into his cup.

Briefly, the coroner's lips twisted with revulsion. He turned to Ryll and raised a hand. "Sorry about all this, Ryll," he said.

She nodded. "I know, Mickey. It's a horrible situation."

The coroner trudged off toward the van, shoulders rounded. By this point, Gordon had abandoned his grief and worked himself into a frenzy. He stormed toward the lodge, planting himself in front of Ryll and Carmen.

Jake stepped closer, ready to intervene if things took a violent turn.

Chief Wade didn't budge.

Carmen's placid expression never faltered, which further enraged Gordon. His face turned an interesting shade of dark purple, and he pointed a stubby finger at her. "You did this." He cocked a thumb over his shoulder to Polly and Martin. "They told me you threatened my mother, and now she's dead. You killed her. Or you had your disgusting snakes do it."

"Stepmother," Carmen said.

"What?" Gordon blustered.

"You said mother. But she was your stepmother."

"Are you correcting my word choice when my father's wife—a woman I cared for—has been killed?"

Carmen didn't respond. Instead, she closed her eyes and lifted her face to the sky. Her lips moved in a silent mantra.

Gordon stomped his foot and turned his ire on Ryll. "As for you and your ridiculous Moonglow Ranch, your days here are numbered. My father and I will sue you for…for criminal negligence. It won't be long before the whole place belongs to us."

Ryll recoiled, and Carmen's chanting turned audible. Her words sounded like a mixture of a prayer and a song, though the lyrics were indecipherable—almost as if she were talking in tongues. Gordon paled, and fear flashed across his face. He stumbled backward, distancing himself from the psychic.

After a moment, Carmen's strange chanting stopped. "I cannot see everything. Not yet," she said. "The spirits will direct me to the answer when they see fit. What they have told me is this: the murderer stands among us."

We all froze for a moment, as if the spirits Carmen referenced had pressed a pause button. Woody sat motionless at my heel. Carl was quiet in his carrier.

Then, with an almost tangible whoosh, the world started moving again. Gordon shook himself as if waking from a dream and squared his shoulders. "I don't know what witchcraft you're up to, Carmen, but it won't stop the inevitable. My father and I are powerful men, and we're coming for you."

He turned to the police chief. "I want that woman arrested. Today."

"Which one? Carmen or Ryll?" Polly asked.

"Either. Both. I don't care. Just get it done."

Without waiting for a response, he stormed across the yard to Martin's car. He got into the passenger seat, slammed the door, and faced straight ahead, arms crossed like a sulky child.

Martin shifted from one foot to another, not meeting anyone's eyes. Polly scanned the group with a smug expression, then marched to the car. Martin followed, and a moment later, the three of them left the ranch.

The coroner's van departed just after them. Chief Wade lingered for a moment, watching the vehicles depart. Then he sidled over to Carmen and drew himself to full height. His belly bulged, causing a button to finally pop off his shirt and land at his feet. *Bingo*, I thought.

The chief ignored the button and looked at Carmen. "I expect to have you in custody before the sun sets."

Beside me, Lynn bristled. "On what evidence? You can't take a person into custody because some rich man's son orders you to."

"She could sue you for false arrest," Summer said.

"Or harassment," Renata added.

"Besides," Lynn said, "you told us earlier you believed the death was an accident."

The police chief looked confused for a moment, then scowled. "Yeah, well, I'll wait for Mickey's findings, but as soon as he rules this a murder, I'm coming for you. Until that time, all I got to say is, don't leave town."

He started toward his car. Even though we'd all decided to stay anyway, Jessica raised a fist. "Listen, mister, I watch enough *Dateline* to know you can't demand that."

Chief Wade didn't turn back. He wiggled his fingers and whistled. "Let's go, Jake."

The young officer scooped up the errant button and started after his boss. I jogged to catch up with him. "Don't you get tired of him talking to you like that?" I whispered. "We teach people how to treat us, Officer. If you ever want the man to respect you, you'll need to stand up for yourself."

He hurried toward the car, glancing at me again over his shoulder. Maybe I'd planted a seed in the poor boy's mind.

"Good for you," Tonya said. "The chief treats that kid like a dog."

Woody huffed in response, and Tonya patted his head. "Sorry, Chief. Wrong analogy. In your world, treated like a dog is something to strive for."

He licked her hand to indicate he accepted her apology. Meanwhile, I chewed a thumbnail as I watched Carmen gazing at the sky. Was she right? Had Eleanor indeed been murdered—and, more important, was the killer among us?

13

After the lawmen left, the spectators scattered. My friends went upstairs to finish getting ready for the hike. Colby and the ranch hands headed off toward the corral. The lodge employees returned to their duties, and Carmen headed off to Crystal Clear, her psychic shop in town.

Mom, Tonya, and I were already dressed for the hike, so we sat in the rockers on the deck. By mutual unspoken agreement, we put aside talk of murder. Hummingbirds fluttered around the feeder near the stairs. Woody pounced after a chipmunk he had no intention of catching.

"Where's Lydia?" I asked Tonya. "She keeps missing the action."

Tonya rolled her eyes. "She decided to join us on the hike, so she went up to change. I expect she'll show up dressed in business-casual attire."

Mom cleared her throat. "Tonya, far be it for me to give unsolicited advice…" Tonya and I looked at each other, trying to stifle a giggle.

"I heard that, girls," Mom said. "Anyway, I know you've had a tumultuous relationship with your mother over the years…"

"Tumultuous I'll give you. But *relationship* is a stretch."

Mom nodded sympathetically. "It's true your mother wasn't there for you in the ways you would have liked. But Tonya, at least she was there. And she's here now. Doesn't that say something?"

Tears welled in Tonya's eyes. Mom leaned over and touched my friend's cheek. "You've built a wall around your heart, dear, and I understand that. Truly I do. But life is short, honey. I'd hate for you to be left with regrets. You'll never have the mother you dreamed of, perhaps, but you can try to accept this one as she is. She loves you the best way she knows how. And here you are on the precipice of a new life with David. Wouldn't you like to start it with forgiveness in your heart?"

Tonya's tears spilled over, and Mom wiped them away with her thumb. I marveled at my mother—so compassionate and wise. She could be so caring and tender, but still know when to call you out. My heart swelled with love and gratitude. I knew there'd been times I'd taken my parents for granted. Now, I vowed never to let that happen again.

Tonya sniffled. "Jeez, I already forgave David for sending her here. How much absolution can one woman be expected to give?" My best friend leaned back in her rocker and sighed. "Maggie, you've been more of a mother to me than Lydia ever was. I don't know how to have a relationship with her. But I respect you. If you say I should try, I will."

"Let go of expectations and past hurts, dear. Easier said than done, I know. But how does one eat an elephant?"

"One bite at a time," I said.

As the three of us chuckled, Lydia stepped onto the deck. She wore white pocket shorts that hugged her hips, a tight pink t-shirt, a wide-brimmed cheetah print safari hat, a leather sling bag, Versace sunglasses, and hiking boots that probably cost more than my townhouse. To her credit, the boots didn't sport heels. Her makeup was impeccable. I couldn't believe the woman was in her late sixties. Though I'd never say it to Tonya, I realized I was looking at an image of my best friend in twenty-five years.

"You're wearing actual hiking clothes," Tonya said,

sounding genuinely surprised.

"Well, you said we were going on a hike."

"Yes, but…Never mind." She shot a glance at my mother. "I'm happy you decided to join us, Lydia. Mom."

Lydia's face wreathed into a broad smile. "Me, too, TeeTee. What fun we'll have, tramping through the wilderness, risking life and limb in the forest primeval. I have my canteen and my snacks, and I'm ready for adventure."

Tires crunched on the gravel road, and a red Jeep Wrangler pulled into the parking area. Audra jumped out and grabbed a backpack the size of a Volkswagen from the back seat.

"Who's that?" Lydia asked.

"Audra," Tonya said. "She led us on the horseback ride yesterday. Guess she's our trail guide on today's hike."

Lydia's pink-lipsticked mouth turned down in disappointment. "I assumed our guide would be that strapping cowboy I met yesterday—Colby, was it?"

Tonya gave a little snort. "And there she is, the mother I remember so well."

"What?" Lydia said. "I just like some nice scenery on my hikes."

***

Ten minutes later, we were all finally ready to set out. Ryll came onto the deck to make sure we had water, hats, and sunscreen. Valerie and Haley distributed box lunches. I'd tucked Carl into his carrier, and Woody stood at attention, awaiting the adventure. We started across the property toward the forest path. As we passed the corral, Colby trotted over to meet us. Lydia adjusted her shorts and peeked over the rim of her sunglasses admiringly.

Colby took off his cowboy hat and bowed. "Have a good hike, ladies."

Lydia giggled. Tonya gave her the side eye. This relationship fix might take longer than Mom hoped.

"Thank you," Audra said. "And you have a good time busting broncos, or whatever it is you're doing today."

Colby's laugh was warm and seductive. His blue eyes twinkled. "Would you care to bust a few with me when you return?" he asked.

She smacked his arm. "My mama would tan my hide. She warned me to stay away from boys like you."

He gave her a mock pout, and she strolled toward the start of the path. Colby turned his gaze to Lydia. "You're looking fetching today, Mrs.…."

"Ms.," she said. "But please, call me Lydia."

"Lydia, then." He smiled. "See you around the ranch."

He took off back toward the corral, with Lydia's eyes glued to his tight-fitting jeans. "That cowboy is one prime hunk of man," she said breathily.

The dirt path that led through the trees was narrow at first, forcing us to walk single file. For the first twenty minutes, we didn't speak much—just listened to the birds chirping and boots crunching across fallen pine needles. Sunbeams pierced the thick branches, dappling the ground like sequins. I took a deep breath, letting the clean, crisp air fill my lungs.

The path widened, and we continued on in pairs. Mom and I walked side by side behind Tonya and Lydia, and we all chatted about light topics such as the ranch, the weather, the healthy food.

"Well," Lydia said, "the landscape is divine. Especially the human kind back at the corral."

"He's thirty years younger than you, Mother," Tonya said.

"Age is mind over matter, dear. If neither of us minds, it doesn't matter."

I chuckled, and my mom grinned. Tonya, though, had clearly had enough. "Audra," she called to our guide, who walked a few feet ahead of us.

Audra looked at us over her shoulder. "Everything okay?"

"We're fine," Tonya said. "I just have a quick question: are you and Colby Trent an item?"

"An item?"

"She wants to know if you two are dating," I translated.

Audra guffawed. "No way. I wasn't kidding when I said Mama would jerk a knot in my tail. Colby is a flirt, and cute, so I don't mind flirting back once in a while. But he has no interest in me. Trust me on that."

I frowned. "Why not? You're outdoorsy, in great shape—seems like you could run rings around him physically. And you're cute, too."

Jessica burst out laughing. "Callahan Cassidy, if you weren't dating Sam, I'd think you were hitting on this woman."

I felt myself blush, but Audra grinned. "I'll take the compliment, thanks. But looks and fitness aren't the issue with Colby. It's…" She rubbed her thumb against her fingers. "Let's just say he's into older women with nice, plump bank accounts."

Lydia's face brightened. Tonya's darkened.

"Anyway, here's our first stop," Audra said. "I think you'll be impressed. We'll break here for fifteen minutes. Drink some water, maybe eat a snack. The next leg of the hike will take us about an hour, so rest up."

Ahead of us, the branches drooped across the end of the path, like an arch leading to paradise. When we passed beneath, we emerged into a broad, grassy meadow. At the center was the lake I'd seen yesterday on our horseback ride. The water was robin's egg blue, and the sun sparkled across it like miniature diamonds. A smattering of fuzzy clouds reflected on its surface. A gentle breeze rustled through the tall grasses. A hawk glided above us, occasionally dropping to the water's surface.

"Ahh," Mom said simply.

"Couldn't have said it better myself," I said.

Woody whined until I released Carl from his carrier. I pulled out two small bowls and filled them with water. The two of them lapped at it for a few seconds before scampering off to cavort in the meadow.

Audra came up next to me and frowned. "Do you feel comfortable letting them run off like that? What if they don't come back?"

"They will," I said. "Years ago, I found Woody living on the streets, and we've been together ever since. Carl came to live with us after life as a stray. Now, they stay because they choose to. We're a family. We'd never abandon each other."

"Okay, then." She smiled and watched them for a moment before joining the rest of the group a few yards away. I pulled out my camera and took a dozen shots of the lake, the mountains, the wildflowers. The sun floated midway between the horizon and straight overhead, providing challenging lighting. But I was up to the task. Satisfied that at least a few of my shots would translate into canvases worthy of display, I sat on a boulder and relaxed as I watched the creatures gallivant.

Lynn joined me, resting her elbows on her knees as she gazed across the meadow. "Beautiful, isn't it?"

"Gorgeous," I agreed.

We let a few seconds of silence pass. I was certain we were thinking about the same thing, but neither of us wanted to broach the subject.

Jessica walked over and plopped down on an adjacent stone. "The rest of them over there are singing the praises of meditation. We're already scheduled for a session this afternoon, for crying out loud. Do we have to worship it all day? Please tell me you two are thinking about something more interesting. Like how to catch a killer."

Lynn smiled. "How'd you guess?"

"I'm smart that way. So, are you two prepared to label Eleanor's death an accident?"

Neither of us hesitated before shaking our heads. "No way," Lynn said. "Too many incongruities. The locked stall door. The syringe. I'm pretty sure even that lunkhead police chief doesn't really believe it's an accident."

"He was practically prepared to handcuff Carmen and haul her off to jail," I said.

"He was trying to keep Gordon Simonson happy," Lynn said. "Or Gordon's father, anyway. From what I can tell, Allen Simonson is the source of all the power around here. The mayor quivers at any mention of him."

"Why do you suppose he wasn't on the scene?"

"Before you came out, I heard Gordon tell the mayor his father was en route home from a business trip."

We pondered that for a moment, then Jessica said, "You don't think Carmen committed the murder…?"

Lynn shrugged. "Can't say. For one thing, we don't know the cause of death yet. As for Carmen, she gives off a weird vibe, but that could be a façade. I mean, don't you have to come across as mysterious to be a psychic?"

I couldn't get a read on Carmen, either. She might be a gifted actress. On the other hand, she'd revealed a secret Tonya hadn't disclosed, and I still couldn't figure out how she'd pulled that off.

"Callie, you don't really believe she can see the future or read people's thoughts, do you?" Lynn asked.

I wrinkled my forehead. "Of course not. Don't be ridiculous. She's just very good at playing her role. That doesn't make her a murderer, though."

Lynn drummed her fingers on her knee. "We need a little background on the woman. I'd like to know her history, where she came from."

"Chief Wade told you to stay out of it. Threatened you, in fact."

"Pish. If I took a step back every time some man told me to, I'd be drowning in the Pacific Ocean right now."

Jessica and I grinned. Lynn was a woman after our own hearts.

Audra's voice rang out. "Five minutes, everyone."

I scanned the meadow and spotted Woody's tail pointing up from the tall grass. I gave a loud whistle, and the creatures came running. Well, Woody came running. Carl sauntered over as if it was his idea.

After tossing them treats, I eased Carl back into his carrier and slipped it over my shoulders. When I reached down to pat Woody's head, a movement in the grass a few feet away caught my eye.

It was a slithering movement. One I'd seen just this morning. "Eek!" I squealed.

Audra dashed over, and I pointed a shaky finger toward the edge of the path.

She spotted the snake and crouched to examine it. Feeling a little braver with Audra between me and the serpent, I leaned in, too.

The snake was yellow-brown with a bit of amber in its pattern, and at least four feet long. It was the image of the snake I'd seen in the stable. For a crazy moment, I wondered if the snake had pursued me with malice in his reptilian heart.

Woody edged forward for a closer look, but I snatched him by the collar. "No sir. If that snake bit you, there's no way I'd be able to carry you back to the lodge."

Audra rose and brushed her hands on her pants. "Well, ladies, you've now met one of our Colorado bullsnakes. He looks intimidating, but he's non-venomous and nothing to be afraid of. In fact, he's one of the good guys. He helps keep our rodent population in check, so we owe him our appreciation."

Hmm. If this guy was non-venomous, and if—as I believed—he was the same type of snake in the stable, that eliminated snakebite as a potential cause of death.

Audra clapped her hands. "Gather your things, everyone, because we're pushing ahead. But a word of caution: this fella isn't alone out here. So watch your step. Their bite wouldn't kill you, but I doubt you'd enjoy it."

14

orty-five minutes later, we'd hiked to the top of what Audra referred to as a hill. From the way my lungs burned and my calves screamed, I'd have characterized it as Pikes Peak. But the reward was worth the effort. The view was spectacular. Colorful wildflowers blanketed the meadow. In the shadow of the mountains, a herd of mule deer grazed peacefully. Jaybirds dipped and soared above us, chasing the puffy clouds across the sky. Picture perfect—especially for a photographer.

After I'd released Carl from the backpack carrier, poured water for the creatures and gulped some myself, I strolled across the meadow and took pictures. When I returned from my impromptu photo shoot, blankets had been spread in a circle on the ground, each with three or four box lunches waiting for hungry hikers.

"Nice of you to join us," Tonya said. "I thought you said no work this week."

I swung an arm toward the gorgeous landscape. "This doesn't feel like work. Besides, a girl's gotta eat."

"Perfect," Audra said. "Because it's time for lunch."

I joined Mom, Tonya, and Lydia on a blanket. Half expecting to find a green mystery concoction, I peered cautiously inside my lunchbox, only to be greeted with a normal-looking turkey and avocado sandwich on whole grain bread, fruit salad, chips, and even a cookie.

"Chips?" I held one up to Summer. "I'm not complaining, but what happened to healthy eating?"

"Honey, those are baked sweet potato chips," she responded. "Good for the heart. Quit wrinkling your nose and try them."

I sniffed the chip and took a tentative nibble. It didn't rival my usual fatty, salty brand, but it wasn't bad. Ignoring Summer's I-told-you-so expression, I ate another.

We'd worked up an appetite on the hike, so we ate in agreeable silence for a few minutes. As I chewed, I scanned the ground for signs of my snake stalker, which inevitably led my thoughts to the stable. The body. The murder.

After I'd devoured my sandwich and chips and started on the fruit, I cleared my throat. "So, Audra, why don't we address the elk in the meadow?"

She gave me a quizzical look, clearly not understanding my play on the elephant-in-the-room reference. I didn't bother to explain. "I'm sure you heard about Eleanor Simonson's death."

Audra dropped her eyes. "Yes. How sad."

"Did you know her?"

"Of course. Everyone in town knew Eleanor. She made sure of it. As did her stepson."

"Not the nicest people?" Lynn asked.

"You can say that again." Audra shifted on her blanket. "But I shouldn't be talking trash about a woman who just died. Mama'd be hotter than day-old road kill if she heard me."

"We'll keep your confidence," Lynn said. "Right, everyone?"

"What's said on the mountain stays on the mountain," Jessica said.

"We only want to figure out if there's anything we can do to…well, to mitigate the fallout," I said. "This could destroy Ryll and Fritz's business before it officially starts. Not to mention the danger to Carmen, since Gordon is demanding her arrest."

Audra's jaw dropped. "Oh no! I didn't know they were calling it a murder. And Gordon is blaming Carmen? Impossible!"

"Sounds like you know Carmen pretty well," I said.

"Enough to believe she's not capable of killing anyone. She's devoted to helping and healing. I've been to see her several times—for psychic readings, tarot, and healing meditation." She pulled a silver chain from inside her shirt, revealing a shiny blue crystal. "From the moment she gave me this—well, sold it to me—my life changed for the better. This crystal keeps me calm and centered."

Summer smiled serenely, but I was skeptical. How on earth could a rock hold power over someone's life? Still, now wasn't the time to debate the actuality of psychic powers. "Last night, before she, well, you know, Eleanor indicated she wanted Carmen run out of town. Do you know why?"

"From what I heard, Eleanor thinks a new age shop damages the character of the town." She winced. "*Thought*, I should say. She wanted Carmen out, and she usually got what she wanted. Until today."

We were all silent for a beat, but I couldn't let the opportunity to ferret out more information pass. "What was it she wanted most?" I asked. When Audra hesitated, I added, "Whatever you can tell us about her could be useful in clearing Carmen's name and helping to save Moonglow Ranch."

Audra studied her fingernails. "I mean, it's not as if Eleanor confided in me or anything. Mama and I are much too low on the totem pole to move in her circle. In fact, I wouldn't say the Simonsons were friends with anyone in town—except maybe Martin and Polly. Not even them, really. Eleanor just used them, far as I could tell. As mayor, Martin has a little power, and Eleanor manipulated Polly into pulling his strings."

"How do you mean?" Lynn asked.

"Oh, if Eleanor wanted the town council to change a

regulation, she just told Polly about it. She and Polly saw to it that Martin made it happen. Things like that."

"Sounds as if Eleanor ran the town, then," I said. "Where does her husband fit into the picture?"

Audra snorted. "Allen's barely in the picture here in Mustang. Never home. Rumor has it the marriage was on the ropes. We heard he was having an affair, and Eleanor's, um, relationship with a certain cowboy was common knowledge. The only duct tape holding the marriage together was how much money splitting up would cost."

Aha! That confirmed my early suspicions about a relationship between Eleanor and Colby. But while marital troubles might explain Eleanor's temper, I still didn't understand why she'd directed her ire at the Bauers.

"Audra, Eleanor seemed to have it in for Ryll and Fritz," I said. "What was her problem with them?"

She shook her head. "Eleanor wanted Moonglow Ranch to fail. She got into the mayor's ear and made it clear she wouldn't rest until the Bauers were out of business."

Summer bristled. "But why? My aunt and uncle are the nicest people, and that ranch is their life's dream. What harm were they doing Eleanor Simonson?"

"It wasn't them personally." Audra wrinkled her nose. "Keep in mind, I'm only repeating what I've heard. Mama's done some bookkeeping for the Simonsons, and she's friendly with a few of their staff, so she gets the scuttlebutt. The story goes that Eleanor was quite an equestrian when she was younger. Her daddy paid for lessons and gave her a horse. She loved that time in her life. So when she and Allen bought their place in Mustang, she figured she'd recapture the happiness of her youth by getting some horses of her own."

Audra took a sip from her thermos before continuing. "But when she broached the subject with Allen, he refused. Apparently, he didn't want..." She made air quotes with her fingers. "...'nasty, smelly beasts' anywhere near his home. That's when Eleanor began plotting to get her hands on the Bauers' property. She figured Allen couldn't object if the stable and the horses were housed on the adjacent property. And as a bonus, she planned on keeping Colby on as her own personal stud—er, ranch manager. She made an offer to Ryll and Fritz, but as you can guess, they declined. Eleanor was livid. She was so used to getting what she wanted. So she began to plot against them."

It was all making sense now. If Eleanor could exercise her influence over Polly and Martin to get the county to deny the guest ranch license, Ryll and Fritz would find themselves in dire financial straits and be forced to sell. Eleanor could scoot in the back door and snatch up the property.

But something else Audra had said niggled in my brain. Eleanor had been *quite an equestrian*. My memory flashed on the syringe we'd found near her body. Could Eleanor have known enough about horses to inject them and make them sick temporarily without causing permanent damage? Surely the woman hadn't been that black-hearted.

Mom clapped her hands. "Enough talk of death and doom. May I remind everyone that we're here to celebrate our bride-to-be?"

I winced. Mom was right. Eleanor's murder had already cast enough of a shadow over our week-long party. Time to put it aside.

"You're right, Mrs. Cassidy," Audra agreed. "On that note, I have a surprise."

She dug around in her backpack, brought out a stack of plastic wine glasses, and went around the circle distributing them. Then she took a bottle of champagne from an insulated carrier, popped the cork, and filled our glasses with the bubbly liquid.

"I suppose this is tomato-beet-spinach champagne or some such," I muttered.

"No, but it's brut—low sugar and low calorie," Audra said. I sighed.

When everyone had champagne, Audra beckoned Tonya to join her at the center of the blanket circle. "Tonya, from all of us at Moonglow Ranch, congratulations. May your marriage be a long and happy one."

We raised our glasses in a toast, then took a sip. The dry champagne made my throat tingle, and the bubbles tickled my nose. Who cared if it was low sugar?

"Now," Audra said, "I'm told Callie will say a few words."

I got to my feet and stood next to Tonya. Ryll had prepared me for this weeks ago, so I had my monologue memorized.

"I'm saving the good speech for the wedding reception, but here are my second-string words of wisdom. Marriage is a sacred event, a beautiful burden and a blessing. At least, so I'm told, never having entered into the institution myself."

"Your day's coming," Jessica called out.

"No doubt about it," Summer added.

"Yes, well, we'll see." I turned back to Tonya. "My dear friend, heart of my heart, soul of my soul, despite my rocky start regarding your relationship with David, I've come to believe you two are meant to be together. You'll make each other incredibly, madly, deliriously happy. But through it all, I hope you know that I'll always be here for you, smooth seas or rough, sunshine or storms." I gestured to the women surrounding us, all smiling up at Tonya from their blankets. Our beloved crew. "We all will. A life partner is a wonderful thing. But don't forget, we were your life partners first."

"But that doesn't mean we'll be chipping in for your wedding," Lynn said.

"Or moving in to your house," Renata added.

"And that's a good thing for all of you," I said. "Because this woman snores."

Tonya smacked my arm, and I pulled her into a tight embrace. Mom lifted her glass. "To the bride," she said.

"To the bride," everyone repeated. Woody barked joyfully, and Carl added a contented purr.

As Tonya and I moved to resume our spots on the blanket, Lydia rose. "As mother of the bride, I'd like to say a few words, too."

Tonya looked uncomfortable, but she stayed put. I sat next to Mom as Lydia put an arm around Tonya's waist and looked at the group. "No mother could ask for a better daughter. Beautiful, smart, talented—my baby is the total package. And now she's found the man of her dreams." She paused and gazed at her daughter. "TeeTee, I haven't been around much, and I'm not the best mother you could have had. But darling, I love you, and I'm so very proud of you."

She hugged Tonya then. Over her mother's shoulder, my friend's face reflected her surprise—and a touch of pleasure.

When the clapping was done, Audra said, "All right, time to pack up and head out. My instructions were to have you back at the lodge no later than four."

"We need to prepare for tonight's meditation session," Summer said. Jessica rolled her eyes. Summer nudged her in the ribs. "What? You love my meditation sessions."

"Of course I do." Jessica gave Summer a sweet smile.

Audra went around the circle again, collecting trash in a reusable bag that read, Leave Nothing Behind. We shook out the blankets and rolled them up, returning them to her oversized backpack. Carl had made his way into his carrier on his own. "Good kitty," I said. He responded with a contemptuous glare. "Forgive me. I seem to have forgotten about your disdain of condescending praise."

15

Two hours later, we emerged from the forest and made our way toward the corral, where a half dozen horses gathered around a metal feeder munching on hay.

"Looks as if they have their appetites back," Renata said.

Summer nodded. "Aunt Ryll said they've been rebounding fast."

The image of the syringe beside Eleanor's body popped into my mind again. I suspected someone had injected the horses with a substance that caused their temporary stomach problems, but how could I know for sure? I wondered if the police chief had even bothered to send the syringe in for testing.

As we drew closer to the stable, raised voices drifted from around the corner—Ryll and Fritz engaged in intense conversation. A few steps more and we could make out the words.

"I can't believe this happened," Fritz said. "I'm gone for a few hours and chaos breaks out."

"You're acting like it's somehow my fault," Ryll snapped.

"Of course not. But didn't I warn you it was a bad idea to have Carmen move onto the property in the first place? And for what it's worth, you've never hidden the fact that you despised Eleanor."

"That doesn't mean I wanted her dead," Ryll shot back. "And as for Carmen—"

We looked at each other. Summer cupped a hand to her mouth. "Yoo hoo, Aunt Ryll and Uncle Fritz! We're back!"

As we rounded the corner, the two of them stepped away from each other and plastered fake smiles on their faces.

"Perfect timing!" Ryll said. "Valerie and Haley just brought out the afternoon snacks."

"How was the hike?" Fritz asked.

"Lovely," Mom said. "Beautiful scenery and the perfect amount of exercise."

"We did see a snake, though," I added.

Audra chuckled. "Callie faced down a treacherous bullsnake. Thank goodness we escaped."

"Well, I'm glad you enjoyed yourselves," Fritz said. "Now, if you'll excuse me, I have a ranch to tend. Enjoy the afternoon." He shot a worried look at Ryll before striding into the stable.

"I need to run, too," Audra said. "Thank you for being such energetic and cooperative hikers. I'll be seeing you again later in the week."

We thanked Audra and said our goodbyes. Ryll gave us an apologetic smile. "Sorry you stumbled into our…discussion, ladies. As you can imagine, we've both been under a lot of stress. Our friend Mickey, the county coroner, just called with news. He's ruling Eleanor's death suspicious."

"It wasn't the snake bite that killed her, I guess," I said.

She shook her head. "He said the puncture wounds occurred post-mortem, and the snake that inflicted them was non-venomous."

I flicked a bead of sweat from my temple. Murder I could handle, but all this talk of snakes nauseated me. "What does the coroner believe happened?"

After a brief hesitation, she said, "I doubt Chief Wade wants me sharing this, but I no longer care what that man wants. He hasn't bothered to contact us since this morning. If Mickey hadn't called…" She waved. "Anyway, Mickey said the cleft on Eleanor's forehead—the one probably caused by Spirit's hoof—likely occurred after she died as well. It's a different injury he believes caused Eleanor's death—one we couldn't see because she was lying on her back. He's calling in the medical examiner to perform the autopsy, but Mickey's preliminary conclusion is that Eleanor was the victim of blunt force trauma to the back of her head. He believes someone struck her with a heavy object, knocking her unconscious. The blow caused a subdural hematoma that resulted in a quick death."

"So she didn't regain consciousness before she died?" I asked.

Ryll stared at me. "He didn't say, and I didn't think to ask. He just told me it didn't take her long to…to…"

Her voice trailed off, and we fell silent, visualizing how the terrible scene must have played out. A couple of things I knew none of us could picture, though: the weapon used and, more importantly, who wielded it.

Ryll drew a breath. "That's all we know at the moment. I shared the information because you deserve to know what's happening, but I hope you'll be able to put it aside so we can keep to our program. I'm sure you're hot and tired from your hike, so if you'll head to the pergola, the overhead fans will cool you off while you enjoy iced tea and snacks. Afterwards, perhaps you'd like to go to your rooms to shower. Summer's meditation session will be at five-thirty in the living room, followed by dinner."

We smiled and thanked her and strolled off to the pergola—everyone but Lydia, that is. She declined the offer of snacks in favor of a visit to the corral, where Colby and the ranch hands were filling water troughs. Tonya shook her head as she watched her mother go.

I ate a few of the snacks—melon prosciutto skewers and cucumber sushi—and poured myself a glass of mint iced tea. Then I told the group I was taking the creatures inside for food and water of their own. The three of us headed through the lodge and into the kitchen.

Valerie stood at the food prep island chopping vegetables, while Haley rummaged through the refrigerator. Georgia, the head housekeeper, sat at the table sipping from a coffee mug.

"Hi," I said. "Is it okay if I feed Woody and Carl? I promise we'll stay out of your way."

"Of course," Valerie said. "You're not in the way. We'd enjoy the company." With a hand holding a silver bladed knife, she gestured toward the table. "You've met Georgia, haven't you? Georgia, this is world-famous photographer Callahan Cassidy."

I set my glass on the table and waved. "World famous is a stretch. I own a little gallery in Rock Creek Village, that's all. And please, call me Callie."

"I've heard about you, Callie." Georgia's voice was smoky and pleasant, like a lounge singer's. "Welcome to Moonglow Ranch. We have stunning views around here. Perhaps you'll make us famous."

I grinned, then stooped to release Carl from his carrier. He stretched, licked a paw, and began grooming his face and ears. I found the pet food in the mudroom and filled their bowls. Woody gobbled the food as if it was his first meal ever. Even Carl deigned to take a few delicate bites. Fresh air gave us all voracious appetites.

While the creatures indulged, I joined Georgia at the table. "Would you like some coffee?" she asked.

"No, thanks," I said, pointing to my glass. "Iced tea hits the spot after a long hike."

Haley carried a coffee pot to the table and refilled Georgia's mug. While the woman added cream and sugar and stirred, I studied her. She had round cheeks, red lips, and the most stunning head of white curls I'd ever seen. Age lines etched themselves in her ivory skin, and her rough, powerful hands painted the picture of someone who didn't shy away from hard work.

When she finished stirring her coffee, she tapped her spoon on the rim of the cup. "You and your friends came for a bridal shower, but you've gotten more excitement than you bargained for."

"Now, Georgia," Valerie said. "Don't be hammering our visitor with your gossipy tongue. Let her be."

"Humph." Georgia lifted her chin. "I'm only making conversation. It's not as if Callie is oblivious to what happened. In fact," she added, "you're the one who found her, am I right?"

"I'm afraid that's true."

"I heard it's not the first dead body you've discovered."

I shifted in my seat. "Well, I suppose that's true, too."

Georgia leaned back and took a sip from her mug. "Eleanor Simonson. Woman like her dead in a pile of manure. A fitting end, if you ask me."

Haley fumbled her fork, and it clattered to the floor.

"Georgia!" Valerie hissed. "That's enough."

She shrugged. "What? I'm just saying what everyone else is thinking. Our guests got a taste of Eleanor's nastiness. Isn't that right?"

I thought back to Eleanor bursting into the living room, interrupting the palm reading event and yelling at Ryll and Fritz. Nastiness was a good way to describe it. "She didn't make the best first impression," I said. "Still, I wouldn't say she deserved what happened to her."

"Then you didn't know her. That woman rubbed everyone the wrong way, including her own husband. You know what they say about karma."

Woody finished eating then trotted over, curled up at my feet, and fell asleep. Carl jumped into my lap and watched Georgia with curious eyes.

Valerie and Haley were busy with dinner preparation. I didn't want to come across as nosy, but Georgia was a wellspring of information. How could I pass up the chance to question her?

"People hated her, huh?" I said, keeping my voice low.

"Oh, sugar, you have no idea. The Simonsons' housekeeper is one of my dearest friends, and the stories she's told me would curl your toes." She fanned herself. "They could write a soap opera about that woman's doings."

Georgia spent the next few minutes listing the people Eleanor had wronged—the town's grocer, contractors who'd done work on her house, Carmen. And she'd had several volatile run-ins with her stepson, Gordon.

"On top of that, the evil woman was determined to get Moonglow Ranch shut down. Eleanor Simonson was like a dog with a bone. When she wanted something, she didn't let go until she got it."

"She sounds unpleasant," I said.

"Ha. That's like saying a hurricane supplies a refreshing breeze."

Across the kitchen, Valerie cleared her throat. "All right, Georgia, let's dispense with the gossip. How do you think Ryll would feel if she overheard you?"

Georgia sighed. "Party pooper."

I got up and took my empty tea glass to the counter. Haley took it from me and put it in the dishwasher. I turned back to Georgia. "Just one more question," I said. "Why do you suppose Eleanor was in the stable in the middle of the night?"

Haley flicked her eyes toward Valerie. I had the feeling the young woman had something to add to the conversation, but didn't want to irritate her mother. I let it go. For now. Maybe later I could get the girl alone and pump her for information.

Or maybe I wouldn't need to. "Oh, that's easy," Georgia said with a wink. "She came for Colby. The two of them had been knocking boots for weeks."

Haley blushed. Valerie tossed a sponge at Georgia, smacking her in the arm with a wet thump.

"She asked!" Georgia said.

Then the door swung open and Ryll entered the kitchen. We froze. She squinted at us suspiciously. After a moment's silence, she said the guests had finished eating and gone upstairs, and she needed help clearing the leftover food and dishes.

Valerie, Haley, and Georgia followed her through the door. As the creatures and I left the kitchen and went upstairs, I considered everything I'd learned. The tidbit about Colby and Eleanor wasn't much of a shock, especially given what Audra had said about the cowboy's preference for older women and lust for money. Interesting that Eleanor had been killed just yards from Colby's quarters, though. Did that make him a suspect? And in light of the alleged affair, I also had to wonder about Eleanor's husband. Gordon had said his father was out of town, but how did we know that was true?

I felt an all-too-familiar surge of adrenaline. Now, if only I could figure out how to balance a murder investigation with a bridal shower.

16

For the next couple of hours, the bridal shower took precedence. Once we'd freshened up and dressed in stretchy pants and loose tops, we gathered in the living room, where Summer had arranged yoga cushions on the floor.

Forty-five minutes of deep breathing did little to achieve the goal of centering me in the present moment. I tried, I really did. But without my permission, my mind started creating a mental checklist of everything I needed to investigate. I wouldn't be able to do it alone—not if I wanted to make a success of Tonya's party, too. Thank goodness Lynn was here and the two of us could team up.

When at last the final chime tolled, everyone else appeared peaceful and relaxed, but I felt as if I'd consumed fourteen cups of coffee. My nerves jangled, and I realized from bitter experience that the only way I'd achieve serenity was through action. As we headed in to dinner, I pulled Lynn aside and made a date to talk later.

The meal passed in a haze. Around me, the others chattered and laughed, but I was so consumed with thoughts of murder that it was as if I was watching them on television in a silly sitcom. I wasn't even totally conscious of whatever healthy food I'd been served. As I poured myself a third glass of wine, Mom reached over and put a cautionary hand over my glass.

Dessert made an impression, though—lemon panna cotta with vodka blueberry syrup. I rolled the sweet delight over my tongue. For that moment, I was centered in the present.

When everyone completed the final sips from their glasses and swipes of their napkins, they rose from the table and ambled outside to relax around the firepit. When Lynn and I held back, Tonya ambled toward us, rubbing her hands together. "Ready to solve this thing?"

I lifted my palms. "What are you talking about?"

"Oh, please. I know that look. You're in investigation mode. And I want in."

I shook my head. "No way. The pall over your bridal shower is bad enough without you getting dragged into the sleazy details."

"Sleazy details are my life's pleasure, sugarplum. As you said, it's my bridal shower, and my wish should be your command. Besides, occupying my mind with crime will keep me from obsessing over Lydia and her escapades. And, of course, it'll make a great story."

Lynn and I looked at each other and shrugged. The three of us headed upstairs and closed ourselves in the room Tonya and I shared. Woody wagged at the sight of us, and even Carl appeared semi-happy.

I sat on my bed, while Tonya and Lynn sat across from me on Tonya's bed. First, we replayed the coroner's findings. Then I filled them in on what Georgia had told me about Colby and Eleanor, which earned me two sets of raised eyebrows.

"Now I'm really concerned about Lydia," Tonya said.

Lynn winced. "Well, not to make it worse, but I think we have to assume that Eleanor Simonson was murdered."

"I concur," I said, and Tonya nodded.

"But how do we prove it?" Lynn slapped a hand on the bed. "The fact that this town's police chief is being so self-important makes me furious. We don't know if he's even collected any evidence. We could do so much more if we worked as a team."

"At least you had me take pictures of the scene," I said. "Maybe they'll offer us a clue."

I retrieved my camera from the bag and turned it on, using Wi-Fi to upload the photos to my laptop. Then I squeezed in between Lynn and Tonya. Carl climbed onto my back to peer at the screen. We scrolled through shots of Eleanor lying on the stall floor and close ups of her forehead wound. If only I'd been able to get shots of the fatal injury…but we had no way of knowing. From this angle, I couldn't even see evidence of the wound to the back of her head. I sighed and clicked to a picture of the puckered puncture wounds on her calf and shuddered.

Then we got to the photo of the syringe lying near Eleanor's outstretched hand. Lynn tapped the screen. "I can't figure out how that fits in, but my gut tells me it's important."

I nodded in agreement. "Chief Wade must have sent it in to have the contents tested."

Lynn reached for her bag and pulled out a small legal pad and pen. "Surely he did. Something to check on."

I snapped my fingers. "Remember how Audra said Eleanor had once been an equestrian? She knew about horses. I've been wondering if she was injecting Ryll and Fritz's herd to make them sick."

"An interesting theory," Tonya said. "But why? What would she gain?"

Lynn added the question to her list. "Well, we know she wanted to stop the ranch from opening. Sidelining the horses might have been one step toward that goal."

"True," Tonya said. "But you know what that means. If Ryll and Fritz discovered what she was up to, it gives them motive."

I blew out a breath. "That seems excessive. If they caught her in the stall, why not just call the police?"

"Maybe it was an impulsive act," Lynn said. "They saw Eleanor preparing to injure a horse and went into protective mode."

A good point, but I wasn't ready to pin this on the Bauers. Too many other people had motives as well. "Let's start a suspect list. It'll help us organize our thoughts."

Lynn flipped the top page on her pad and titled the new page SUSPECTS. "First, we'll put Ryll and Fritz," she said. "Then Carmen, since Gordon is so insistent on her guilt."

"Remember, too, that Eleanor and Gordon both mentioned Carmen's snakes," Tonya added. "Could she have set one of her pets loose in the stall?"

Lynn raised her eyebrows. "Hmm. Definitely something to look into. Any thoughts on her possible motive?"

"Well, we heard Eleanor threaten to ruin her business and run her out of town," I said.

"That would do it." Lynn scribbled a few words on the notepad and looked up at us. "Okay, so we have Ryll, Fritz, and Carmen. Who else?"

Tonya stirred. "Based on the tidbits of gossip from Georgia, I'd say we need to add Colby." Did I hear enthusiasm in her voice?

Still, she wasn't wrong. "The proximity of his cabin to the stable would have made it easy for him to get in and out," I said. "I can't figure out a motive, though. Wouldn't he be derailing his own future gravy train?"

"It's something else to research," Lynn said, writing a note. She tapped the pen against her chin. "What about that Gordon character? He seems sketchy to me. One of those entitled silver spoon guys who'd go to any lengths to keep himself cushioned in the lap of luxury."

"And his reaction when he saw the body being wheeled out..." Tonya added.

"A fine performance," I said.

Lynn added Gordon's name to the list. "I don't know much about Allen Simonson, and according to Gordon, he wasn't even in town at the time of the murder. But the rumor about the Simonsons' troubled marriage means we at least need to confirm his alibi. After all, the spouse is the primary suspect in any murder case."

I chewed the inside of my cheek, thinking. "We're a little over our heads because we don't have background on any of the players."

"I can call Phil first thing in the morning," Tonya said, referring to her associate editor. "He has access to *The Gazette's* databases. I bet he can find time to look into Carmen's past—especially if I tell him he might get a story out of it. He can run a check on Colby, too." She tapped a finger against her lips. "Do you know their last names?"

"Colby's is Trent," I said, recalling my conversation with Georgia. "But I never heard Carmen's."

"How many psychics named Carmen can there be?"

"He could research Ryll and Fritz, too," I said with a pang of guilt. How would Summer react if she knew we were looking into her beloved aunt and uncle?

Tonya sensed my concern. "We might discover something that will help eliminate them as suspects."

Lynn dug inside her pocket and pulled out her phone. "Raul's been champing at the bit to get involved in this, pardon the horse pun. Let's get him on FaceTime. I'm sure he'd be happy to help us with Allen and Gordon Simonson."

FaceTime, eh? She couldn't just call or text him? I had a suspicion Lynn's ulterior motive involved getting a glimpse of her partner's face. I didn't blame her. With his olive complexion, deep brown eyes, and glossy black hair, Raul was nice to look at. Objectively speaking, of course.

The phone jangled twice, then Raul appeared on the screen. "Well, if it isn't my partner, the one who left me stranded on Boring Island while she finds herself immersed in a murder case. Calling to gloat?"

She grinned. "Naturally. And I have a couple of conspirators here to gloat alongside me."

Tonya and I pressed our cheeks in next to Lynn's face. "Hi, Raul," Tonya said.

"Evening, Detective Sanchez," I said. "Are you keeping everyone safe in Rock Creek Village?"

"You know it," he said. "Why, just today I jump-started a stranded tourist's car and lectured a twelve-year-old that stealing a treat from the Fudge Factory was just one step away from a life of crime."

Tonya and I waved and moved off the screen. "You may not see us, but we can still hear everything," I called. "No talking smack about us."

"Never," he said. "So, what's up, partner? Are you stymied? Need me to come to the ranch and take care of things?"

"Not on your life," Lynn said. "I've got this…" Tonya and I both cleared our throats. "Sorry. *We've* got this. We just need a hand with the grunt work, and you sprang to mind."

"Hardy har har," he said. "I'll be glad to help, assuming I can squeeze in your menial tasks between the menial tasks I'm already seeing to."

Lynn told him what we needed, and Raul whistled. "You're talking about Allen Simonson, the oil guy? The millionaire—wait, *billionaire*—who owns an entire block of downtown Denver, as well as his own jet?"

Lynn raised her eyebrows. "I mean, I realized he was well off, but—"

"Well off? Some detective you are, Clarke. Governor Crandall—you've heard of him, right?" Lynn rolled her eyes at his sarcasm. "He may be elected to the highest office in the state, but he has said that Allen Simonson holds more power. Behind the scenes, anyway."

"Then it shouldn't be too hard to research him," Lynn said. "Even for you."

"I don't know much about Allen's son." Raul ignored the jab just as she'd ignored his. Their casual teasing told me something about the ever-growing closeness of their relationship. "But I can dig into him. You want financial information? Social?"

"We'll leave it up to you to sift the wheat from the chaff," she said.

"Not that we're allowed any wheat here," I muttered.

Lynn smirked. "Just pass along whatever you think might be relevant. If possible, try to uncover Allen's schedule over the past day or two. Gordon says he was out of state yesterday, which would alibi him, but—"

"But a man who has his own jet isn't bound by a recorded schedule," Raul said. "Yeah, I'm on it." There was eagerness in his voice, the thrill of the hunt, and I identified with it. As much as I loved my quiet life running a village photo gallery, there was something about a murder investigation that got the adrenaline flowing in a way nothing else could. That sensation was the only thing I missed from my old life as an investigative photojournalist.

Lynn and Raul chatted for another minute or two before disconnecting. I got the sense their sign-off might have been more intimate if Tonya and I hadn't been in the room. When Lynn dropped her phone onto the bed beside her, I noticed a slight flush in her cheeks. Lynn caught Tonya and me staring at her. "What?"

"Don't give us that innocent act," Tonya said. "What's the scoop?"

"I have no idea what you mean."

"We recognize the signs," I said. "You and Raul are on the verge of taking this partnership to a different level."

"There's no denying it, honey," Tonya said. "You've got smitten written all over your face."

Lynn tried for an expression of cluelessness, but she couldn't maintain it. A huge smile wreathed her face. "All right, yes. I find Raul fairly attractive. I imagine most women do."

Tonya laughed. "*Fairly attractive*? Admit it—you think he's hot."

Lynn flushed again, and her eyes went dreamy. "Well, maybe I do. He's funny, too. And smart. And such a good detective."

"Oh, my." Tonya fanned herself with her hand. "You've got it bad."

Lynn held up a hand in a stop motion. "But I'm not doing anything about it. For one thing, I don't want a relationship interfering with my job—"

"Those things can be navigated," I said. "I'm sure you could work out the parameters."

"I also have two little girls to consider. I wouldn't want them to build expectations, only to have them dashed. They've been through a divorce, and I need to be a hundred percent sure of a relationship before I drag them into something new."

I didn't believe anyone could ever be a hundred percent certain, but I kept my mouth shut. She'd get to the jumping-off point before too long. Because as she talked about her partner, I could see Tonya was right— Lynn had it bad. And from the way Raul's eyes had lit up when he talked to her, he reciprocated the feeling.

That thought brought Sam into my mind, and I smiled. Six months ago, I might have envied Lynn and Raul. But now, Sam and I were in a good place—more than good. I flashed back to our last conversation, the one interrupted by the beach babe in the bikini, and the jealousy returned. Then I remembered his words just before we disconnected: *Love you, beautiful. Can't wait to have you in my arms again.* And the jealousy dissolved into a pool of affection. Mostly, anyway.

17

The three of us rejoined the group at the firepit and spent the next hour talking about Tonya's wedding. She and David planned a Rock Creek Village ceremony, though they hadn't yet set a specific date. She thought a winter wedding would be stunning. David, though, was pushing for fall, arguing that an exchange of vows against a backdrop of shimmering gold aspens would be breathtaking. Privately, he'd told me he just didn't want to wait any longer than necessary to marry the woman of his dreams. That endeared him to me even more.

Once we'd chimed in our opinions—four for fall, three for winter—we sat in silence for a while, staring up at the sky. The moon was waning, just a sliver of light in the cloudless black sky, and I let the day's stress drift from my bones. Carl lay in my lap, purring as I ran a finger down his spine. Beside me, Woody pressed his nose against my dangling palm, and I stroked his thick fur.

Mom's gentle voice broke the quiet. "Summer, thank you for suggesting Moonglow Ranch for Tonya's shower. The place is magnificent. Your aunt and uncle are delightful people."

I slitted my eyes open and looked at Summer, who beamed in delight. She sat cross-legged in the Adirondack chair, her long, blond hair twisted into a single braid that fell across her shoulder. "I'm so glad you're enjoying it, Maggie, despite…well, you know."

"Let's not mention that tonight," Mom said. "Why don't you tell us more about Ryll and Fritz? You seem quite close to them."

"Ryll has always been like a second mother to me," Summer said. "Don't get me wrong, my own parents are wonderful. I love them, and they adore me. But Aunt Ryll and I have a unique connection. We're alike in ways my mother and I are different."

Jessica reached over and squeezed her wife's hand. "Summer's mother and father are accountants," she said, as if that explained everything.

"Business types," Summer said. "As I'm sure you can tell, my aunt took a different path. She and Uncle Fritz met in the Peace Corps. They've had some…well, rough patches in their life together, but they're good people. The best."

"It's funny," Jessica said. "Ryll and Fritz's daughter Autumn is more like Iris, Summer's mom. In fact, Autumn works at Iris' accounting firm on the west coast. It's as if Ryll and Iris' babies were switched at birth."

Another silence fell over the group. I noticed Lydia twisting a ring on her finger, looking like she wanted to say something. After a moment, she did. "I'm pleased to hear you speak of your mother so affectionately, Summer, despite your unique personalities. We don't have to be birds of a feather to love each other, do we? We just have to accept each other."

She looked at Tonya, who shifted in her seat, then leaned over and gave Lydia a peck on the cheek. "You're right, Mother." She winked at my mom. "Life is too short to let our differences come between us."

"Exactly, darling," Lydia said. Then a door slammed at Colby's cabin, and Lydia's eyes flicked that direction. "And too short to let opportunities pass."

***

Soon after, the gathering broke up. Jessica and Summer went upstairs to chat with Ryll and Fritz in their apartment. Lynn left to sit by the pool and call her daughters, who were with their father for the week. Renata headed to her room to phone Ethan, her boyfriend and now my full-time partner in the gallery. Mom made her way to her room to call Dad, and Tonya departed to call David, taking the creatures along with her.

I stayed outside near the now-extinguished fire and tried Sam on FaceTime.

"Hi, beautiful," he said when the call connected. He was leaning shirtless against a pink padded headboard, his hair damp from a shower. He looked so good, so at ease, that I longed to be snuggled up beside him.

I glanced at my watch and made a face. "Sorry it's so late. I forgot about the time difference."

"No problem," he said. "It's not that late. It's just that we're in Florida. Folks here bed down as soon as the sun sets. Plus, Elyse and I had a full day, and we both needed alone time."

"Full day?" I asked. "You mean sunning yourself at the beach with the *Baywatch* babe?"

He smiled, and the tiny lines around his eyes and mouth crinkled. I felt a rush of warmth, a desire to put my lips on each of those lines.

"Wait, you're not jealous, are you?" he asked.

"Well, if I'm being honest…I mean, you have to admit the woman is gorgeous. Your parents couldn't have moved in next door to a wrinkly septuagenarian? I think they did this on purpose."

"My parents adore you, Callie. They keep saying they wish you could have joined Elyse and me."

I didn't respond. We both knew his parents had never entirely forgiven me for leaving Sam long ago for college in Texas—and waiting twenty-five years to return.

He diplomatically changed the subject. "So, are you

going to tell me about the dead woman in the stable, or do I have to get the details from *The Gazette*?"

"I was trying to tell you earlier, but you had to go frolic in the waves with Ms. Florida. How did you hear?"

"I called Snow Plow Chow earlier to talk to Jamal, and he'd heard the news from Butch. And from Mrs. Finney. And Frank."

I grinned. News traveled at lightning speed in Rock Creek Village. I spent the next few minutes giving my boyfriend the few details he hadn't gleaned from Jamal, his assistant at the cafe, via my father the former police chief, as well as Mrs. Finney, the owner of Rocky Mountain High coffee shop who used to work for the CIA, and Frank, the current Rock Creek Village chief of police. When I finished, Sam smiled wryly. "I'm sure you and your team of sleuths will have the case wrapped up in the next day or so."

"I'm not enjoying this, if that's what you're implying. In fact, I feel terrible that it's putting a damper on Tonya's shower."

He snorted. "Are you kidding? She lives for this kind of thing almost as much as you do. But that's enough talk of murder. I want to tell you how much I miss you and how I'm going to show you when we're back together again…"

The temperature seemed to rise ten degrees. We murmured to each other for a while, and when we finally hung up, I sat for a moment, just letting myself be happy, reveling in the fact that I was, for perhaps the first time in my life, deeply in love. The breeze brushed my cheeks. I leaned my head back and stared at the stars. All was right with the world.

Except for the dead body, of course.

The lodge's front door creaked open, and I saw Valerie make her way to the wooden swing at the end of the deck. She sat, shoulders stooped, staring at her hands clasped in her lap. I realized she hadn't noticed me in the shadows beside the firepit. As I was about to make my presence known, the door opened again, and Haley joined her mother on the swing.

I knew I should get to my feet, clear my throat, say hello. Something. Instead, I lurked in the shadows, priming myself to eavesdrop. Maybe it wasn't right, but I couldn't resist the opportunity. People who worked behind the scenes were often privy to insider information. I was only trying to help, after all.

I waited. And waited. The two of them didn't speak for several minutes. When they did, their voices were so hushed that I couldn't make out their words. Since being sneaky wasn't getting me any intelligence, I did the honorable thing after all—I stood up, walked across the yard, and climbed the steps.

"Hi," I said, lifting a hand. "What a lovely evening."

Valerie gave me a weak smile. "Oh, Callie, we didn't see you there. Sorry if we disturbed you."

"Not at all. I just finished a call to my…my boyfriend." As a middle-aged woman, it seemed strange to refer to Sam as my boyfriend, as if we were still mooning teenagers. But until I came up with a better word, it had to suffice.

I frowned at Valerie's troubled face. "Not to pry, but are you okay?"

Haley put a protective arm around her mother. "She's worried about her job. She loves Moonglow Ranch, but with everything that's happened…"

"We'll be fine," Valerie said. "I pray Moonglow survives this…incident. But even if the worst happens and Ryll and Fritz are forced to sell, there are other jobs."

As Haley leaned back, Valerie pushed the swing into motion. "I'd just hate to see them lose everything. They don't deserve the obstacles others have put in their way."

"Neither do you, Mom," Haley said. "You've worked so hard in your life. This was supposed to be your last job—a place where your talents were truly appreciated."

A tear trailed down Valerie's cheek. She stopped the swing and brushed it away. "Well, I'm not giving up hope. I'm going to proceed as if it's life as usual here, and that means I need to get to bed. The alarm goes off at five so we can get breakfast started." She stood up. "I hope you'll forgive us for this little display of emotion, Callie. You're a guest here, and I didn't intend to burden you."

"It's no burden." I paused, weighing my next words. "I'm sure you know my friend Lynn is a detective. My past, too, has provided me with…an investigative skill set, I guess you could say. We want to see this case solved, for everyone's sake. If you have any thoughts, any insights, please let us know. I don't mean to speak ill of your police chief, but…"

The side of her mouth curled. "Chester Wade. He's…well, I believe the man is in over his head."

"We got that impression." I lowered my voice. "It also appears he may be more interested in keeping Gordon Simonson happy than he is in solving the case."

Haley huffed. "Gordon's a jerk. He's the one everyone should suspect."

"Why do you say that?" I asked. "Do you have information that implicates him?"

Her mother looked at her sharply, and Haley dropped her eyes. "No, I just meant…I don't like him. Most of us around here don't."

Valerie's posture stiffened, and I realized my window of opportunity had slammed shut.

"Like I said, we need to be off to bed." She walked stiffly to the door, her daughter behind her.

The atmosphere had turned chilly in a heartbeat, I reflected. I had a strong sense that Haley held a nugget of information that could shed light on the case. Tomorrow, I'd find a way to get her away from her mother.

18

As I headed to my room, I noticed Mom's door was ajar. I peeked inside and found her sitting in a leather armchair reading a book with her feet crossed on an ottoman. I stepped inside and looked around. With its wooden beams, braided rag rug, and galloping mustang lampshade, the room oozed dude ranch vibes. The bunk beds displayed plaid sheets and handmade quilts.

"Which one of these are you sleeping in?" I asked, pointing from the upper to the lower bunk.

"Last night I slept low. But who knows? Tonight, I'm feeling daring. Maybe I'll make the climb." She patted the lower bunk, and I sat. "I spoke to your father this evening. He said to tell you to stay out of the murder investigation."

"Absolutely. I'm focused on Tonya's bridal shower. No time to think of anything else."

"Exactly what I told him." She paused. "So. We haven't had a chance to talk about Carmen's big reveal last night."

"You mean Tonya and David's plan to adopt?" My gut clenched. I'd been trying to push thoughts of it aside until I had time to process my feelings.

"Doesn't sound like it's imminent yet, but yes."

"Did you know?" I asked. It wouldn't have surprised me if Tonya had confided in her. They'd grown very close over the years. And I knew my mother would never have broken her confidence.

"No, darling. It was as much of a surprise to me as to you. How do you feel about it?"

I considered my response. "I think the two of them will make great parents. The world will be a better place with kids in it raised by Tonya and David."

Mom gave me that probing look of hers. "There's a *but* in your voice."

I took a deep breath. "I don't want to admit it, even to myself, but I guess I'm a little hurt that Tonya didn't tell me herself. Selfish, I realize."

"No, sweetheart. Normal. Selfish would be trying to make her feel bad for keeping it between her and David."

"I'd never do that. Not intentionally."

"Of course not. Because you love her. You want her happiness almost as much as you want your own."

I nodded. "I do."

"Be sure to tell her that," Mom said. "Tonya has a lot on her emotional plate right now: a wedding, a change to her entire lifestyle, her mother's reappearance, and possibly motherhood herself. She may not verbalize it, but she needs your support now more than ever."

My mother was the most intuitive, intelligent woman I'd ever known. Rising from the bed, I leaned down to kiss her cheek. "I love you, Maggie Cassidy. You're the best."

"Ditto," she said, touching my cheek. "Pleasant dreams, darling."

I chuckled to myself. If Tonya's snoring reached the same fever pitch it had last night, that seemed unlikely. But I'd try to stay positive. Optimism was my middle name.

When I opened the door to our room, I found my three roomies dozing—Woody and Carl on my bed, and Tonya tucked beneath her own covers. She stirred and mumbled, "Turn out the lights."

"Already? It's only ten-thirty. I thought you'd be up for girl talk. Or even a game of Truth or Dare."

She groaned. "I need my beauty sleep, Callie." She flipped over to face the wall, and within seconds, the snoring began.

I changed into pajama pants and one of Sam's t-shirts. After brushing my teeth, I padded to my bed, nudged Woody aside, and climbed between the sheets. Screwing my eyes shut, I said a silent plea to the sandman, but he ignored my request. Twenty minutes later, I gave up.

Ambient light from the window frosted the room. Woody's sleepy snuffles harmonized with Tonya's snores, creating a clamorous aria. On the pillow above my head, Carl breathed in and out rhythmically. Everyone slept but me, it seemed.

And one other person, I realized. Above the crescendo of sleep sounds, I heard footsteps creaking on the stairs. I remembered the same sound occurring last night. Maybe Valerie needed to take care of something in the kitchen, or Fritz was making sure the place was safely locked up.

Then Carl lifted his head, alert to the sound, and hopped over to the window. Front paws on the windowsill, he emitted a curious chirrup that made me sit up and peer through the glass.

In the pale light of the crescent moon, I could barely make out the figure below. A woman, I thought, making her way down the steps. She peered furtively up at the lodge, and I glimpsed her face.

Lydia.

She hurried across the yard to Colby's place, her pale blue silk robe fluttering behind her. As I leaned my forehead against the glass, I spotted a bottle of wine clutched in one hand. When she reached the porch, she tapped on the door and was ushered into the cabin.

Yikes. I glanced over at Tonya, now sprawled on her back with one arm thrown across her face. She'd be mortified—and furious—over her mother's escapades.

It didn't take me two seconds to decide against waking

her. What would be the point? But I faced a tougher choice about whether to tell her at all. I didn't want yet another incident spoiling this ill-fated bridal shower week. On the other hand, the last time I'd concealed information from my best friend, it had threatened to cost us our friendship.

No, I'd learned my lesson. I'd have to tell Tonya I'd seen her mother sneaking over to the ranch manager's quarters for what could only be a late-night tryst. I'd do it first thing tomorrow.

19

When Tonya shook me awake, it felt as if only minutes had passed. But when I wrenched my eyes open, it wasn't moonbeams that greeted me but the full rays of the sun.

"Rise and shine, sleepyhead." My friend wore a floral-patterned skirt, a pink sleeveless button-up blouse, and low-heeled sandals. She looked fresh as a daisy.

The clock on the nightstand read eight-fifteen. The last time I'd looked at it had been three-thirty. I calculated I'd gotten five hours of uninterrupted sleep—better than I'd expected, but not enough to alleviate my crankiness. "Stop suffocating me with your chipperness," I grumbled.

"Someone needs coffee." She pinched her nose. "And a shower."

"I smell fine. Leave me alone."

She laughed. "I'll expect you cleaned up and dressed in twenty minutes. It's a gorgeous morning, so you can eat breakfast outdoors."

"So bossy," I muttered, heaving myself to a sitting position. "What's the rush?"

"Everyone else has eaten, and they're off doing stuff. Renata, Lynn, and Jessica went for a run. Your mom, Summer, and Ryll are doing yoga." She paused. "No sign of Lydia yet. I assume she's still in bed. Like you."

My eyes flew open as I remembered last night. If Lydia was still in bed, I could only wonder whose. I looked out the window and caught sight of Colby in the corral. That didn't mean Lydia wasn't still snuggled up in his bed, but it rendered it less likely.

I needed to tell Tonya what I'd seen. But not before I had some caffeine whizzing through my veins.

Tonya took Woody and Carl downstairs, leaving me to shower and dress. Always motivated by a deadline, I finished in fifteen minutes. Downstairs, the lingering aroma of breakfast wafted through the lodge, and my stomach rumbled in anticipation. Perhaps the ranch's healthy fare agreed with me after all.

On my way to the front door, I passed the living room, where the yogis twisted into a painful looking formation. Mom flashed me a serene smile. The woman was sixty-eight years old and still contorted her body in ways that didn't seem possible.

Outside, Tonya sat at the table beneath the pergola. The creatures sprawled nearby, snoozing in the sun. I plopped into a seat across from my friend and took a gulp of coffee. Ahh...I dug into the generous portions of turkey bacon, avocado toast, and scrambled egg whites.

Tonya grinned as I wolfed down the food. "I'd say the fresh air has given you an appetite, but I suppose it's not unusual for you to eat so voraciously."

I wiped a dribble of salsa from my chin and tossed Woody the last bite of bacon. "Is that a fat joke?"

"Not a chance. You're slimmer and in better shape than I've seen you since high school."

I flushed at the praise. I'd told myself I was past the age of caring about my appearance, but deep down, I knew that wasn't true. Though I no longer chased the body shape and fresh-faced gleam of my early twenties, I still wanted to look good.

Especially after the glimpse I'd gotten of Isabella.

I tossed my crumpled napkin onto the plate, preparing to deliver the news of Lydia's antics. Tonya's face was turned to the sky, her eyes closed. A small smile played on her lips. I hated to disrupt her contentment. Even more, though, I hated the idea of another rift between us.

Possibly sensing what was about to come, Woody and Carl rose in unison and trotted off around the corner of the lodge. Cowards.

I reached across the table and covered Tonya's hand with mine. "I need to tell you something."

Her fingers stiffened beneath my palm. "Uh oh. That doesn't sound good."

I sat back. "It's no big deal, really. Just…"

"Out with it. Your hemming and hawing only makes the suspense worse."

"Okay. Last night, after you were asleep, snoring like a buzz saw—"

"Stop right there. I do not snore, and I will sue you if you continue to slander me."

I snorted. "Anyway, last night, after you were sleeping as silently as a mime, Carl woke up and clambered to the window, and I looked outside, and…well, Tonya, there's no easy way to say this. I saw your mother hightailing it over to Colby's cabin."

Tonya looked blank for a moment. Then her jaw tightened. Her hand clenched into a fist on the table. "Every time," she said.

"Every time?"

Her eyes flashed. "Every time I give that woman the benefit of the doubt, she does something like this." She gazed into the distance, quiet for a few moments. Then she waved. "Whatever. I will not let her spoil this for me. I'm as happy as I've ever been, and I will not permit Lydia Fredericks to ruin it. She can do as she likes. Makes no difference to me."

I cocked an eyebrow. Was Tonya lying to me, or to herself? Either way, in this case, the lie could be a positive form of self-protection. It might even evolve into the truth. If Tonya could truly stop caring and, as my mother had advised, accept Lydia for who she was, warts and all, it would go a long way toward her peace of mind.

She turned back to me with a sad smile. "I appreciate you telling me, Callie. I'm sure it would have been simpler to keep quiet, but that's not how friends treat each other, right?"

"Right," I said.

"You forgot to say it," she said, laughing. "Remember what we talked about? How I expect to be addressed?"

My lips curled up. "Ah, yes. Goddess. You're always right, goddess."

"Perfect. Now, speaking of how friends treat each other, I owe you an apology."

"I accept."

"You haven't even heard what I'm apologizing for."

"Doesn't matter. There's nothing you could do that I wouldn't forgive you for." I knew now it was an essential truth of our friendship. Whatever happened between us, forgiveness would always follow.

"Oh, Callie. Beneath that tough exterior of yours beats the biggest heart I know." She fidgeted with her engagement ring for a moment. "Listen, I know you must have been pretty shocked when Carmen said that about David and me possibly adopting. I don't know how she guessed that. David and I swore we wouldn't tell anyone until we'd made a final decision. Anyway, I'm sorry you found out the way you did. I should have—"

I raised a hand to stop her. "Tonya, you have nothing to be sorry for. You're planning a life with David, a family with him. I get that. I don't expect to be part of any decisions the two of you make. The only thing I expect is that I'll be permitted to spoil your future kids rotten. I want to be known as Fun Aunt Callie. If you can promise me that, we're good."

Tonya lunged forward and pulled me into a fierce hug. "Then we're good," she whispered in my ear. "I love you, Callie Cassidy."

"Back at you, Tonya Stephens. Or should I start calling you Tonya Parisi?"

She laughed. "No, I'm sticking with Stephens. I'm a diehard feminist, remember? Now, let's take your dishes inside and—"

Suddenly, we heard Woody from the side of the lodge—a tense, urgent barking so unlike his laid-back nature. Then Carl darted around the corner, summoning our presence. Tonya and I hurried after him.

We found Woody standing rigid, his tail raised and the hair on the scruff of his neck standing up. His attention was fixed on the latticed crawl space beneath the lodge. I exhaled a breath I hadn't known I was holding. The creatures had apparently chased some smaller animal into hiding. "What is it, boys? A chipmunk?"

Carl reached a paw up and scratched my shin so hard it left a mark. I frowned. "Not a chipmunk, then. Something more serious?"

The cat stared at me as if I were daft before scurrying toward a hinged door in the lattice framework. I bent over and peered into the semi-darkness. "You don't expect me to go in there, right?"

He shot me a disdainful look and arched his back. Tonya put her hands on her knees and looked into the gloom. "Well, someone has to."

I straightened and crossed my arms. "I'm not convinced that's true, but if so, you go."

"No way. I'm wearing a skirt. You're in shorts. And your creatures are the ones making the fuss."

"But these are my nicest shorts," I whined. "Dressy, even. I plan to wear them to your luncheon today. And I have on my good shoes. Besides, it's dark in there."

"Callie Cassidy, you spent your career chasing stories in much worse conditions. What have you become?"

"Back then, I was dressed for it," I muttered. But I kicked off my shoes, dropped to my knees, and yanked the small door open on its hinges. A musty scent drifted out, and shadows pooled inside a space large enough to hide an entire family of chipmunks.

Or snakes.

I shuddered at the thought and came to a decision—I wasn't going in there.

Tonya squatted beside me and turned on her phone's flashlight, holding it to the lattice framework. The beam glinted off a silvery object, and I squinted at it. Once I figured out what it was, I chuckled in relief and looked reproachfully at Woody and Carl.

"You got us worked up over a shovel?"

Woody barked again, and Carl followed up with a commanding yowl. I stared at them. Something about this simple tool had the animals in a tizzy. I turned back to the door and reached out my arm. The shovel lay a couple of feet beyond my grasp. It wouldn't take much effort to get to it. Just a few shuffles on my knees into the musky, dark space…

"What if there are snakes?" I murmured.

"Oh, don't be silly," Tonya said. "Still, if you see something slither, back the heck out of there as quick as you can."

"Thanks for the pep talk. You'd make a great life coach."

She nudged my rear end. "Quit stalling."

I grunted and gingerly placed one hand inside the crawl space. The ground felt cool and moist beneath my palm. There was probably mold in here, infiltrating my lungs with every breath. And for what? A stupid shovel?

Another poke at my posterior propelled me forward. I lifted a knee and planted it a few inches ahead. A silky substance brushed across my forehead. A spiderweb. I cringed. Where there were webs…

Ugh. *Just get it over with*, I told myself. I stretched my arm out. Close, but not quite. One more crawl and I should be there.

Then my knee landed on something slimy. I jerked up and bashed my head against the steel beam above me. When I instinctively lifted my hand to my scalp, I lost my balance and tumbled onto my side. Remembering the slimy thing, I scrambled back onto my knees and skittered forward. Tonya aimed her flashlight at the spot I'd vacated. What I'd suspected was a snake turned out to be a small piece of discarded rope. My resulting cackle sounded suspiciously like impending hysteria.

Despite the possibility of mold, I took a few deep breaths to slow my heart rate. A second look showed I was close enough to grab the shovel by its handle. Clutching it, I scooted backward—back into the sunshine and fresh air. I tossed the shovel to the side and plopped onto my rear end, panting as I assessed myself.

My shorts were covered with mud. In fact, the entire left side of my body was coated. My hands were dimpled with embedded pebbles. I glared at the creatures. "All this for a stupid shovel?"

Then I heard Tonya gasp. She pointed to the shovel's metal blade. "Is that…?"

I leaned on one hand and studied the shovel, then nodded in confirmation. "Blood," I muttered.

Carl responded with a triumphant meow.

20

While I stood guard over the shovel, Tonya dashed inside to retrieve my camera so we could document what we'd discovered before summoning the police. When she returned, she had our friends in tow, as well as Ryll and Fritz. "Nothing I could do about it," she said. "Yoga ended, and the others just returned from their run."

To be honest, I was glad to see them—especially Lynn. Hands clenched behind her back, she bent to get a look at the shovel. "It's blood, though I can't confirm it's human." She sighed. "Guess we'd better get Chief Wade out here."

"Do we have to?" Jessica said.

Lynn eyed me. "Could you get a few pictures before he arrives?"

I held up my camera. "I'm on it."

As Lynn stepped aside to make the call, Ryll leaned in for a closer look. "Does it belong to you guys?" I asked her, snapping the camera's shutter.

She shrugged. "Can't be sure. One shovel looks like another to me. When I see a shovel, it's usually covered in horse poop. But it's a logical conclusion that it's from here on the ranch."

Fritz said, "We have four. I'll run over and see if any of them are unaccounted for."

He jogged off to the stable as Lynn pocketed her

phone. "Chief's on his way. I hope Officer Jake comes with him. The kid grasps investigative technique better than his so-called boss."

There was nothing more for us to do, so we gathered in the pergola to await the so-called pros. Lynn remained near the corner of the lodge to keep an eye on the shovel, as if the killer might sneak out of the forest and abscond with it. Ryll went inside to ask Valerie and Haley to bring out a few jugs of iced tea.

"And maybe a few of those muffins," I called. Apparently, groping around in the dirt for a potential murder weapon hadn't suppressed my sweet tooth.

Fritz returned, his forehead creased. "Only three of the shovels are there now. So it's gotta be one of ours."

No surprise, and truthfully, it didn't mean much—not in terms of trimming the suspect list. Anyone could have accessed the stable.

I closed my eyes and let myself visualize the scene. *The killer—the face and figure hazy—witnesses Eleanor entering the stable. The person follows her inside, watches as she lets herself into Spirit's stall, sees Eleanor remove a syringe from her...hmm.* There'd been no sign of a purse. Or keys. Or a car. Why hadn't I considered that earlier?

Eleanor might have walked over from her property. From what I'd heard, the Simonsons' house wasn't that far from here. Traipsing through the woods in the dark of night didn't seem her style, but what did I really know about the woman or her style?

Still, would she have come to the ranch without a single belonging—other than a syringe?

It was something I'd need to run by Lynn later. But for now, back to the visualization. *Eleanor has the syringe in her hand. The killer sees it...* Was that the impetus for the attack—someone wanting to stop Eleanor from injecting yet another horse? Or did the assailant follow her into the stable, intending to kill her?

That was a key question, and the answer would create

different subsets of suspects. If the killer caught sight of the syringe, maybe the motive involved saving the horses, or the ranch itself. If the syringe was a coincidence, we were looking for a different motive for Eleanor's murder.

Mentally, I returned to the scene in the stall, watching as Eleanor entered and pulled out the syringe. *Then the killer acts. He...or she...grabs a nearby shovel.* A weapon of opportunity, or had the killer decided on it as a murder weapon in advance?

Shovel in hand, the killer heads into the stall. Eleanor looks up, confused. She exchanges a few words with the interloper. Then she turns her back on the killer. Did that indicate a lack of fear?

The person raises the shovel overhead, and with a heavy swing, cracks the sharp edge of the blade onto the back of Eleanor's skull. Eleanor falls to her knees. Did she see the killer before she died, eyes wide in final understanding? Did she cry out for help? Or was she rendered unconscious right away?

Details we might never uncover.

Then what? *The killer crouches to verify that Eleanor is dead. Perhaps the person even flips her onto her back. From the corner of the stall, Spirit shuffles and neighs. Fearful that the horse will attract unwanted attention from the lodge, the killer hurries out now, leaving Eleanor sprawled in the hay, and... stops to latch the door?* Why would the killer take the time to latch the door?

Then Spirit rears up, and his hoof crashes onto Eleanor's forehead. Was it pent up fear that caused his reaction? I flashed on the memory of the snake gliding out of Spirit's stall just before I discovered Eleanor's body. Horses were terrified of snakes, right? So that would make it a perfect storm of timing—murder, snake, trample. Unless...

Did the killer toss the serpent inside the stall, hoping to elicit just such a response and possibly mask the murder as a gruesome accident?

I shook my head—still so many questions.

The police car pulled onto the property, lights flashing but sirens silent. The chief stepped from the passenger side, and Officer Jake emerged from behind the wheel.

The chief hitched up his pants and strode toward the pergola. Jake trailed a few steps back.

Chief Wade gave us a cursory glance before his eyes found Lynn near the corner of the lodge. He spat tobacco juice into the ever-present cup and held up a finger. "You all stay put."

He ambled over to Lynn. "Where's this shovel that has everyone in a dither?"

Lynn started around the corner. "Just point me in the right direction, little lady," he said. "No need to trouble yourself."

"It's Detective Clarke." Lynn's voice was a low growl. "And I never consider proper investigation of a crime to be troublesome."

With an expression that made it clear she wasn't giving in, she continued around the corner and out of sight, giving the officers no choice but to follow her.

I bounced on the balls of my feet and looked at Mom. She gave me an encouraging nod, so I placed my camera on the table, told the creatures to stay, and trotted off after Lynn. I'd been the one to rescue the shovel from its hiding place, so I had a right to be included. At least, that's what I told myself.

The chief bent over the shovel, hands on his knees, still clutching his spit cup. He turned at my approach and signaled to Jake, who stepped in front of me. "Stay back, ma'am. Please."

I stopped in my tracks and craned my head so I could see past the young officer's shoulder. After a cursory examination, Chief Wade wrenched himself up, his back cracking with the effort. He looked at me. "You the one who found this?"

"Yes. It was in the crawl space."

"So we're gonna find your fingerprints on it?"

"On the handle, yes. Not on the blade."

"If this turns out to be the murder weapon, you've mucked up the evidence."

I put my hands on my hips. "Now you're interested in forensic evidence? It didn't concern you yesterday. Did you even bother to send the syringe in for analysis?"

He ignored me. "Shoulda left it where it was. Didn't you say you were an investigative journalist or some such nonsense? I'd a thought you'd know that."

I gritted my teeth. "First, I didn't know it was a murder weapon when I recovered it. Second, if it weren't for us, you'd likely never have found that shovel. I imagine the killer would have retrieved it as soon as possible, wiped it clean, and returned it to its spot in the stable. If they didn't dispose of it, that is."

A trail of brown saliva dripped down his chin. I could see the wheels turning in his head as he tried to figure out what to do next.

"Jake," he said at last, "get on in there and see if there's any more evidence. Something this little lady missed."

Jake's face paled. "You want me to go in there?"

"That's what I said, boy. You deaf?"

"No, it's just..." Jake swayed on his feet. "I'm...well, I'm claustrophobic."

"Claustrowhat?" Chief Wade bellowed. "I don't give a good goldarn. Get your butt in there. That's an order."

Jake's eyes darted about, his breathing coming in quick rasps. Just as I thought he might refuse the chief's order, a resolute expression came into his eyes, and he dropped to his knees and crawled inside. When it was clear the chief wasn't going to offer any help, Lynn used her phone to light Jake's path.

Meanwhile, Chief Wade turned to where the rest of the group had gathered at the side of the lodge. "Fritz! Ryll! Get over here."

When they drew near, the chief pointed at the shovel. "That yours?"

Fritz nodded. "Pretty sure."

"Guess you realize this makes you suspects. Prime suspects."

Inwardly, I rolled my eyes. The man wasn't even doing a passable impression of a TV detective. "Come on, Chief," I said. "Everyone had access to that shovel."

He glared at me. "Guess I'll say who's a suspect."

Without abandoning her post at the crawl space, Lynn said, "The Bauers never lock the stable. Eleanor got in with no problem. Anyone could have followed her inside and killed her." She paused. "Listen, Chief, it may be time to call in the county sheriff."

The man's face turned purple. "Are you threatening me, little lady?"

Lynn's face took on a hue that matched his. "If you don't stop calling me that, you'll find out what a threat is. I'm Detective Clarke. I suggest you don't forget it again."

"Whatever you say, *Detective Clarke.*" The sarcasm dripped from his tongue, along with tobacco juice. "But I shouldn't need to remind you I'm Chief Chester Wade, and here in Mustang, I run the show. If you want to be in charge of something, I suggest you head back to Stony River, or wherever it is you came from."

Before Lynn could respond, Jake backed out of the crawl space and lifted his empty hands. "Nothing there except spiders and a decomposing chipmunk."

I grimaced. I'd seen more dead bodies than I cared to remember, but the thought of being in proximity to a chipmunk corpse made me queasy.

Lynn fumed. Chief Wade rolled his shoulders. Then he pointed his spit cup toward the shovel and addressed Jake. "Bag that thing up and bring it to the car. I'll send it to forensics for evidence."

Then he stared at Ryll and Fritz. "I'm not taking you two in. Not yet. But you need to stay in town." He looked past them to the rest of the group. "All y'all need to stay local. Hear me?"

We all knew he couldn't enforce that demand, but I didn't even bother to remind him he had no such authority. But as he started off to the car, a thought occurred to me. "Chief Wade, wait. Before you set your sights on Ryll and Fritz, you need to consider other potential suspects. Allen Simonson, for example. Where was Eleanor's husband at the time of the murder?"

Beneath his expression of irritation, I glimpsed a seed of doubt. "That's police business, little lady. Meaning it's none of yours."

Meaning he hadn't spoken to the victim's husband, I deduced. Was Allen Simonson still off the grid? I glanced at Lynn, and she gave me a subtle nod. Someone needed to find out where Allen was—now and two nights ago.

Once the chief had stormed away, I looked at the young officer, who seemed worried. "We've never had a murder in Mustang," he said. "At least, not as long as I've been on the force."

"So you're not sure how to take care of the evidence," Lynn said, her voice sympathetic.

Jake shot a glance toward his boss's back and nodded. "I don't think he knows either."

"You don't have any evidence bags, I assume?"

"I doubt it." His eyes fell to the shovel. "Nothing big enough for this."

"I'll go to the kitchen and get plastic wrap," Lynn said. "You can use it to wrap the blade and the handle. That should do the trick."

She trotted off, returning a short time later with an industrial-sized package of plastic. Officer Jake secured the shovel in its folds. After casting a grateful look at Lynn, he carried the tool to the car, where the chief sat in the passenger seat, tapping away on his phone. Once Jake secured the shovel in the trunk, he climbed into the driver's seat and pulled down the gravel road.

We were silent for a moment, watching them go. Then Lydia emerged from the lodge. She noted the departing police car, then the group of us gathered solemn-faced near the deck.

"What'd I miss?" she asked.

21

I hurried upstairs, stripped off my mud-caked shorts, and took a quick shower before slipping into the spare outfit I'd packed—my all-purpose little black dress. It was functional, I supposed, but not a summery frock like everyone else would be wearing. Oh, well. I wasn't a fashionista of Tonya's caliber, nor was I intended to be the center of attention at this gala.

Before leaving the room, I filled Woody and Carl's water bowls, gave them each a pat on the head, and told them to behave. Woody grinned at me, but I swear Carl did his eye roll thing.

When I made my way to the deck, I stopped in my tracks and did a double take. Sitting in a rocker next to my mother was none other than Mrs. Finney, my coffee-shop-owning-former-CIA-agent friend. Her curls nestled against her scalp like a periwinkle Brillo pad. Purple was her signature color, and today she wore a tie-dyed blouse, lilac slacks, and matching Keds. Though she'd never revealed her exact age, I figured she had to be at least seventy. She still possessed the strength and agility to pin a perpetrator to the ground, as I'd witnessed the first week she came to Rock Creek Village. I'd quickly grown to adore the woman—as we all did—and now the sight of her lifted my spirits.

She looked up and held out a hand. I took it, wondering if she expected me to kiss it. Instead, I gave it an awkward little shake.

"Mrs. Finney," I said.

"Yes, dear, it's me," she said in her faux British accent.

"What are you doing here?"

She arched a frizzy eyebrow. "I believe you invited me."

"Yes, of course I did. You said you couldn't leave Rocky Mountain High."

"Pish," she said. "When I heard of your little intrigue, I knew my skills would be of better use here. At any rate, I've trained Mr. Purdy. He is capable of overseeing the shop for a few days."

Ah, Mr. Purdy. The man—supposedly a stranger to Mrs. Finney—had shown up on a tourist bus a few months ago and ended up at Rocky Mountain High. As the story went, he'd fallen in love with our village and its coffee and instructed the bus driver to go on without him. He'd been a fixture in town since then.

I frankly found the story dubious. The man's demeanor suggested that he had skills of his own, and I suspected the two of them shared a top-secret past. I had yet to verify my conjecture. Mrs. Finney wasn't talking, and even Preston Garrison, my former boss at *The Washington Sentinel* and Mrs. Finney's longtime friend, remained tight-lipped. But I wasn't giving up. I'd uncover the truth if it killed me.

Whatever the backstory, it wasn't much of a surprise that she'd entrusted Mr. Purdy with her precious coffee shop.

"So, Mr. Purdy is in charge," I said, teasing her. "How long has he been in training?"

"Never you mind, dear. We have more important items on our agenda. I need to be brought up to speed on your investigation."

"Well, it's not *my* investigation. But before we get into that, where are you staying? I thought Ryll said she didn't have any available rooms."

Mom rocked in her chair. "She's rooming with me, of course."

"But your room has bunk beds."

Mrs. Finney's eyes pierced mine. "Callahan, your mother and I are both in excellent shape and perfectly capable of climbing a ladder. And if you must know, we flipped for it. I won, so I get the upper bunk."

"You won and selected the top?"

"Those who climb higher see farther." Her face lit up, and she reached into the bag at her feet to pull out a notepad and pen. "That's one for the cups."

I chuckled. Along with the purple attire and the British accent, profound axioms were one of Mrs. Finney's trademarks. From the time I met her, she'd dispensed wisdom in the form of unique—sometimes indecipherable—sayings. When she opened Rocky Mountain High, it was only natural to make them part of her brand. Every few weeks, she ordered in paper coffee cups graced with a new adage. People lined up to get a glimpse of her latest truism.

As Mrs. Finney closed her notebook, the rest of our group stepped outside. After a series of squeals at the sight of Mrs. Finney and hugs all around, we set off toward town. Renata could only fit six in her Suburban, but Mrs. Finney offered to drive, too. Lynn and I jumped into her Mazda sedan so we could discuss the murder on the way.

By the time Lynn and I had filled Mrs. Finney in on the details, including the suspect list we'd drafted, we'd arrived at the restaurant, a Victorian-style home on one corner of the town square. Painted butter yellow, the two-story house flaunted ornate gables, steeply pitched rooflines, and a tower topped with an iron finial. It looked out of place in this small Western town, as if it had been plucked from a different era.

We crossed the wrap-around porch and entered the restaurant. The interior was something out of a gothic novel. Wallpaper patterned in burgundy and gold surrounded us. A pictorial tapestry of a fox hunt hung on one wall. China place settings and linen napkins covered a cherry wood dining table. To the side of the room, buffet tables held silver serving dishes.

Tonya clutched my forearm. "This is just perfect, Callie. Who knew you were so fancy?"

"As much as I'd love to take the credit, I confess Ryll was the one who planned this. I just suggested a luncheon in town."

Dressed in a cinched-waist, floor-length Victorian gown, the restaurant's proprietor, paradoxically named Miley, greeted us. She instructed us to choose our seats at the table, grab our appetizer plates, and head to the buffet for the first course.

I had to admit, the place made me tense. I felt like Jake probably had when the chief ordered him to bag the shovel—out of my element. As Tonya had hinted, "fancy" was not a regular word in my vocabulary. I had no idea what constituted an appetizer plate, so I watched Tonya and followed her lead.

At the buffet, tented cards indicated the offerings in each serving tray. The appetizer table held salmon mousse canapés, sweet potato crostini with marshmallows, rosemary crackers with cut vegetables, and roasted red pepper hummus. On an adjacent table, the main course selections included cucumber sandwiches topped with dill, chicken salad croissants, bacon and feta cheese quiches, and a pina colada fruit salad. But it was the dessert table that drew my attention, with its apple cinnamon tarts, black-bottom brandy bites, mini chocolate wafer cakes, and even a flowing chocolate fountain. I breathed a sigh of relief.

Once I'd filled my appetizer plate and taken my seat, I relaxed into the event. Even though I didn't know a dinner fork from a dessert spoon, I knew how to eat. And despite its ritzy presentation, the food was scrumptious.

As we ate, we took turns extolling Tonya's many virtues. Mom noted her compassion. Summer spoke of her quiet spirituality. Jessica mentioned perseverance and resilience. Renata told us how welcoming Tonya had been when she moved back to the village. Lynn outlined her journalistic talents. And Mrs. Finney made us laugh with a story about Tonya's prankish humor.

When Lydia's turn came, she brightened. "My daughter is always the most beautiful woman in the room. I'm proud to say she inherited my genes."

Then it was my turn. "There's so much I could say about my best friend, but today, I'll focus on her ability to accept and forgive. She sees past a person's flaws and faults to unearth what's best in them. I'm grateful to have been a recipient of those qualities more than once."

Tonya stood and put a hand to her chest. "My friends," she said, her voice choked with emotion. "My family. It means so much to me to have you all here. I sometimes say that when I found David, I discovered the love of my life. But that's not entirely true. You're the loves of my life, and for that, I am blessed."

Mrs. Finney raised her mimosa glass. "Here's to the bride."

Around the table, glasses raised and clinked. "To Tonya," everyone chanted.

"Didn't we just do this on our hike?" Jessica said. "How much love must we rain on this woman?"

"However much it is, it won't be enough," I said. "But now, let's concentrate on dessert."

"Hear hear," Jessica said.

We laughed and headed off to the dessert table to fill our plates—the smallest ones in the setting. I didn't know what etiquette rule dictated that, but it meant I'd be making several trips.

22

After dessert, I grouped everyone together, adjusted the settings on my classic Nikon film camera, and asked Miley to take a group shot. Then I took portraits of Tonya with each individual in the group. Finally, I turned the camera over to Mom, who shot a picture of Tonya and me with our arms wrapped around each other. I foresaw hours of darkroom time to get these printed, but I loved the control I had on a photo made from film.

Afterward, we thanked Miley and the waitstaff for a superb lunch and left the restaurant. Our plan was to squeeze into our bathing suits and spend the afternoon at the Moonglow Ranch pool, soaking in the sun and relaxing.

As we headed to our cars, we noticed Polly and Martin exiting a small building a few doors away: Crystal Clear Psychic Shop. Carmen's home base.

Polly glowered when she caught sight of us and stomped toward us. Martin's head swiveled as if he were searching for an escape route, but at a single dirty look from his wife, he clumped along behind her.

"How nice to be out celebrating when my friend is lying in the morgue." Polly lifted her knuckles to her mouth and choked back a manufactured sob.

She looked straight out of a 1950s TV show: a black mid-length dress, low black pumps, and a black pillbox hat with a net veil.

She stretched her hand toward her husband, palm

upturned. He stared at it blankly. "Martin," she hissed. "Give me your handkerchief."

He dug around in his pocket and retrieved a white cloth, which he dutifully handed her. As she reached beneath the little veil and dabbed nonexistent tears from her eyes, he patted her shoulder and mumbled, "There, there, honeybun."

After a moment of pretending to compose herself, Polly threw back her shoulders and sniffed. "Well, I suppose you might as well enjoy your visit. It'll be your last. The mayor and I will see to that."

She tossed her head and gave us a look I remembered seeing on the face of every snotty high school girl I'd known. Then she pivoted and marched off, leaving us gaping. Martin followed like a tired but well-trained dog.

"That was entertaining," Mrs. Finney said. "I presume that was Mayor Finkle and his congenial wife you mentioned earlier."

I nodded. "Looks as if they paid a visit to Carmen, and I doubt they were there for a reading. Do you think we should...?"

"Indeed I do," Mrs. Finney said, and Lynn agreed.

I told the rest of the group to go on ahead and we'd join them soon. Tonya narrowed her eyes. I realized she wanted to go on the adventure, too, but her presence as the honored bride-to-be was required at the pool. I assured her she'd be the first to know about any dirt we dug up.

"All right," she said grudgingly. "But remember, my forgiving nature only extends so far. Don't test me."

"Been there, done that," I said, chuckling. "Won't happen again, my goddess."

They piled into Renata's Suburban and pulled off toward the ranch. Mrs. Finney strode down the sidewalk, with Lynn and me behind her. I felt like we were characters in a Western movie, making our way through the dusty streets of the town toward the saloon.

We stopped in front of Crystal Clear's plate glass window to peer inside, but couldn't see much. Mrs. Finney pulled the door open, and a bell tinkled as we entered. Despite the bright sunshine outside and the front wall of glass, the shop lay in shadow. I examined the window, which had been covered with a smoky liner to dull the exterior light. The result was a mysterious yet soothing ambience. The sweet, musky aroma of patchouli floated through the air. Wooden shelves lined the walls, each covered in the tools of Carmen's trade. One wall held an array of crystals: some standing alone, others hanging from necklaces, embedded in bracelets, decorating keychains, or vividly portrayed on book covers. On another row of shelves, patrons could select from tarot cards, silk turbans, incense sticks and trays, oils, candles, stones, and so much more: anything a New Age aficionado's heart could desire.

A whoosh of a thick velvet curtain revealed Carmen, whose taut posture made her appear ready to do battle. Her stance relaxed when she saw the three of us. "Oh, it's you," she said. "I was afraid the mayor and that miserable wife of his had returned with more threats and ultimatums."

My first thought was, if she was such a good psychic, how come she didn't know ahead of time who'd come calling? But my second thought, the one that lingered, was, how dare Polly and Martin Finkle harass this woman?

In her peasant blouse, flowing layered skirt, and bare feet, Carmen didn't present as a threat against society. Today she'd tied a bright blue scarf around her forehead, and it descended the length of her silver hair. A necklace of copper-colored coins tinkled when she moved.

Mrs. Finney held out her hand. "Good afternoon, Carmen. I'm Mrs. Finney, a friend of these ladies and the others visiting Moonglow Ranch. I'm pleased to make your acquaintance."

For a moment, Carmen looked surprised. Then she took Mrs. Finney's hand in both of hers and grasped it tight. I admired the unique pattern on the leather bracelet encircling Carmen's arm from her wrist to her elbow.

Then the bracelet squirmed, and a head popped up.

I couldn't help myself. I squealed.

Carmen released Mrs. Finney's hand and held up her wrist. "I see you've noticed my friend Pietro. Don't be frightened. He's a pygmy python, gentle as a lamb. He means no harm."

The snake's head moved languorously from side to side as he appeared to study us. He was perhaps a foot and a half long, though curled as he was around Carmen's arm, it was difficult to tell. His slender body was beige with a brown diamond pattern so perfect I couldn't believe it was real. *Amazing what nature creates,* I thought, my awe almost edging out my trepidation.

Mrs. Finney gestured to the snake. "May I?"

Carmen appraised Mrs. Finney and nodded. "From the moment I saw you, I sensed a kinship." She uncoiled the snake from her wrist and placed him in Mrs. Finney's upturned hands. Lynn remained stoic, but I took an instinctive step back, then another, until I'd backed myself against the door. I watched as the snake locked eyes with Mrs. Finney, flicking his long tongue in and out. She must have passed his assessment, because he gracefully curled around her forearm.

"He likes you," Carmen said, gazing at Mrs. Finney with respect.

Mrs. Finney turned toward us, brandishing her serpent-covered arm. "Most snakes are not dangerous to humans. When they strike, it's only in self-protection. If they don't sense a threat, they can be docile and even pleasant."

Carmen smiled. "I have three others in the back. They make magnificent companions. Pietro here has been with me the longest." She reached out and stroked him.

"Twelve years now, isn't it, my friend?"

"Snakes carry significant spiritual meaning," Mrs. Finney continued. "People even contend they possess healing power."

"Indeed," Carmen said. "They represent wisdom, creativity, even fertility." Her eyes danced as she looked from Lynn to me. "Perhaps the two of you should hold him."

I held my hands up in a no-thanks gesture. "Fertility isn't something I'm interested in."

"Me either," Lynn said with a chuckle. "My two girls are plenty."

To my horror, Mrs. Finney lifted the snake to her face and brushed him across her cheek. "His skin is silky as a baby's bum." She held her arm toward us. "Feel."

Lynn touched her index finger to the snake's scales. "Smooth and sleek."

I shrunk back and shook my head. "Callahan Cassidy," Mrs. Finney said. "Are you trembling? Why, you're ten thousand times the size of this creature. What happened to the brave woman who used to go toe to toe with criminals and heathens?"

It was like saying, *I double dog dare you.* I knew I should be well past the peer pressure stage, but I wasn't. I took a tiny step forward and held out a finger. The snake watched me, and I swear he rolled his beady eyes. When I made contact, I jerked back, then reached out again. His muscular back was dry to the touch—not the slimy texture I'd expected.

"Feeling especially fertile now?" Lynn asked.

"Ha ha."

Mrs. Finney returned the snake to Carmen, who watched as he coiled around her arm again. Then she gestured to the curtain. "I doubt you came here for a lesson in ophiology. Why don't you join me in the back room? I think we'll find it a more comfortable place for you to conduct your interrogation."

23

C armen pulled back the red velvet curtain and ushered us into the back room. A round wooden table covered with a crimson cloth dominated the space. On it lay the tools of Carmen's trade, many of which she'd displayed during our interrupted session at the lodge—a crystal ball, tarot cards, a small satin pillow. The patchouli scent was stronger here, courtesy of the thin curl of smoke rising from a single incense stick standing in a stoneware holder, its tip a glowing ember.

Flames glimmered from at least twenty round votive candles placed around the small room. The only other light glowed from a tall lamp in the corner, its shade draped with a long silk scarf. The resulting mood was one of suspenseful anticipation—as if something life-changing might happen in this room.

Six chairs encircled the table. Five were plain wooden seats. The sixth, placed at the back to face the curtain, was an ornate affair of carved mahogany, topped with a red velvet cushion. It looked like a throne, and it belonged to the queen of the shop.

As Mrs. Finney, Lynn, and I gathered at the table, Carmen sailed toward a large glass tank at the back of the room. There she uncurled the snake from her arm, cooing as she placed him gently inside. Three other snakes writhed over to greet their brother, and Carmen stroked each of them. My stomach roiled. My tender moment with Pietro a few minutes ago hadn't been enough to banish my lifelong serpent repulsion.

"Aren't you going to put a lid on that?" I asked, hearing the squeak in my own voice.

"My snakes are not the creatures we need to fear in this town. Or in this world."

I figured there was truth in those words, so I suppressed my objection. Still, I sat where I could monitor that tank. At the first sign of a snaky jailbreak, I'd lead the charge out the front door.

Carmen settled onto her throne, looking like a tiny but powerful monarch. Solemnly, we folded our hands on the table. Such was Carmen's compelling presence that I felt as if I'd gained an audience with the pope rather than an interview with a palm reader. I understood how she created believers of those who came to her.

She breathed in and out rhythmically, then said, "What are you seeking?"

"Only the truth," Mrs. Finney said.

"Ah, but what is the truth? Isn't it something different for each of us? Our perceptions, our worldview, our expectations—these things generate a variety of truths."

Mrs. Finney gave her a deferential nod. "I concede your point, Ms...."

With a wry grin, one that said, *I know what you're up to*, she responded, "Just Carmen."

Mrs. Finney dispensed with the wiles and got to the point. "Do you have a last name, Carmen?"

"Do I have a name at all? I am a shifting, changing being, one who eschews outer labels. Only to appease others do I identify myself by name. At present, my appellation is Carmen."

"All right, Carmen," Mrs. Finney said. "Perhaps I should have said we are seeking facts."

Carmen waved her fingers above the incense stick, pulling its scent toward her. Lynn shifted in her seat. When the psychic turned to us, the ember from the incense reflected in her eyes. "It is a fact that the woman who died, the one who called herself Eleanor, spent much of her life planting seeds of hatred and distrust. It is also a fact that the karma she dispersed came back to her." She looked at each of us, as if challenging us to disagree. "That is my interpretation of the facts."

We were silent for a moment. Carmen placed her palms on the table. "What you really want to know, though, is whether I killed her."

Mrs. Finney didn't even blink. "Did you?"

"No. It is not my place to destroy any living creature, no matter how abhorrent."

I leaned forward, resting my elbows on the table. "Carmen, you appeared at the stable just after I discovered Eleanor's body. You told me you'd been 'called' to the ranch. What did you mean by that?"

She closed her eyes and sighed. "The visions come to me unbidden. Sometimes in dreams, sometimes during meditation. It is both a blessing and a curse."

I found myself losing patience with the psychic's theatrics. "Listen, Carmen, a woman was murdered. Regardless of whether it resulted from karma or bad juju or whatever, Amaryllis and Fritz Bauer are in the hot seat. At best, they're in danger of losing their business. At the worst, they could go to jail for murder. So it's time for you to tell us everything you know—or envision. Who do you believe killed Eleanor Simonson?"

The psychic regarded me with…what? Amusement? Irritation? Respect? "My visions are vague and subject to interpretation. My spiritual sources don't approach me to offer confessions. That's not how this works."

"Well, to be honest, I'm not getting the idea it works at all. Perhaps you need to consult these unaccommodating spirits of yours and demand a few answers." I stood, ready to take another, more tangible tack. "In the meantime, do you have a bathroom I can use?"

"Of course. But Callie, you won't find what you're looking for."

"I'm looking for a toilet and a sink. Does your bathroom have those?"

Her mouth twitched, and she pointed down a narrow hall. "Second door on the left." As I stomped off, I heard her voice floating behind me. "The medicine cabinet opens from the right."

***

The bathroom was nothing special—a coat-closet sized room with the usual accoutrements. As Carmen had anticipated, I peeked in the medicine cabinet, finding a few prescription bottles without labels. No names to identify her. There was a hairbrush I supposed I could snatch for DNA, if I had the time to wait for test results—or anyone to conduct the test. Otherwise, I came up empty. To be honest, I wasn't even sure what I was looking for.

Without even using it, I flushed the toilet. Then I let the water run in the sink. I rubbed my hands around a bar of vanilla-scented soap and thought about Carmen. She was such a tiny woman, creeping up in age. But I'd seen wiry muscles in her arms and a fiery resolve in her eyes. And she sure knew how to handle a snake.

My mind wandered back to the scene of the murder and the bullsnake that slithered out of Spirit's stable. Could Carmen have carried it to the stable—or summoned its presence? I closed my eyes and let the scene play in my mind. *At the lodge, Eleanor threatens to drive Carmen out of town. Somehow, maybe through one of her so-called visions, Carmen knows Eleanor will return to the stable later that night. So she waits, biding her time. When Eleanor arrives under the cover of night, Carmen follows her into the stall, bashes her with the shovel, latches the door, and tosses a snake over the gate, knowing it will cause Spirit to rear up in fright. Then, the psychic glides unseen out of the stable, only to return after someone discovers the body...* That someone being me.

When I pulled myself back to the present, I caught my reflection in the mirror. The theory was a long shot, I figured, but no more so than any of the others we'd suggested. I shook the excess water off my hands and dried them on a plush cotton towel. When I returned to the seance room, the other three women stood silently near the folds of the curtains. The interview had come to an impasse. Mrs. Finney and Lynn exited through the curtain. When I moved to follow, Carmen stopped me with a thin, papery hand.

"Did you find what you were looking for?" she asked.

"I found the toilet. My bladder thanks you for your hospitality."

She regarded me solemnly. "Remember, Callie, I've glimpsed your future. When you are ready to see it for yourself, come find me."

24

After we'd settled into Mrs. Finney's car, I leaned across the front console and looked at Lynn in the passenger seat. "So? What did you think?"

She shrugged. "I think it was a bust. We learned nothing new—not even the woman's last name."

"Her last name?" Mrs. Finney said. "I doubt Carmen is even her legal first name. The woman has a history; I'm certain of that. I suspect she's a bit of a nomad, scuttling from place to place, alighting just long enough to wear out her welcome, then flittering on to the next location."

"You're saying she's a con artist?" I asked.

"Well, dear, I'm not trying to shatter any belief you might have in her supernatural powers, but yes, I'm guessing she makes her living scamming the hopeful, the desperate, and the gullible."

I frowned. Mrs. Finney was reiterating what I believed, but still...part of me longed to believe in Carmen's magic. I mean, if the woman didn't have visions, how had she been privy to Tonya and David's adoption discussions?

"Okay," I said. "So without a last name—or maybe even a true first name—what's our next move?"

"Well, Carmen had to have filled out a lease agreement. If we could get our hands on that, we might discern her true identity."

Mrs. Finney clucked her tongue. "Girls, I'm just not convinced Carmen is worth spending so much energy on."

"You don't think she belongs on the suspect list?" I asked.

"She could have killed Eleanor, I suppose. She seems to possess the physical strength, as well as the cunning. But my instinct tells me we should look elsewhere."

As I pondered Mrs. Finney's instinct, which rarely steered us wrong, Lynn's phone buzzed with a text. "It's a message from Raul," she said. "He has information and wants to FaceTime."

She pressed a button and held the phone up so we could see the screen. Raul looked out at us from his desk at the station.

"So I'm lucky enough to get all three amigos," he said with a grin. "Mr. Purdy told me you'd gone to Mustang, Mrs. Finney. Couldn't stay away from the action?"

"Whatever do you mean?" She smiled sweetly. "I'm here for a bridal shower."

"Uh huh. Listen, I don't blame you. I wish I was in on the action myself. But from Rock Creek Village, all I can do is provide the brains while you contribute the brawn."

"Quit stringing us along, big shot," I said. "Did you find any information or not?"

"Of course I found something." He picked up his notebook and flipped through the pages. "For starters, Gordon Simonson was mired in financial difficulties."

"Hmm," Lynn said. "I notice you said *was.*"

"Excellent observation, partner. A week ago, just as he was about to succumb to bankruptcy, the man received an influx of cash—the source of which I traced to his late stepmother."

"Eleanor Simonson gave Gordon a bunch of money?" I asked. "How much are we talking about?"

Raul glanced at his notes. "Just over a quarter of a million. But I didn't say she *gave* it to him."

I frowned. "What do you mean?"

"The money was intended as payment for Gordon's stock holdings in his father's company."

There were a few beats of silence as we digested the information. "That company is worth a fortune," Lynn said.

"Even if the boy was in financial trouble, selling his stock seems counterproductive," Mrs. Finney added. "Besides, how would his father react?"

"Here's something else to consider," Raul said. "The sale, scheduled to be finalized tomorrow, would have made Eleanor the company's largest minority shareholder. She'd control just under fifty percent of the company."

"That's a lot of power," I muttered.

Raul turned another page and continued. "As for dear old dad, he appears to be on the up and up. Except no one knows where he is."

"He's gone off the grid?" I asked.

"From what I could gather, Allen went to New York City on a business trip last Thursday, and he planned to return to Mustang yesterday. He left New York, but I can't find a record of his return to Colorado. When you own a personal plane, I guess you can be spontaneous. I've put out some feelers, but so far, I haven't been able to track down his alternate flight plan."

"I mean, he must be aware his wife is dead, right?" I said. "You'd expect him to get back as fast as he could…"

"Technically," Lynn mused, "if no one's heard from him in days, he has no alibi for the night of Eleanor's death—at least not one we know of."

"Bingo, partner. And as you know, he's a powerful man with untold resources. That means you three need to watch your backs. At least until I can finish solving your case for you."

We said our goodbyes, and Lynn disconnected. "How anxious are you guys to get to the swim party?" she asked.

"Did you have something in mind?" I asked.

"I'm thinking this might be a good time to pay a visit to Gordon Simonson. If nothing else, he might disclose his father's whereabouts."

***

After driving down a well-tended winding road, we arrived at the Simonson home. Bracketed by stands of large pine trees, the place was a two-story, log-and-stone construction the size of Versailles. Okay, not quite, but the place was palatial, with wrap-around balconies on both floors.

The property stretched toward the mountains, with a similar view to that of Moonglow Ranch. In fact, if you stood on the second-floor balcony and looked over the copse of trees that separated the properties, you'd just be able to glimpse Moonglow's stable—probably a great source of frustration for the dearly departed Eleanor. On the other hand, perhaps she reveled in the everyday sight of her young stud in the corral.

We used the elaborate brass knocker and moments later the door swung open, revealing a slender woman in a tailored herringbone patterned skirt, a black silk blouse, and sensible black pumps. Fifty-something, I estimated from the light wrinkles on her forehead and subtle streaks of gray in her shoulder-length blond hair. Administrative assistant, maybe.

She arched a thin eyebrow. "May I help you?"

I cringed, realizing we'd barged over here willy-nilly, not even bothering to rehearse a story. Without hesitation, Lynn reached into her bag and pulled out a leather wallet, flipping it open to display her badge and credentials. As she held them out for inspection, she discreetly placed her fingers over the words *Rock Creek Village*.

"Good afternoon," she said. "I'm Detective Lynn Clarke, and I'm here to speak to Gordon Simonson regarding his stepmother's death."

The woman examined the badge, her eyes flitting from

Lynn to me and then to Mrs. Finney. "These are my associates," Lynn said. "Ms. Cassidy and Mrs. Finney."

I was glad my muddy excursion beneath the lodge had forced me to change into my black dress. The woman's gaze skittered over me, and I surmised I'd passed muster. But Mrs. Finney, in her purple attire, gave her pause.

"And you are?" Lynn asked quickly, preempting a question.

"Ms. Clemens," she said, folding her hands primly. "I'm Mr. Simonson's administrative assistant. Mr. *Allen* Simonson, that is." She lifted her chin, proud to be serving the big boss instead of his erstwhile son.

"Well, Ms. Clemens, we're pressed for time, so if you could just summon Gordon for us..."

After a moment's indecision, Ms. Clemens gave Lynn a curt nod and stood back to allow us to enter. "If you'll wait in the Great Room, I'll see if Mr. Simonson is available."

"Please tell him Detective Clarke said it would be in his best interests to *make* himself available," Lynn said.

Ms. Clemens walked away briskly, heels tapping as she ascended a polished wooden staircase. I grinned at Lynn. When I'd first met her, she was a detective on loan to Rock Creek Village, assigned to a murder case. Her cool demeanor had irritated me at the time, but now I found it endearing. And useful.

"Can you believe this place?" she whispered. I followed her gaze across the room. It was the size of a basketball court, with subtle and tasteful decor—a less-is-more strategy conveying a sense of wealth and refinement. A dormant stone fireplace dominated one wall. Facing it, an arrangement of leather couches and chairs spoke of casual gatherings, with friends discussing the stock market while they indulged in vintage wine and expensive hors d'oeuvres.

It was the opposite wall, though, that took my breath away. Fully glass, it looked out over the meadow, the lake, the trees, and the distant mountains. I could only imagine the pink and orange hues of the sun setting over the range—a photographer's dream.

Once I'd mentally oohed and aahed, I let my eyes wander over the rest of the place. I assumed the kitchen and dining room lay beyond the stone arch at the back of the room. But my interest settled on an open barn-style door near the arch, leading into what appeared to be an office containing a messy desk strewn with papers. I stepped closer and saw a huge framed portrait of Gordon Simonson himself, wearing a navy blue golf shirt and brandishing a sparkling gold trophy.

I sneaked a peek at the empty staircase and tiptoed toward the office, ignoring Lynn's worried expression. "Just taking a quick look," I whispered as I passed her.

The office was decorated in a gaudy, rococo style. The gigantic, Louis XIV-style desk spoke of a man who was, shall I say, overcompensating. A leather golf bag stuffed with clubs leaned against the wall.

I made a beeline for the desk, knowing my window of opportunity was short. But where to begin? The disheveled piles of papers didn't seem to abide by any organizational strategy, so I plunged in. Shuffling through the stacks, I read "Collection Notice" on one piece of paper. Another read, "Third Attempt at Contact." If we hadn't already known of Gordon's financial troubles, his desk would have made it obvious.

My eye fell on a manila envelope. Flicking a glance over my shoulder, I saw Lynn pacing, chewing her thumbnail, while Mrs. Finney stood beside the door, humming. I pulled the envelope out and, finding it unsealed, carefully opened the flap. Inside, my fingers grasped the edges of a smooth, thin sheet. Any decent photographer would recognize that surface without seeing it—a piece of glossy photo paper.

I jiggled the photo from the folds of the envelope and almost gasped. The image had been shot with a telephoto lens, and I suspected the photographer had been hiding in the bushes like a paparazzo. It was just the sort of snapshot you'd find in a tabloid newspaper.

The light was low, either dawn or, more likely, dusk. The backdrop was a wooden building I recognized—Moonglow Ranch's stable. The subjects of the photo, a man and a woman, were locked in a steamy embrace. Her fingers were tangled in his hair, and she'd thrown her back as if in rapture. His lips pressed against her slender neck. One hand rested on her back and the other on her backside.

The woman I recognized as Eleanor Simonson. The man, of course, was our own Thor lookalike, Colby Trent.

25

Mrs. Finney's humming rose to a not-so-discreet crescendo, and I knew my time was up. I shoved the photo back into the envelope, tucked the envelope beneath the stack of papers, and scampered toward the far wall, where I pretended to study Gordon's portrait.

Lynn attempted to introduce herself, but Gordon ignored her and stormed into the office. "What do you think you're doing?" he asked.

I pasted an innocent expression onto my face. "Oh, Mr. Simonson, I noticed this portrait of you and just had to see it up close. That trophy, well, it's stunning. But I can't make out the wording. What did you win it for?"

He gave me a dubious look, but his ego overcame his suspicion. "Nine hole champion at the 2012 Cascade Springs Golf Tournament," he said, puffing out his chest. "I won by four strokes."

"Wow, that's impressive." Probably a vanity affair he'd paid to win.

As Gordon engaged in nostalgic self-congratulation, I looked him over. Stretchy shorts, pasty white legs covered in matts of brown hair. White undershirt barely covering a swelling belly. Damp, thinning hair sticking up like a chia pet's. The towel around his neck indicated he'd just gotten out of the shower.

After a moment, I could see the recognition dawning. He spun and looked at Lynn.

"I was told a detective was here to talk to me." He

pointed from Lynn to me. "But I've seen the two of you before. You're guests at Moonglow Ranch, where Eleanor was murdered."

"I'm Detective Clarke," Lynn said, flashing her badge again. "My associates and I are assisting with the investigation into your stepmother's death."

Gordon didn't bother to look at Lynn's credentials. "Yeah, right. As if Chester would allow that." He gestured to Mrs. Finney. "I guess this is your bodyguard."

If you only knew, I thought. Mrs. Finney stared at him with an intensity that melted the smirk off his face.

Lynn pulled a small notebook from her bag and opened the cover. "Mr. Simonson, in the course of our investigation, we've learned that you were preparing to sell your shares of your father's company to Mrs. Eleanor Simonson. Was your father aware of that transaction?"

The blood drained from Gordon's face. For a moment, I feared he might pass out, but he rallied. "That's a bald-faced lie. If you repeat that publicly, I'll sue you for libel."

"Slander," I said.

He swiveled to face me. "What?"

"Libel means written defamation. Slander is spoken. Detective Clarke said the words aloud. She didn't publish them. So you'd have to sue her for slander."

He shook his head in confusion. Behind his back, Lynn gave me a quick grin before continuing her interrogation. "We have documentation of the transaction, Mr. Simonson, so there's nothing to be gained by denying it. Here's our question: why did you sell? Was your stepmother blackmailing you?"

Gordon inhaled sharply. "Why would you even say that? I simply had no further use for my shares of the company, so I agreed to sell to her. Keep it in the family. My stepmother had nothing with which to blackmail me. When it came to damaging information, I was the one holding the cards."

Lynn raised her eyebrows. "What do you mean?"

He hesitated, but then I saw calculation creep into his eyes. I'd seen that expression before—always on the face of a narcissist. Gordon Simonson had just told himself he was the smartest person in the room, and now it was time to brag.

"I had the dirt on mommy dearest. You'd better believe it. Eleanor enjoyed playing with her boy toys, especially the cowboy who lived next door. But I had evidence of their affair. No judge on earth would give her any of my father's money in a divorce settlement if she was caught cheating."

He leaned on his desk. "Now, I've grown bored with this conversation. It's time for you to leave."

"Just a couple more questions," Lynn said, jotting something in her notebook.

"I said leave!" Gordon roared. "It wasn't a request. I want you out now."

None of us moved. He reached over to the bag leaning against the wall and yanked out a golf club—a formidable-looking driver with a head the size of a grapefruit. Though I was certain it could do some damage, I couldn't get too worked up. The whole scenario reeked of bad melodrama.

I crossed my arms. "What are you going to do, tee off on us? Three women invited into your home by your father's administrative assistant? They'd arrest you for assault."

He lifted the club, trying to appear imposing. "I'll say you trespassed and threatened me. Chester Wade would have my back. But if you leave now and don't say a word about that stock sale, I'll forget this incident ever happened."

Just then, we heard the front door open. With Gordon sidetracked by the sound, Lynn dropped her notebook to the floor and, fast as lightning, grabbed Gordon's wrist and twisted it until he screeched in pain. The golf club clattered to the floor. Mrs. Finney lunged forward, swung her foot behind Gordon's knees, and knocked his legs out from under him. He landed on his backside with a thud. Then Mrs. Finney sat on him, and any air left in his lungs whooshed out.

"What were you saying earlier about a bodyguard?" she asked. She didn't get an answer.

A moment later, a tall, sophisticated-looking man in an expensive suit stood in the office door. I recognized Allen Simonson from pictures in *Forbes*. The prodigal husband had returned.

Behind him loomed a beast of a man holding two suitcases. The guy was at least six-foot-five and two eighty. Now here was a legitimate bodyguard. I mean, the man's muscles had muscles.

Gigantor dropped the bags and lurched past Allen toward Mrs. Finney and Gordon, skidding to a halt when his boss held up a hand. "It's all right, Creed," Allen said.

The senior Mr. Simonson took a moment to assess the situation. His eyes took in the club on the floor, Lynn standing to the side with her arms crossed, me likely looking guilty and nervous. Finally, his gaze rested on Mrs. Finney perched atop Gordon like a bird in a nest. Allen's mouth twisted, and I could see he was stifling a laugh.

My first reaction was shock. This man had walked into his home, discovered his son splayed out on the floor, bested by a plump older woman, and this was his response? Then I looked at the scene with fresh eyes and couldn't resist a smile of my own. It was almost a farce.

A split second later, Allen turned to Gigantor, all traces of humor gone. "We're fine here, Creed. Take my bags upstairs. I'll call if I need you."

Without comment, the man grabbed the suitcases and backed out of the room. One look at Allen convinced me he didn't brook dissent from many people. He walked over and helped Mrs. Finney to her feet.

Then he reached down and grasped his son's hand. Gordon groaned as Allen pulled him off the floor. When he saw the stern set of Allen's mouth, Gordon dropped his eyes.

"Get upstairs and make yourself presentable," Allen said to his son.

"But Father, don't you want to know—"

Allen held up his hand in the same authoritative way he'd done with Creed. It was a gesture that said, *Don't mess with me.* And those blue eyes blazed with barely concealed rage. *Ruthless beneath a veneer of civility*, I remembered from the *Forbes* article.

Gordon hung his head and shuffled toward the door. But then Allen snapped his fingers. "Before you go, pick up your toys."

He pointed to the club lying on the floor. Gordon glanced at us, embarrassed. He retrieved the club and put it in the bag, exiting the office without another word.

"Ladies, I hope you'll forgive my son's behavior," Allen said. I was certain Gordon was still within hearing distance and that Allen intended to further humiliate him. The dynamics in this family wouldn't inspire any parenting books—unless they were shelved in the "not to" section.

"Please explain what business the three of you have in my home." His tone remained friendly, but his eyes still smoldered. I knew he expected to be obeyed, or there would be repercussions.

For the third time since we'd arrived at the house, Lynn pulled out her badge. "We're assisting with the investigation into your wife's death, Mr. Simonson." She hesitated. "Someone has informed you, I assume."

He dropped his eyes, but when he lifted them, his expression was placid. "Of course. There is no detail in my life of which I'm not immediately informed."

"We're sorry for your loss," Lynn said.

He waved. "I expect I'll be hearing that ad nauseam

over the next few weeks. Thank you, though. And please, call me Allen."

Lynn nodded. "Allen, if I may make an observation, you don't appear especially…"

"Emotional?" he asked. "Not my style. If it's emotion you're looking for, talk to my son." He inspected Lynn. "You're very young, Detective. People grieve in different ways, as I expect you'll learn when you gain some experience."

At Allen's version of "little lady," Lynn stiffened. I decided it was my turn to wrestle with the boss man. "Mr. Simonson…Allen…no one here in Mustang seems to have heard from you since your wife died. Your son told Chief Wade you were scheduled to return yesterday, but you were delayed. Would you mind telling us where you've been?"

He turned to me and studied me coolly. After a moment, he tilted his head. "Now I have it. You're Callahan Cassidy, the photographer. Sundance Studio, Rock Creek Village. I do business with Bradley and Tim, and I follow them on social media. They've raved about your work."

He was referencing the two social influencers who had given my business a tremendous boost over the past year. I felt myself flush under the praise, and I realized that was likely his goal. A master of manipulation. "Thank you," I replied. "If we could return to my question…"

"Ah, yes. Where in the world was Allen Simonson?" His smile carried no trace of humor. "I can't imagine that my whereabouts are any concern of a photographer. One who happens to be in the company of a detective outside her jurisdiction. As well as a…?" He turned to Mrs. Finney. She didn't say a word, just graced him with one of her wise smiles.

Allen rocked back on his heels and addressed Lynn. "I'm a bottom-line guy, Detective, and here's my bottom line. I don't believe you have any authority here, but in the event I'm mistaken, I'm instructing you to address further questions to my attorney." He reached into the interior pocket of his designer suit coat, opened a leather case, and pulled out an embossed card. "Here's his information."

She took the card, studied it for a moment, and tucked it into her pocket. "One last thing," Allen said. "I'm hoping we don't need to make an issue of my son's actions today. The boy is impulsive even in the best of times, and with the added stress of his stepmother's death…well, he simply lost control. He didn't mean any harm. Never does."

"I'm fine with letting this go," Lynn said. "That is, if my associates agree."

Mrs. Finney and I both nodded. "Appreciate that," Allen said. "I can assure you, Gordon will be dealt with appropriately."

He sounded like the father of a teenager who'd been skateboarding on private property. What was he going to do, ground the man? Take away the keys to his car? Gordon probably lived in a perpetual state of puberty.

"So we're done here." Allen summoned Ms. Clemens, who appeared as if by magic. "Please show these ladies to the door."

She walked out of the office, and we followed her through the enormous Great Room. As she opened the front door, Allen stuck his head out of the office. "Ms. Cassidy? Callahan?"

I turned back to him. "Yes?"

"I've been considering a formal portrait. Perhaps I'll commission your services. I'll be in touch."

He disappeared into Gordon's office, and another line from the *Forbes* article popped into my head: "Simonson is the type of businessman who will hug you tight as he's stabbing you in the back."

I shivered. That might be exactly what he was trying to do with me.

26

During the short trek back to Moonglow Ranch, Lynn, Mrs. Finney, and I concluded Gordon was a rich punk. Impulsive, as his father said, and capable of killing his stepmother. Allen, on the other hand, presented himself as refined, intelligent, and well-bred. It was difficult to picture him getting his hands dirty by bashing a shovel into his wife's skull, but it wasn't beyond the realm of possibility. Besides, he had his own personal Gigantor at his beck and call. I felt certain that guy knew where all the bodies were buried.

As we turned into the ranch, it occurred to me that the afternoon had flown by, and we'd all but missed the pool party. I grimaced, feeling as if I'd once again botched my priorities.

As soon as Mrs. Finney pulled to a stop, I jumped out of the back seat and hurried past the lodge to the pool. Woody let out a welcoming bark, and Tonya, sunning herself on a lounge chair, shaded her eyes with her hand. Fortunately, she gave me an amiable smile that assured me there were no hard feelings.

"Well, look what the cat dragged in," she said. Beside her chair, Carl arched his back, and Tonya reached down to pat his head. "Sorry, fella. Didn't mean to insult you."

Woody bounced to my side, as excited as if I'd been gone a week. I took a seat near Tonya's lounge chair and ran my fingers through his fur while I waved at Summer and Jessica, who were lying on floats in the pool. I blew a kiss to Mom on the pool's edge, her feet dangling in the water. Near her, Renata sat reading a magazine, wearing a bikini that would have made Ethan's eyes water. Then my eyes found Lydia, and I did a double take.

Stretched out on a lounge chair, Tonya's mom wore a one-piece bathing suit, red with sparkling white rhinestones. The suit was cut high on the sides to emphasize her long legs. Her toenails, painted a seductive red, flashed in the sunlight. She stretched her arms above her head, displaying her ample bosom, and glanced toward the corral, where Colby and the ranch hands were rounding up the horses.

I leaned toward Tonya. "Has she been doing that all afternoon?"

"Except the times she strolled around the pool in heeled slippers. Oh, and once when she noticed Colby coming toward the lodge. Then she got in the pool just long enough to get wet, got out, and ran a towel across her body. Very slowly." Tonya rolled her eyes. "I know you and Maggie said I should give her a chance, but I'm telling you, it's hard."

I tutted as Lynn and Mrs. Finney joined us. "Never mind," Tonya said. "Distract me from the madness with a recap of your shenanigans. We've been on pins and needles, wondering if the three of you solved this thing."

"Nothing like that," Lynn said. "But we did gather some interesting information."

Jessica and Summer got out of the pool and sat on towels beside us. Mom and Renata moved chairs over so they could listen, too. Only Lydia stayed put, seemingly disinterested in the ongoing murder investigation.

The three of us took turns sharing the details of our visits to Carmen and the Simonsons. When we finished, the group mulled over the information. Then Summer sighed. "I didn't expect you'd have it wrapped up today, but I was hoping for something more definitive." She glanced at the lodge and lowered her voice. "Aunt Ryll is trying not to show it, but this is taking a toll."

Mrs. Finney reached over and squeezed Summer's fingers. "I can only imagine the depth of your aunt's trepidation. It must be difficult for her to see her lovely ranch in peril."

"As I've said, this place is her life's dream. A place where people can come to meditate, heal, bond with nature, and have fun doing it. And now those awful people are making it impossible." Her voice rose. "I'm beyond furious."

We stared at Summer in shock. I'd rarely seen our yoga and meditation guru angry. Jessica put a hand on her wife's shoulder. Summer noticed the concern on our faces and took a breath. "Sorry. I'm so close to my aunt, and I'm feeling especially protective of her. Emotional outbursts won't help, though. They'll only send more negative vibes into the universe, and we don't need that."

In one enviably fluid motion, she rose from her cross-legged position and squeezed the water from her braid. "Anyway, Aunt Ryll asked me to watch the time. We should head inside to get cleaned up before dinner."

She helped Jessica up, and everyone began wrapping towels around themselves. Lydia shimmied into her lacy black cover up and heeled slippers, her eyes never wavering from the corral.

"Would you mind staying behind for a minute?" Tonya asked, signaling to me, Lynn, and Mrs. Finney.

We settled back into our chairs, and when everyone was out of earshot, Tonya reached into her bag and pulled out her phone. "I heard from Phil. He looked into the names I gave him. He couldn't find anything on Carmen. No surprise, since we couldn't even give him a full name. Turns out there are four hundred twelve psychics who call themselves Carmen, and that's only in the United States."

Mrs. Finney chuckled. "I doubt even The Company could have done much better," she said, referencing the CIA, her former clandestine employer.

"As for Colby…" Tonya wrinkled her nose in distaste. "No criminal record. He's from Wyoming, where his parents still live, as does his younger brother. Colby grew up poor and feral, according to Phil's research, but he's stayed on the right side of the law. When he was twenty-five, he married a woman in her late forties, heiress to a tech fortune. They divorced a year later, long enough to invalidate the terms of the prenup. He walked away with a decent settlement, which he frittered away in no time flat. Since then, he's been ranch-hopping across the West. Apparently, he's a skilled ranch manager, but he can't make enough money at it to be satisfied. My guess is he hooked up with Eleanor hoping to snare rich wife number two—assuming he could persuade her to divorce rich husband number three."

She shook her head. "Makes me even more irritated at Lydia. She's not a member of the one percent, but she's gotten a few large settlements from her own ex-husbands. Colby probably sees her as ripe for the picking. And here she is, drooling over him like a mare in heat."

"It is troubling." Mrs. Finney chewed her lip. "Perhaps I should have a word with this Colby fellow."

Tonya and I grinned at each other, and I knew we were both picturing a similar scenario: Colby tied to a rickety wooden chair, a lone lightbulb hanging from the ceiling above him. Mrs. Finney smacking the handle of a horse whip in her palm as she circled the chair. She'd handle Colby, all right.

"Much as I appreciate the offer, I think we'd best leave him be," Tonya said. "We don't want to scare the boy into leaving town under the cover of night. He's on our suspect list, and we can't afford to lose him."

Lynn frowned. "He's on the list, yes, and he belongs there—for the time being. But I'm having trouble figuring out his motive."

"That is problematic," Mrs. Finney agreed. "What would this Colby fellow gain by murdering his wealthy paramour? If his primary goal involved wrangling the woman into marriage to gain access to her fortune, killing her only upends his plan."

"Maybe it wasn't premeditated," I said. "Maybe when they met up in the stable, Eleanor said she wanted to break things off, and that infuriated him. Or maybe she'd found something in his past we haven't yet uncovered, and she was using it to blackmail him."

Lynn snapped her fingers. "What if he saw her preparing to inject a horse, figured out what she'd been doing, and in a moment of righteousness, bashed her over the head to protect Spirit?"

"Hmm," I said, considering the idea. Colby cared for the horses, I believed, but I didn't see him as a "right fighter." Then another thought popped into my head. "Why didn't Colby hear any noise that night?"

Lynn tilted her head. "What do you mean?"

"His cabin is close to the stable. Even if Eleanor had sneaked in, shouldn't Colby have heard Spirit whinnying, or when he reared up in fright? Come to think of it, didn't Ryll mention that Colby was always up before dawn, tending to the horses? Why was he so late getting to the stable yesterday? If he'd kept to schedule, he'd have found the body instead of me."

"You're right," Lynn said. "Someone needs to interview Colby Trent."

"I've already offered to have a word with the young man," Mrs. Finney reminded us.

The corner of my mouth turned up. "Indeed you did, Mrs. Finney. But I'd suggest we hold off for the time being. I want to talk to the ranch hands first, do some reconnaissance. It's easier to snare a bug in the spider web if it doesn't see you coming."

Mrs. Finney tittered. "Why, Callahan Cassidy, you're starting to develop axioms of your own. That one is a bit dark for the cups, but keep trying, dear."

Tonya cleared her throat. "Do you want to know the

rest of the information I uncovered or not?"

"Don't you mean *Phil* uncovered?" I asked.

"My employee, my instructions. I'm entitled to take credit. Any man would, in my position."

"Point taken."

Tonya scrolled through Phil's email. She looked around to make sure no one was listening. "This regards Ryll and Fritz," she whispered. "I didn't want to discuss it in front of Summer. She's feeling a little fragile."

The three of us leaned forward, our curiosity piqued. Always one to appreciate an audience, Tonya paused for dramatic effect. "Today, if you don't mind," I said.

"All right, all right. Amaryllis Simmons and Fritz Bauer were arrested together back in the early seventies—"

"Who wasn't?" Mrs. Finney interjected.

"And charged with felony assault on a police officer," Tonya finished with a flourish.

My mouth dropped open. Summer's sweet, peace-loving hippie relatives had committed assault? Lynn appeared equally stunned.

Only Mrs. Finney didn't seem surprised. She sat back and folded her hands. "You girls aren't old enough to know about the early seventies, but I was a young adult back then. Let me tell you, anyone who didn't work for The Man was likely arrested at some point for opposing his dictates. It was a time of protest and demands for change. Sometimes those demands got…heated. The police hauled off dozens of protestors at a time and charged them with assault or resisting arrest. I'd guess the charges against Ryll and Fritz were later dropped, or reduced to a misdemeanor."

My brow furrowed. "But Mrs. Finney, you worked for…" I swiveled my head and whispered, as if there were spies hiding among the pine trees. "You worked for the CIA. You *were* The Man."

She graced me with that wise smile of hers. "I'm not *that* old, dear. I didn't join The Company until the eighties. Besides, a person can believe in and support the causes the protestors espoused and still work in law enforcement. In fact, it's one of the few ways to affect real change."

I gazed at my friend with admiration. Mrs. Finney was tight-lipped about her past, and I could only imagine the stories living in that head of hers. I'd make it one of my goals to extract them, one by one.

Meanwhile, Tonya had continued scrolling through Phil's email. "Sure enough. Says here they pled guilty to misdemeanor disorderly conduct and got sentenced to probation and a hundred hours of community service. Soon after, they signed up for the Peace Corps."

"Regardless of the plea deal, the mere fact of a felony charge could damage their business, especially in a place like Mustang. I'd guess that's the dirt Eleanor had."

"It would explain her confidence that she'd get Moonglow Ranch closed," Lynn mused. "But why wouldn't she just confront them with the information, or make it public? Why go to the trouble of getting the mayor involved?"

My mind spun with questions, but I slapped my hands against my knees and stood. "I've had enough for now. I'm exhausted, and my brain is tangled in knots."

Tonya smiled wryly. "You outslept us all today. How can you be tired?"

I was about to point out it was her snoring keeping me from a sound sleep, but I remembered why we were here in the first place and how badly this bridal shower had gone awry.

"You're right," I said, slinging an arm around her. "Must be middle age catching up with me. Nevertheless, I'm going upstairs to shower. I hope that'll help reset my synapses."

"Good idea," Lynn said. "We need your synapses operating full throttle if we're going to solve this case and save Moonglow Ranch."

27

As soon as I'd showered, Tonya took her turn in the bathroom. Experience had taught me my friend wouldn't be out soon, so I decided to give Sam a call. I tapped his FaceTime icon and waited as my phone attempted to connect with his. No answer, but just after I hit the End Call button, a text appeared.

At a neighborhood party, it said. *After that, movies. Call you tomorrow?*

I sighed. Sam was having so much fun—without me.

Sure, I responded. *Love you.*

Love you, too, beautiful.

I fell back against my pillow, picturing Sam tanned from the beach, his lips curved in a sexy smile, his fingers running through his thick mop of hair.

Then I pictured his new friend Isabella, who was undoubtedly attending this same neighborhood shindig.

I chewed my lip, knowing full well I should leave it alone but unable to fight my baser instincts.

I pulled up Instagram.

Though I rarely used the site except for business purposes and Sam didn't even have an account, his daughter did. I pulled up Elyse's page and, as anticipated, discovered a collage of vacation photos. A lot of selfies, many of them with her dad and grandparents. Very sweet. Then I found photos from the infamous beach outing, including one of Sam and Isabella on adjacent beach chairs, toasting the camera with cans of soda.

When I scrolled through today's posts, I found images

of a well-attended outdoor block party. Old folks abounded, a few with walkers, one in a wheelchair, but all looking vigorous. They'd cordoned off the cul-de-sac and gathered around tables covered with homemade casseroles and desserts.

I scrolled until I found what I secretly knew I was looking for: a picture of Sam and Isabella standing off to the side. He wore khaki cargo shorts and a white polo shirt that accentuated his tan, and she wore a tight red sundress which fell at least five inches above the knee, revealing firm thighs. Heeled sandals emphasized muscled calves, and the low neckline of the dress emphasized...other assets. The woman had muscles and curves in places I could only dream of.

My pulse quickened. Using two fingers, I enlarged the photo so I could further torture myself. Isabella and Sam stood practically hip to hip. She'd thrown her head back in laughter and rested a hand on his arm. I tried to assess the look on Sam's face but couldn't decide whether he was enjoying the attention or uncomfortable with it.

Most likely enjoying it, I decided. But that might be my current mood talking.

The remaining photos revealed little else of interest. I tossed my phone onto the nightstand and draped an arm over my eyes. The flicker of jealousy I'd experienced could bloom into a blaze if I fed it. The question was, did I want to feed it?

My therapist had told me most humans lean toward negativity and are attracted to drama. Misery draws our attention like a magnet. But by developing insight, as well as positive self-talk, and especially by divulging those feelings to a caring listener, we could often avoid being consumed by those negative feelings.

It was worth a try. After a few meditative breaths, I repeated to myself that I was overreacting. Sam was merely being friendly to his parents' neighbor. No big deal. I was friendly with Raul. People could be friendly with other attractive people without it leading to impropriety.

Was this working? I couldn't tell. When I heard Tonya turn off the shower, I wrenched myself off the bed and slipped into a cute outfit I'd packed—emerald green capris, a loose peasant blouse, and a comfy pair of flats. I poofed my dark shoulder-length hair, dabbed on lip gloss, and took one last peek at the mirror. I was certainly no exotic beauty like Isabella, but I was pleased with what I saw. Maybe I'd even catch Colby's eye and shoot a selfie that showed him laughing at a witty comment I made. Maybe I'd post it on Instagram. Maybe Elyse would show her father…

So much for positive self-talk.

When Tonya emerged from the bathroom—every bit as stunning as Isabella—I plastered on my happy face and followed her downstairs to dinner. Afterward, we engaged in a raucous game of charades, mostly topics befitting a ribald bachelorette party. Throughout the game, I noticed Tonya watching me, assessing. I tried my best to get into the spirit of things, but I just couldn't shake my mood. When the game ended, we gathered around the firepit to roast marshmallows and make Valerie's healthy version of s'mores.

Tonya pointed her stick at me, a white blob oozing from the end. "All right, sugarplum, spill. What's got you in a funk?"

I shrugged and forced a smile. "Nothing. I'm great."

Jessica snorted. "Oh, please. You're easier to read than a Dr. Seuss book. Something's been chewing you up one side and down the other all night."

"You're among friends, Callie," Summer said. "Talk to us."

Renata pressed her marshmallow between two homemade graham crackers and watched the slab of dark chocolate inside melt. "I recognize that look. It's a relationship issue."

"Ugh," Lynn said. "Relationship issues are the worst. In my experience, it helps to vent."

I snatched a graham cracker from the wooden bowl and offered it to Woody, who sniffed the unfamiliar treat before taking it in his teeth. He gulped it down and looked up at me with gratitude.

I regarded the faces around the fire. I'd never been one to relish vulnerability, but these women were my friends. My family. So I danced outside my comfort zone and told them about the gorgeous neighbor and the unfamiliar—and unpleasant—feelings she evoked in me.

"I've never been a particularly jealous person," I said. "I mean, occasionally another photographer got an assignment I wanted, and I'd be irritated. But in relationships? I can't remember feeling this way. Not even in high school."

"It's because you've never experienced this level of commitment before," Summer said. "When we fall in love, even the most serene among us grapples with jealousy from time to time."

"Even you? I'm surprised."

"Even me. In case you haven't noticed, which seems unlikely, Jessica is gorgeous. Add in her vivacious personality, and people are drawn to her. When you see others reacting to your partner's attractiveness, it's only human nature to want to protect what you have."

Jessica pointed at Summer. "My yoga guru here is surrounded every day by fit clients in tight clothes, so yes, I'm jealous once in a while, too. But I know she loves me, so the jealousy never gets the best of me."

Tonya nodded. "It's a mixed feeling. That quick rush of jealousy tells me I have something special. But then it seeps away fast because, well, I know I have something special."

"You all have a different problem than mine." Lydia poofed her hair and preened. "I find myself on the opposite side of the equation. Other women are always jealous of me. It makes it difficult to maintain female friendships. But it's a burden I'm forced to bear."

"Maybe if you stopped trying to steal people's husbands and boyfriends, they'd like you better," Tonya mumbled.

"What was that, TeeTee?" Lydia asked.

"Nothing, Mother."

Then Mrs. Finney chimed in. "A spurt of jealousy might be a good thing, but in my opinion, it's important to tame the beast before it devours you. I'm thinking of a man I knew in Belgium. I believed he was *the one*, as people say. Then I found him *in flagrante delicto* with a young Dutch tart." She pursed her lips. "That was the last time I saw the man. Second to the last time, actually. And that's all I'm prepared to say about that."

We all laughed, a bit nervously, I thought. Our friend Mrs. Finney was an enigma.

Next, Renata weighed in. "I agree with Mrs. Finney. Jealousy is all well and good until it gets out of control. Jeffrey…" We engaged in a mutual shudder at the mention of Renata's ex, who had met an untimely demise last winter when he was murdered at our local hockey rink. I instinctively glanced at the scar on my wrist. "…Jeffrey's jealousy contorted into a need to control my entire life. He wanted to pre-approve everything I did and everyone I interacted with. It didn't make for a happy marriage, and that's putting it mildly."

We sat in silence for a moment, listening to the fire pop. From what I was hearing, my jealousy was normal and not a sign of something broken in a relationship—or in me—as long as it was controlled.

Tonya leaned back and crossed her legs. "We haven't heard from you, Maggie. Have you ever grappled with the green-eyed monster?"

"Of course," Mom said. "You all know what a hunk Butch is."

Every woman in the group nodded enthusiastically. I

cringed. This was my father they were referencing.

"I'm not blind to his sex appeal." Mom's eyes took on a dreamy cast. "And oh, my, back in the day…When Butch was chief of police and put on that uniform, women swooned. Some even threw themselves at him." She cast a sidelong look at Lydia, who avoided her gaze. "During the early years of our marriage, I admit to jousting with jealousy. Butch did, too. You may find this hard to believe, but I was considered a bit of a catch back then."

"Oh, please," Tonya said. "You're still a catch. You're a gorgeous woman, Maggie Cassidy. Inside and out." Lydia cleared her throat, but Tonya ignored her.

Mom brushed the compliment away. "As the years wore on, Butch and I learned to communicate. We developed a level of trust that transcended the jealous impulses. When a couple reaches that stage, they've formed a bond that provides them with an insulating sense of security and love. We're each other's best friends, life partners, lovers." Her face flushed. "Jealousy has lost its power."

I looked at my mother in awe, thankful for parents who set such a high standard for relationships. "Your jealousy is natural, Callie," she said. "But I'm a hundred percent sure there is no basis for it. Sam has loved you for as long as I can remember. A pretty young thing in Florida won't put even a tiny dent in those feelings. Rest easy."

A wave of warmth flooded me, washing away the lingering drops of negativity. My mother and my friends were right. Sam and I had something I hadn't even known I'd dreamed of all these years.

"Speaking of resting easy," I said with a yawn, "I'm going up to bed. I haven't slept much the past couple of nights, and all this girl talk has worn me out."

"Not sleeping well?" Mom said. "Why?"

I squirmed in my seat, unwilling to mention Tonya's

snoring again. "Everything that's going on, I guess. Can't get my brain to stop racing."

"Well, darling, let's go up together. I might have something that will help."

"I'm off, too," Mrs. Finney said. "To paraphrase John Muir, the top bunk is calling, and I must go."

The others stood as well, and we said our goodnights and parted at the top of the stairs.

Mom led me into her room, where she handed over a set of earplugs and a single sleeping pill. Once I'd changed into my pajamas, I crawled into bed, ears stuffed and pill swallowed. Tonya was on the phone with David, but even her murmurings didn't pierce the fog. I fell into an immediate and deep sleep.

Sometime later in the night, Carl patted me on the lips with his paw, dragging me from dreamland. I tried to brush him away, but he persisted. At the end of the bed, Woody groaned and curled into a ball. Finally, I sat up, groggy and foul-tempered. "What do you want, cat?"

Once he was sure he had my attention, Carl hopped onto the windowsill. When I leaned forward and looked past him, I saw a figure stepping onto Colby's front porch. Clouds had drifted across the silver sliver of a moon, and I couldn't make out details, but I could guess who I was seeing. It had to be Lydia, making another nightly foray to the pleasure dome.

I dropped back onto the pillow, and despite Carl's irritated hiss, fell back asleep at once.

28

I awoke before seven, bright-eyed and bushy tailed. Literally. As I pushed Carl's tail off my face and spit stray hairs off my tongue, I had a hazy recollection of our midnight encounter and the figure at Colby's door. I peered over at Tonya, sleeping quietly for a change. For all I knew, the whole thing could have been a dream.

Woody indulged in a full-body stretch, while Carl ambled to the corner of the bathroom to use his litter box. I pulled on a pair of shorts and a t-shirt, and the three of us left the room, closing the door behind us. Except for Lydia's, the doors were ajar, indicating everyone else had gotten an even earlier start than me.

Downstairs, I peeked into the den to find Summer leading Mom, Ryll, and Mrs. Finney in a downward dog. I hurried off before they spotted me. Outside, the rest of my friends were stretching quads and calves to prepare for another run.

Pulling her ankle toward her tush, Jessica called to me. "Come with us, Callie. It'll be good for you."

"Yeah, grab your running shoes. We'll wait," Renata said.

"Running shoes?" I responded with a grin. "Never heard of them."

Lynn laughed. "It's a short run today. Only a few miles. You'd survive."

I waved them off. "Thanks, but I'm going to enjoy the quiet of the morning." Beside me, the cat had started hacking up a hairball. "With Carl."

Once the women took off down the road, I stood on the deck, breathing in the fresh air. The sun had been up for an hour, but today its presence was muted by a layer of slate gray clouds, which cast a lovely glow over the ranch. I reached for my camera but realized I'd left it in my room.

Before I headed up to retrieve it, I took the creatures to the kitchen for their morning meal. As we approached, the sound of giggling filtered through the door.

Inside, Valerie, Haley, and Georgia stood behind the kitchen island, looking captivated. And no wonder. Colby Trent was leaning against the wall, regaling them with a story about his time as a rodeo cowboy. Clad in tight jeans and a pearl buttoned shirt, his Stetson rested lazily on his brow.

Woody and Carl pushed past me. Valerie and Haley startled when they saw us and quickly returned to their tasks, as if they were children who'd been caught with their hands in the cookie jar.

"Sorry to interrupt," I said. "Okay if I feed the creatures?"

With a genuine smile, Georgia turned her attention from Colby to the animals.

"Absolutely," she said. "But tell me, why do you call them the creatures?"

"Because if I call them pets, it makes Carl crazy."

Georgia gave me a quizzical look. "It's like this," I explained. "I found Woody as a puppy years ago on the streets of D.C. When I took him in, I told people I'd rescued him, but in truth, he'd rescued me. I hadn't realized how lonely I'd become until we found each other. When we moved to Rock Creek Village, a stray orange tabby came into our lives. The three of us are…well, we're a family. To call them *pets* seems to, I don't know, shift the balance of power. I don't own them. We choose each other."

Carl purred his approval and rubbed against my ankles.

Woody licked my hand.

"Makes perfect sense." Georgia took a seat at the table. "Come here, you wild and gorgeous creatures. Let me love on you." Woody put his head on her knee, giving her hand a slurp. Carl surprised me by jumping into Georgia's lap and allowing her to stroke his back.

Colby turned to me and tipped his hat. "Mornin', Mizz Cassidy," he said. "That's a nice story. Kind of feel that way about the horses. And my lady friends, of course." He winked in Valerie and Haley's direction, and the lines around his mouth crinkled. The man had charisma— enough to cause someone, likely Lydia, to pay him multiple late-night visits. Even Eleanor's death hadn't put a crimp in his prowling, I realized. My smile faded.

Colby noticed my change in expression. He plucked a grape from a bowl and popped it into his mouth. "Thanks for breakfast, ladies," he said. "This cowboy needs to get back to work."

As he headed out of the kitchen, he whispered, "I'll see you at lasso lessons, Ms. Cassidy. I don't imagine you'll have any problem handling a rope. And I expect you'll be my star pupil with the whip."

I drew back. Colby's eyes danced, and he swaggered out of the room.

When I spun around, Valerie and Haley had returned to their pastry making. Georgia shook her head. "I wouldn't dip my toe in that water even if I was invited," she said. "Though I have to admit, I'd be tempted."

Valerie wore a sour expression, and Haley blushed. I couldn't keep from grinning.

I took the empty bowls from the back wall and carried them to the mudroom, where I filled one with dog kibble, one with cat kibble, and a third with fresh water. When Woody and Carl scampered over to eat, Georgia rose from her chair. "Well, ladies," she said, mimicking Colby's deep drawl, "this cowgirl needs to get back to work."

I prepared to excuse myself as well to retrieve my camera, but then Valerie said she needed to set the table. Pushing a cart covered with plates and glasses, she followed Georgia through the door, leaving Haley rolling pastry into thin cylinders. I remembered Sunday night when the young woman had appeared to have something on her mind. Now I'd have a chance to speak to her alone. The camera could wait.

Leaning a hip against the counter, I tried to look casual. "What are you making?"

"Spinach cheese coils."

"Gluten-free, I assume."

"Yup."

I watched as she kneaded the dough, seemingly disinterested in conversation. I tried again. "They look like Carmen's snakes."

She gave a nervous laugh. "I wish you hadn't said that. I hate snakes."

"Me too. I'm not sure where my phobia came from, but they give me the willies."

Gingerly, she began to roll the dough again. "You'd think I'd be used to them, growing up in Colorado, but whenever I see one, I get as far away from it as I can. How does Carmen tolerate them?"

With that, I sensed we'd established a level of rapport, so I dispensed with the small talk. "Speaking of Carmen, you must have heard the police chief suspects her in Eleanor's death. Detective Clarke and I are…well, we're looking into it, too. The other night on the deck, I got the idea you had information you didn't feel comfortable sharing in front of your mom. Is there something you know that might help us? The faster the murder is solved, the more likely that Moonglow Ranch will survive."

She froze, fingers clenched around a piece of dough. I waited, conscious of precious time ticking away, resisting the temptation to shove a chair in front of the door to keep Valerie out.

Finally, Haley sucked in a breath. "I mean, I'm not sure it's even relevant. And Mom told me to keep it to myself. She thinks my gossip, as she calls it, might make things worse for Ryll and Fritz. And by extension, her."

My pulse quickened. Whatever information Haley had stored in her memory, I wanted it. "How about this: You tell me whatever it is. If it turns out the information isn't important, we'll just forget we even had this conversation."

She studied my face, then nodded. "Okay. It's been weighing on me. I think I need to get it off my chest."

The door opened, and I groaned inwardly as Valerie appeared. She looked at her daughter, then at me. "I forgot the silverware," she said, lifting a tray from the counter against the wall. She lingered, staring at her daughter, who began cutting the crust into small ovals.

"Well," Valerie said at last. "Guess I'll go finish setting the table. Back in a flash."

I figured she'd put an end to our conversation. Instead, Haley seemed to acquire a heightened sense of urgency.

"It's like this," she said, leaning across the island. "I took a walk a week or so ago and found myself at the Simonson property."

She winced. "Okay, so it wasn't completely accidental. Since I got here, I've wanted to see their place up close, so I sneaked through the woods. I knew I was technically trespassing, but I figured if I got caught, I'd act like I was lost. People usually see me as sweet and innocent." She gave me a mischievous grin, and I realized there might be more to this girl than met the eye.

"I stood in the evergreens a few yards from their house, and I could hear two people arguing on an upstairs balcony. I recognized their voices: Eleanor and Gordon."

"Could you make out what they were saying from that distance?"

"They weren't exactly whispering."

"What were they arguing about?"

Her expression held an emotion I couldn't decipher. "Eleanor said she'd see to it that Gordon was out of the will. She'd even make sure he was disowned. And Gordon…he…"

"Go on," I urged.

"He said he'd kill her before he let that happen." Her head dropped. "If I'd only told someone…Maybe I could have prevented Eleanor's murder."

Now I realized the indecipherable emotion was guilt. I hurried around the island and put an arm around the girl. "Not true, Haley. You aren't in any way responsible for that woman's death. Besides, just because Gordon threatened her doesn't mean he followed through."

She looked up in surprise. "So you don't think he's the killer?"

Before I could respond, the kitchen door swung open and Valerie strode through it. She took in her daughter's red eyes, and her face creased with worry.

After a moment, she turned to me. "It looks as if your furry friends have finished their morning meal. Haley and I will have the human breakfast prepared in an hour. That is, if you'll allow us to get back to business."

It was a not-so-subtle dismissal, but I hesitated. I didn't want Haley to feel like I was abandoning her. But when I looked at the girl, her eyes silently pleaded with me to go.

I called to the creatures and left the kitchen, giving Haley one last sympathetic glance.

29

After I'd grabbed my digital camera from upstairs, I headed outside and lost myself in my art. I took pictures of the distant mountains beneath the drifting clouds, random beams of sunlight glistening off the stream behind the lodge, groves of pine trees dancing in the breeze. Before I knew it, a half hour had passed, the runners had returned, and the yoga masters had gathered for coffee on the deck. Late-risers Tonya and Lydia joined us.

"Morning, sunshine," I said, patting Tonya on the head.

She swatted my hand away. "How long have we been friends? You know better than to touch the hair."

"Ooh, someone got up on the wrong side of the bed," I said playfully.

Then Ryll and Valerie came out carrying platters of food, and we all followed them like ducklings to the pergola.

***

After we ate, we were directed to the corral for a lassoing demonstration and lesson with Colby and the ranch hands, named Donovan and Nathan. In the center of the corral stood a metal rendition of a large bull, silver horns protruding from a welded head. I was relieved they didn't expect us to wrestle a live cow.

Colby took the lead, explaining how to hold the

rope—which could also be referred to as lasso, lariat, or riata. Donovan and Nathan took turns dancing around the corral with ballet-like choreography, gyrating the lariat above their heads in a mesmerizing display. Then Donovan took the spotlight, maneuvering his feet and spinning the lasso in circles until a magical moment when the time was right to toss the noose around the fake cow. I found the whole thing fascinating, and it made for terrific photos.

Next it was Nathan's turn. His performance was more practical. In minutes, he'd thrown the lariat across the metal horns and pulled the rope tight.

Finally, it was time for the pièce de résistance, and Colby did not disappoint. He mounted a chestnut brown mare named Beauty, and the two of them pranced around the corral as I snapped photos. Colby twirled the lariat, and with a flourish, lassoed the fake cow. The small crowd burst into a round of applause while Colby leapt off of Beauty and tipped his hat.

"Your turn, ladies," he said, his gray eyes twinkling. "Ms. Cassidy, let's begin with you." He held out a hand as if inviting me to dance.

"Umm…"

"Come on, Callie," Renata called. "Show us how it's done."

Everyone began clapping and stomping until I acquiesced. "Okay," I said, handing my camera to Tonya. "But you should all sign waivers before I start."

Tonya put her eye to the viewfinder and twisted the lens to focus. "These are going to be great on social media," she said.

Before I could object, Colby led me to the center of the corral. I shoved my hands into a pair of thick black roping gloves, then picked up the lasso. Colby positioned my fingers on the rope. I couldn't help but notice the muscular limberness of his hands.

He moved behind me, wrapping his arms around my

shoulders and grasping my wrists. My breath quickened as his biceps pinned my shoulders. "Oh, my," I heard Lydia whisper.

"It's all in the wrists." His warm breath rushed into my ear. "You want to get a sense of the rhythm, the loop, the motion. Move your body into it." He put a hand on my waist. "Rotate here. Hips, thighs."

Just as I was thinking this was about more than roping, he stepped back. I spun the lasso, slowly at first, awkwardly. As I moved faster and felt the rope sliding across my palm, I gained the confidence to lift it over my head. Faster, faster. My torso gyrated, and the muscles in my shoulder rippled.

"That's good," Colby said. "Now, when the loop reaches the outside peak, just above the cow's horns, let her fly."

A couple more spins, then I lofted the lasso toward the cow. The rope landed next to the fake cow's front leg. I exhaled, deflated.

"Outstanding," Colby said.

"What are you talking about? I missed."

"Did you expect perfection on your first toss? No one makes it the first time. But you have the moves. You're a natural."

"I bet you say that to all the women," I said with a smirk.

He winked. "Not all of them. Now, try again."

I gathered the lariat into my hand and swung it again. One twist, two, three. When the knot hit the apex, I let go, watching in shock as the rope fell around the cow's horns.

"Now pull," Colby said. I tugged the rope, and it tightened around the cow's shoulders. I squealed and jumped up and down like a cheerleader. Behind me, the group whooped and high-fived. I turned and took a bow.

Colby gave my shoulders a squeeze. "Atta girl." He looked at the rest of the group. "Okay, who's next?"

Tonya took a turn, followed by Renata, Lynn, Jessica, Summer, Mom, and Mrs. Finney. The only ones who even came close to roping the steer were Summer and Mrs. Finney, so I was especially proud of myself. Maybe if the photo gallery didn't work out, I'd explore career opportunities as a ranch hand.

Lydia had positioned herself to go last. When it was her turn, she stepped toward Colby and said breathily, "My turn, Cowboy."

I couldn't help but think of the two of them…well, liaising. Then I remembered the picture of Colby and Eleanor I'd found on Gordon's desk. The image, uncomfortable though it was, lodged an idea in my head.

I excused myself, saying I needed to visit the bathroom, and exited the corral in the direction of the lodge. With everyone's attention fixed on Lydia's antics, I was sure no one would notice when I changed trajectory and headed to Colby's cabin.

Luckily, his door was unlocked. I scanned my surroundings to make sure no one was watching and entered, closing the door behind me.

I tried to decide how best to proceed. I knew I had little time, but this had been an impulsive decision, so I also didn't have a plan. What was I even searching for? I hoped I'd know it when I saw it.

I scanned the space, which contained a combination bedroom, living room, and kitchen. A bathroom lay beyond a half-open door. For a bachelor pad, the place was unexpectedly tidy. Maybe Colby wanted his residence to look nice for his lady callers. A plaid couch with sculpted wooden legs faced a wooden stand that held a mid-sized flat screen television. A low coffee table was clear except for the remote. A refrigerator, a sink, a microwave, and an oven with a stovetop comprised the kitchen, along with a small breakfast table and two chairs. A full-sized bed, neatly made, took up one corner of the room. A cheap-looking lamp stood on the adjacent nightstand. I walked over and opened the single drawer to find a book—a well-worn copy of Larry McMurtry's *Lonesome Dove*.

I peeked into the bathroom and discovered nothing of interest. As I prepared to write off my little breaking-and-entering escapade as a bust, my eyes fell on a wooden trunk nestled in the corner. I walked over to it, unclasped the metal latch, and lifted the lid.

Bingo.

Inside lay a bizarre treasure trove of ladies' belongings. Low-cut push-up bras, silky panties, scarves, fuzzy slippers, sheer robes, a bikini…even jewelry. A silver chain, a leather bracelet.

It seemed Colby was a collector.

I saw a silky frock that looked familiar. I searched my memory until I placed it—the pale blue robe I'd seen Lydia wearing two nights ago as she made her way across the yard to the cabin. My stomach clenched. Tonya would have a conniption fit.

Still, weird as it was, this discovery didn't tell me anything new. Colby was a womanizer—not exactly breaking news. Though I didn't know if they'd serve a purpose, I figured I should take photos of his stash for future reference. Better to have photos I didn't need than to miss documenting something important.

When I focused the lens on the upper corner of the chest, I saw a piece that made me flinch. A red lace thong—nothing special. Except for the monogram. ES.

Eleanor Simonson?

Again, I wasn't sure it meant much. Georgia and Audra both had indicated Colby and Eleanor were an item. But here, at least, was possible proof. I snapped a picture and decided to leave. I'd already pressed my luck.

As I eased the trunk's lid down, the front door squeaked. Then it banged open, and I flinched at the sight of Colby's muscular silhouette in the doorway. My luck had run out.

30

Colby took a step into the cabin, glowering. "What do you think you're doing?"

"I...I was looking for a bathroom," I stammered, sounding lame even to my own ears.

He clenched his fists and took a step toward me. Then another. "You won't find a toilet in that trunk," he growled.

"No, I..." I felt a flutter of panic. I couldn't come up with anything clever, so I fell back on the truth. I delivered it in the tone of a schoolteacher lecturing her misbehaving class. "Colby, I wish I hadn't had to invade your privacy. But a woman's been murdered. My friend's aunt and uncle are in danger of losing their ranch—or worse. Chief Wade can't find his foot inside his shoe, so I felt compelled to help. I've sensed that you're hiding something. Exploring your place seemed like the best option. I'm only trying to eliminate you as a suspect."

Colby reared back as if I'd slapped him. "A suspect? You think I..." He slammed a fist against the wall. "You're accusing me of killing Eleanor Simonson?"

Suddenly, Lynn and Tonya appeared in the doorway. Lynn quickly assessed the scene, and her hand dropped to where her gun would have been if she'd been carrying.

Since she didn't have it on her, she used her next best weapon: her commanding cop voice.

"Take a step back, Mr. Trent. Now."

Colby's mouth formed an O, and he pivoted toward Lynn. At the sight of her, with her feet planted hip-width apart and her lips pressed together, he complied, lifting his hands in surrender. When he spoke, his voice was pleading. "Listen, you people can't believe I killed Eleanor. I barely knew her."

"Ha! You and I have a different definition of knowing each other." I gestured to the trunk. "Cut the crap, Colby. I found your stash of ladies' lingerie. Either you have a unique wardrobe, or you kept a souvenir from every woman who's been with you."

His face turned red. "You can't prove any of that belongs to Eleanor."

I yanked the lid up and gingerly removed the thong, pointing to the monogram. "Heck of a coincidence."

Colby's countenance changed from rigid to deflated in a millisecond. I even had the fleeting idea he might confess.

Instead, he stared at the floor for a few seconds before making a move toward the kitchen.

"Hold it right there," Lynn ordered.

Colby halted, looking confused. "I only want to get a beer," he said, his voice quavering.

Lynn hesitated before gesturing for him to continue. He opened the refrigerator, pulled out a longneck, popped the top, and chugged half of it. Then he carried the bottle to the living room and slouched onto the couch. "Okay, I knew her."

Tonya snorted. "In the biblical sense, you mean."

He took another swig of beer and wiped the foam off his mouth. "Eleanor and I were having an affair. That may make me a jerk, but it doesn't make me a killer."

Lynn closed the front door. I perched on the edge of the coffee table, my knees inches from his. "Colby, no one here believes you're a murderer," I said.

Lynn made a face, not quite ready to drop the ranch manager from the suspect list. To be honest, I wasn't either, but my intuition told me I'd be more likely to catch this fly with honey than with vinegar.

"It's obvious you're hiding something, though," I continued. "Maybe…were you and Eleanor scheduled to…hook up the night she died? Is that why she was at the ranch?"

He shook his head. "No, that night I had another…" His eyes flitted to Tonya. "I was entertaining another guest."

Tonya frowned. "Are you referring to my mother?"

The corner of his lip turned up. "I don't kiss and tell, ma'am."

Four quick strides took Tonya to the open trunk. I cringed as she pawed the contents, snatched out the pale blue robe, and stalked back to the couch. Steam wasn't shooting from her ears, but I might have noticed a few puffs of smoke.

"What is this? A trophy? How dare you! You…you…well, I'm too much of a lady to finish that sentence."

"Sorry," Colby muttered.

"Sorry? That's all you have to say for yourself, you worthless piece of—"

I shot Lynn a look, and she put an arm around Tonya and guided her to a chair at the kitchen table. When I was sure my best friend wouldn't attack, I continued.

"All right, let's ignore your…exploits for the moment," I said. "My gut tells me you know more about this than you told the cops. The morning I found the body, you didn't register any shock. Your reaction didn't make sense to me at the time, but now…Colby, you already knew Eleanor was dead, didn't you?"

He refused to meet my eyes. He bobbed his knee, and his hands fidgeted in his lap.

"Did you kill her, Colby?" I asked.

"No!" he said with conviction.

"Then you have to tell us what you're hiding."

He was silent, weighing his options. He took off his Stetson and dropped it to the floor before lifting imploring eyes to me. "You can't tell Ryll and Fritz. Please. I can't afford to lose this job."

"I'm afraid I can't make that promise. This is a murder investigation, Colby. There's more on the line here than your job, or your reputation. You've made a mess of that for sure. But here's your chance to do the honorable thing, regardless of the personal consequences."

He leaned his elbows on his knees, tapping the beer bottle with a thumbnail. I kept my mouth shut and waited.

At last, he sighed and sat back. "All right. I saw Eleanor in Spirit's stall. She was dead."

My heart raced. "You mean, before I found her?"

He nodded. "After Lyd…" Tonya stiffened, and Colby winced. "After my guest left, maybe one-thirty in the morning, I was getting ready to go to bed…to sleep, that is…and I heard something. Footsteps. Someone running. I knew it wasn't…my guest, because I'd watched her walk back to the lodge and go safely inside."

"And I thought chivalry was dead," Tonya mumbled.

Colby looked chagrined, but continued. "I went out on the porch, but I didn't see anyone. Then I noticed the stable door was open. I always close it at the end of the day. Always."

"And you were concerned," I prodded.

"There are coyotes around here, sometimes a mountain lion. Leaving the stable door open at night would risk the horses' safety."

He drained the last of the beer and looked with longing toward the kitchen. But Tonya sat between him and the refrigerator, so he stayed put.

"I assume you investigated?" I asked.

"Came back inside and grabbed my rifle first."

Lynn straightened, suddenly on alert. "Rifle? Where's this rifle now?"

Colby looked at her, not comprehending her tone. "Locked in the safe."

He indicated a large metal contraption in the corner. When he saw Lynn examining it, he huffed. "Hey, I'm not going to grab a rifle and shoot my way out of here."

"Of course you're not," I said. If I wanted him to keep talking, I needed him to stay calm, so I stepped into the kitchen and got him another bottle out of the refrigerator.

When I returned, I sat next to him, trying to appear relaxed. Just two friends ironing things out over a beer. "What'd you do after you got the rifle?"

"I headed into the stable and started to walk the corridor to make sure the horses were all right. A few of them had been experiencing stomach problems over the last few days."

He dropped his eyes, and I knew then he was aware of the source of their illnesses.

"I looked in Spirit's stall and...I saw Eleanor." He dropped his head into his hands. "She was sprawled in the hay."

"Did you go to her? Try to help?"

"It was no use. Her head was bloody. I watched her chest, and she wasn't breathing. She was dead. There was nothing I could do."

A spurt of anger rose in my throat, but I swallowed it back. I needed to focus on the end game, so I kept my voice even. "Why didn't you call the police?"

He leaned his head against the back of the couch, closed his eyes, and sighed. "I should have. But all I could think of was how guilty I'd look. See, Eleanor and I had a...well, an argument earlier that day. As far as I could tell, no one overheard us, but I couldn't be sure. Then hours later, she turns up dead yards from my cabin? It wouldn't look good for me."

Withholding evidence doesn't earn you a medal of honor, I thought. "What was the argument about?"

"I told her I was breaking it off with her. She didn't take kindly to that. They never do."

I looked at Tonya, who stared into the distance, her hands flexing on the table. I'd seen that expression before. The calm before the storm. Given half a chance, she'd run over here and use her long fingernails on Colby's face. And I'd be half inclined to let her. But first, we needed to squeeze all the information we could out of the cowboy.

"Why did you decide to end things?" I asked. "From what we've been told, Eleanor was your golden ticket."

He opened his eyes. "Eleanor isn't...wasn't...a nice person."

"That was news to you? I mean, she was cheating on her husband."

"Yeah, but I'm talking about a whole different level. I don't even want to say."

"You've come this far, Colby," Lynn said. "Go the distance."

He hesitated, and Tonya slammed a palm against the table. "Oh for crying out loud, spit it out. I'm tired of sitting here watching your stupid face while you try to figure out how you can spin this to make yourself into a victim."

Colby paled. He looked from Lynn to me, as if wondering which of us would be most likely to protect him if Tonya attacked. I hid a smirk. I'd been going for honey, but vinegar had the motivating effect here.

"I found out Eleanor had been making the horses sick. I couldn't tolerate that."

Ah. We'd suspected Eleanor's culpability, of course, given the syringe lying beside her hand, but here was our corroboration.

"How did you find out? Did Eleanor tell you?" I asked.

He exhaled. "She didn't just tell me, she bragged. Expected me to jump right on board with her plot."

"What plot?" Lynn asked.

"To take ownership of the ranch," he said. "First, she did everything she could to keep the town from granting a license. She cozied up to the mayor's wife and pressured Polly into influencing her husband. That worked for a while, but when the Bauers started making noise about hiring a lawyer, she realized the scheme would fail. So she decided on another strategy."

He paused and chugged the rest of his beer. Tonya squirmed impatiently, but she didn't speak. After a tiny burp, Colby continued. "No one's going to want to visit a dude ranch where the horses are always sick, she said. Eleanor has experience with horses and a friend in Montana who's a veterinarian. She got her hands on a drug that produces digestive issues without causing permanent damage. By the time I found out, she'd already injected a few of the horses. She said she wouldn't stop until she ruined Moonglow Ranch."

The three of us spent a moment processing the information. "I don't understand why you kept this to yourself," Lynn said. "You covered up the fact that Eleanor was committing a crime and endangering those horses—"

He bristled. "Wait a minute. I didn't find out until the day before she died, and when I did, I insisted she stop."

"But she didn't," Lynn said, exasperated. "Didn't it occur to you to go to the Bauers? Or the police?"

"You don't understand. Eleanor threatened to tell Ryll and Fritz about our affair—and also say I was part of her scheme. Even though the last part wasn't true, I was sure they'd believe her over me. They'd fire me, and I'd be blackballed all over the state. This is the only thing I know how to do…"

Well, not the only thing, I thought.

"You realize this gives you a motive for Eleanor's murder, right?" I said. "She was blackmailing you and threatening your livelihood. When you found her in the stable preparing to inject another horse, an animal you cared about, you snapped. You grabbed the shovel and cracked it across her skull."

He leapt to his feet. "That's not what happened!"

Lynn took a step toward us, but I held up a hand. "No one would blame you, Colby," I continued. "In fact, they'd probably consider you a hero, jumping in to save that horse from suffering. And Eleanor, well, she wasn't much of a prize, was she? Not too many people are mourning her passing. You may have done the town a favor."

Inwardly, I shuddered at my own words. But I'd say whatever I had to if it helped us solve this murder.

Colby crumpled back onto the couch. "I screwed up. I get that now. I should have told Ryll and Fritz what Eleanor was doing. And when I found her body, I should have called the police. I made a lot of mistakes. But I didn't kill her. I'm a lover, not a murderer."

Tonya barked a cynical laugh. But as I studied Colby's face, twisted in anguish, I believed him.

"I have only two more questions for you," I said. "How did Eleanor get onto the property? She didn't have her car."

"She liked to walk over for our…meetings," he said. "Trekking through the woods at night heightened the anticipation, she always said."

I nodded. That solved that part of the puzzle. "Last thing. When I found the body Sunday morning, the stall gate was locked. Do you have any idea how that happened?"

He lifted his eyes to the ceiling, remembering. "I latched it myself, I guess. I wasn't thinking, really—just doing what I always do. Does it matter?"

"I suppose not," I said, rising from the couch. "Just tying up a loose end." I headed to the door, and Lynn and Tonya joined me. I met Lynn's eyes. She nodded slightly, agreeing with my unspoken assessment.

"What are you going to do now?" Colby asked.

"Well, we obviously can't keep this a secret," Lynn said. "We'll tell Ryll and Fritz first. Then we'll have to go to Chief Wade. I'm sure he'll want to question you, so I'd advise you to stick around."

He nodded, looking defeated. Then he pointed to the robe in Tonya's hand. "Listen, do you think I could—"

Wow, I thought. *This cowboy is even braver—or stupider— than I'd imagined.*

The look Tonya gave him carried enough ice to freeze a lava flow. He flinched. "Never mind. Don't even know what I was thinking."

31

Outside on the porch, Lynn, Tonya, and I stood for a moment, blinking in the sunshine. The next thing I knew, Tonya was on the move, stalking toward the lodge like a woman on a mission. I shaded my eyes with my hand to see what had elicited such a sense of purpose.

Valerie, Haley, and Georgia had rolled a cart onto the wooden deck and were distributing snacks and pouring lemonade. Lydia sat in a rocker and sipped from a tall glass, oblivious to the approaching tempest.

"Uh oh," I said.

Lynn and I hurried after Tonya but couldn't catch her before she marched up the stairs. She planted herself in front of her mother and flung the silk robe into her lap.

Lydia smiled. "Oh, TeeTee, I've been looking everywhere for this. Where did you find it?"

I hurried up the stairs and took hold of Tonya's arm. She shrugged me off. "Where do you think I found it? The cowboy's cabin, that's where, on top of a pile of women's undergarments."

Lydia opened her mouth but shut it without responding.

Tonya shook a finger at her mother. "I forbid you to enter that man's place ever again."

Valerie let out a tiny gasp, and Georgia grinned. Haley froze, the pitcher of lemonade poised above an empty glass.

Lydia stopped rocking. "Excuse me?"

183

"Stay away from Colby Trent. You're way too old for him. It's…indecent. Embarrassing. Dangerous, even."

Lydia scooted her rocker back and stood, arms folded. "I'm not accustomed to taking orders from my daughter."

"Believe me, I wish I didn't have to issue them," Tonya shot back. "But I'm telling you, stay away from him. He doesn't care about you. He's a gold digger."

"Well, sweetheart, it's my gold he's digging, not yours. And whatever I buy with my money is none of your concern."

A shudder worked its way through Tonya's body, starting with her forehead and ending at her toes. Her lip quivered, and I thought for a moment she might cry.

Instead, she pivoted and stormed across the deck, slamming open the door and disappearing inside the lodge. We heard her footsteps pounding up the stairs.

For a long moment, no one moved. Even the birds seemed to stop chirping. Woody sidled up next to my thigh and whined. Carl scampered onto the deck railing.

Mom stood and touched Lydia's shoulder. "You should go after her," she whispered.

Lydia waved, trying to appear cool, but I saw the tremor in her hand. "She doesn't listen to me. Never has. I've been nothing but an embarrassment to her."

"The two of you have had a rocky time over the years, it's true," Mom said. "But Lydia, Tonya loves you. If you don't go upstairs and make this right, you may never have another opportunity."

Lydia locked eyes with Mom, and after a long pause, she turned and went inside.

"My, my," Georgia said. "You people do liven up the place. It's like *Real Housewives of Moonglow Ranch*."

Ryll raised an eyebrow. "Don't you need to be tending to business, Georgia?"

Georgia nodded, but her smile didn't waver. "Yes ma'am. Ladies, let's go tend to business."

Valerie and Haley followed her inside, while the rest of us tried to recover. Woody flopped onto the deck, panting, and Carl stretched across the dog's back.

Mom resumed her seat. "What brought that on?"

Lynn and I took turns describing our confrontation with Colby. Ryll's face reddened as she listened to the story of decadent liaisons, horse poisonings, and destructive scheming. Once we'd finished, she stared off into the distance. I could tell she was trying to wrap her head around the news.

"All we wanted to do was carve out our little niche," she whispered. "I don't know what we did wrong."

"You did nothing wrong," Summer assured her.

Ryll seemed numb. "It's karma. That's what Carmen would say. Fritz and I have interrupted the celestial flow, and we're paying the price."

"Now, Aunt Ryll, don't be melodramatic," Summer said, her voice gentle. "If anyone interrupted the flow, it was Eleanor Simonson. You and Uncle Fritz just happened to be in the way of her cosmic windstorm. Everything will return to its natural course now. The police will arrest Colby Trent, and you'll open your ranch as you planned." She turned to Lynn and me. "Right?"

The two of us glanced at each other. "The thing is," Lynn said, "Colby denies responsibility, and there's no proof to the contrary. None that we've found, anyway."

Summer's expression darkened. "Okay, then go find some. And if Colby didn't do it, you need to figure out who did. Aunt Ryll and Uncle Fritz shouldn't have to live like this. Not for another day."

***

We knew Summer was right. After a brief conference, Lynn and I reluctantly agreed we were obligated to tell Chief Wade everything. While we were at it, we hoped to wheedle information out of him as well.

Naturally, Mrs. Finney wasn't about to be left behind. She was already peeved about missing out on the drama in Colby's cabin. "I'll drive," she said, without waiting for an invitation. This time, I took the passenger seat, and Lynn climbed in the back for the trek into town.

As we pulled out of the ranch's parking lot, we noticed Fritz standing on a ladder, working on the entry arch. I took that as a good sign. If Fritz was busy making improvements, he believed the ranch would survive.

A few minutes later, Mrs. Finney pulled into a spot facing the police station in the middle of the town square. I twisted in my seat, intending to ask Lynn how we should proceed. But a heavy thud jarred the passenger window. When I swiveled toward the window, I saw a hairy hand pounding on the glass.

Then a face appeared—an angry face, flushed red. Gordon Simonson. He rotated his finger, miming that I should roll down the window.

That didn't seem like an excellent plan to me. The car's electric locks clicked, and Mrs. Finney held her finger and thumb an inch apart in a gesture that told me, *Open the window, but just a little.*

I pressed the silver lever on my armrest, and the window slid open. Feeling brave, I let it go two inches. Gordon put his mouth to the crack. When he spoke, I smelled the whiskey on his breath.

"Ew," I said.

"Get out of the car," he said.

"Not a chance. You're drunk."

"That's ridoclious," he said. "I had one shoot of whiskey. Maybe two. But that's because of you. That stunt you pulled at my house ruined my life."

Lynn leaned across the center console. "Gordon, you're the one who threatened us with a golf club."

He bashed the window again, stumbled back a step, and dragged a shaky hand across the stubble on his chin. His eyes were bloodshot and puffy, and tendrils of thin hair clung to his forehead like octopus tentacles. Though he wore slacks and a jacket, it appeared he'd slept in them.

"My father disheriteted me," Gordon said. "He removed me from his will and fired me from the business. He even took away my allowance."

His allowance? Gordon sounded like an immature teenager—one who'd indulged in way too much alcohol.

"That's not our fault," I said. "You're the one who stirred up trouble. And there's worse trouble coming, too, once we prove you killed your stepmother."

I threw that out there just to bait him, and he didn't disappoint. He slammed his hand against the glass again, then wriggled his fingers into the crevice and attempted to pull the window open. I pushed the lever and rolled it up until the glass trapped his fingers. When he squealed, I lowered the window a half inch, enough to allow him to free his hand.

"You coulda broke my fingers," he whined.

"Don't be such a baby," Mrs. Finney said. "Run along, Mr. Simonson. But don't you dare get behind the wheel. You'll be in the slammer facing a DUI, and I assure you, that won't endear you any further to your father."

Gordon leveled such a look of fury at us that I drew back in my seat. He leaned toward the window. "You better watch your backs, because I'm coming for you."

As he reared back and kicked the passenger door, Jake ran out of the police department, his hand on his gun belt. "Step away from the car, Mr. Simonson."

The officer's voice carried a new, imposing tone that belied his youthful appearance. Gordon did as instructed, lifting his hands. "Wassup, Jake? We were just talking."

Jake stepped between Gordon and the car and peered in at us. "Are you all right?"

"We're fine," I said. "Like he said, we were talking. But he needs to sober up."

Jake nodded, turned to Gordon, and held out his hand. "Keys, please."

Gordon's face turned red again. "You little pipsqueak. If you want my keys, you'll have to come and get them."

Jakes's eyes hardened. "That can be arranged." He took a step toward Gordon. "Last chance. Hand 'em over or you'll force me to take you into custody."

Gordon looked over his shoulder, then back at Jake, likely calculating his odds of getting away if he made a run for it. Drunk as he was, though, he wasn't stupid enough to risk it. He fumbled in his pocket, retrieved his keys, and dropped them into the officer's hand.

Jake closed his fingers around the keys and pointed to a bench on the sidewalk outside the building. "Give me a minute, and I'll get someone to run you home."

Gordon scowled, but he trudged over to the bench and sagged onto it. His chin fell to his chest, and I wondered if he was about to pass out.

Jake leaned toward the window. "Do you want to press charges? If so, I'll book him."

"I don't think that's necessary," Lynn said.

"Unless he dented my car," Mrs. Finney said, huffing.

She unlocked the doors, and we stepped out of the vehicle, watching as she came around to examine the passenger door. "You're lucky there's no damage, you weasel," she yelled. Without lifting his head, he gave her a thumbs up. She responded with a different finger.

Jake smothered a grin. "I assume you're here to see Chief Wade."

I nodded. "We have information he needs."

"He went down the street to get a donut..." Jake paused as I smirked at the cliché. "He should be back in a minute or two. I can take you to the interview room if you want to wait."

"Well, we could talk to you instead," I said.

His expression indicated he was considering it, but he shook his head. "Chief'd have my hide. Best to wait." He paused, seeming to weigh his next words. "There is something you might want to hear. Let's go inside."

32

We followed Jake into a small reception area, where two uniformed officers sat behind a tall counter, discussing Rockies baseball. They gave us curious looks. Jake didn't bother to explain, just told them someone needed to take Gordon Simonson home. They did a quick round of rock, paper, scissors, and the loser rose with a sigh and grabbed a set of keys.

The building was the size of an average three-bedroom house. The reception area contained two shaky-looking wooden desks, a water cooler, and a stand with a coffeemaker and accessories. Jake led us down a hall to an interview room furnished with a card table and four folding chairs. The three of us crammed ourselves into the room and took seats. Jake offered us coffee, but we declined, anxious to hear what he had to tell us before the chief returned.

He hovered near the door, glancing out periodically. "I shouldn't be divulging this information," he said. "But seeing as one of you is a detective, and one of you found the body…" After a quizzical glance at Mrs. Finney, he continued, "I guess you have a right to know. Just…keep it to yourselves, okay?"

Lynn folded her hands on the table. "Whatever you tell us will stay confidential unless it becomes necessary to share the information. Even then, we wouldn't reveal our source. The three of us have taken part in many investigations, including more than a few homicides."

Jake closed the door. He pulled out his notebook and

sat in the empty chair. "First, we got back a report on the contents of the syringe. Naloxone, used as a tranquilizer for horses exhibiting excitable behaviors. The side effects include minor stomach distress. It wears off in a matter of hours and doesn't pose a long-term threat to the animal's health."

"Eleanor had been injecting the horses," I said. Jake raised his eyebrows. "She got the drug from a vet friend in Montana. We can fill you in on the details when the chief arrives."

Lynn leaned forward. "What else do you have?"

"The county lab analyzed the shovel you found under the lodge. The blood matches Eleanor Simonson's, confirming it as the murder weapon. They found Amaryllis and Fritz Bauers' fingerprints, Colby Trent's, and the two ranch hands, as well as several others they have yet to identify."

"No surprise," I said. "I'm sure many people handled that shovel every day."

Mrs. Finney drummed her fingers on the table. "None of this eliminates a single suspect."

"No, but it's led Chief Wade to think—"

The door whooshed open, and the police chief waddled through, half a donut clutched in his chubby fingers. He squinted at Jake. "Heard we had visitors."

"Good morning, Chief," Mrs. Finney chirped. "While we waited for you to come back from your donut run, Jake here was kind enough to fill us in on the local wildlife we might expect to spot on our hikes."

Chief Wade narrowed his beady eyes. Then he shoved the last half of the donut in his mouth and wiped his glazed fingers on his trousers. "What you waitin' for, boy? Get your behind outta my chair."

Jake jumped up, and the chief slouched into the vacated chair, leaving the officer to lean against the wall.

"So, Nancy Drew and friends, to what do I owe the pleasure of your visit?"

"We've stumbled across information we thought you might find helpful," Lynn said. "As good citizens, we felt duty bound to share it."

"Mm-hmm," he said. "Stumbled across it, did you? Because you surely wouldn't go out hunting on your own, not after you were told to stay out of it."

Lynn got to her feet. "Listen, Chief, if you don't want our information, that's fine. I'm sure the county sheriff will be plenty interested."

"Is that a threat, little lady?"

"Take it however you want," Lynn said. "I'm tired of tiptoeing around your enormous ego. We have knowledge that might help you nab a killer. If you're too proud to accept it, so be it."

I swiveled toward the chief to gauge his reaction. His body stiffened and his forehead creased. After a moment, he gestured magnanimously, as if he were a monarch granting a peon permission to speak.

"I'll give you ten minutes. Tell me what's so dadgum important."

Lynn resumed her seat and told the chief about Colby's affair with Eleanor. No response. Then she revealed that Colby had failed to report discovering Eleanor's body hours before I found her. Chief Wade picked at a cuticle, appearing bored.

Finally, Lynn mentioned what Raul had found out about Allen Simonson altering his itinerary. "He was supposed to be home the day Eleanor died, but he didn't show up until yesterday," she said. "No one knows where he was."

"Just because you don't know doesn't mean no one does," the police chief said. "I'm well-acquainted with Allen Simonson, and I've talked with him."

"Where was he?" I asked.

The chief's eyes slid toward me. "The man's whereabouts are none of your business."

Lynn shot me a warning look, and I bit my tongue.

This was her show, and I wouldn't tread on her turf.

"Fine," Lynn said. "Let me tell you what we've learned about Gordon Simonson."

She detailed the incriminating evidence we'd gathered on Gordon, starting with Raul's research on the sale of Gordon's stocks to his stepmother, the photo of Colby and Eleanor I'd seen on Gordon's desk, and what Haley had divulged about the argument between Gordon and his stepmother. I noticed Lynn didn't mention that Gordon had threatened us with a golf club. She'd promised Allen she'd overlook it, and she was a woman of her word.

When she finished, Chief Wade took a toothpick from his shirt pocket and shoved it between his teeth. "That everything?"

Lynn stared at him. "You don't appear surprised by any of this."

"Why would I be? Nothing new here. You forget that I've been busy doing my job."

Jake shifted his feet and frowned. I understood from his reaction that the police chief was lying—or at the very least, exaggerating. He might have talked to Allen, and he likely knew about Colby and Eleanor's affair, but no way was he privy to what Haley had told me.

Lynn leaned her elbows on the table. "Listen, Chief, we've been forthright with you. We've given you evidence to help strengthen your suspect list. I'd like you to reciprocate. We're on the same team. Putting our heads together can only help expedite this murder investigation."

Chief Wade guffawed. Then he scratched his chin and fixed his watery eyes on Lynn. "I realize you think I'm just a backwoods yokel and you're smarter than me. I'm used to being underestimated. But this is my town. My people. And my case."

"Yes, I understand that, but—"

"I notice you didn't mention Amaryllis or Fritz

Bauer—the two people with easiest access to the scene. The ones who had the most to gain from Eleanor's death. It was their shovel that killed the woman. Yet you didn't bother to do any 'research' on them. Could that be because they're related to your friend?"

I couldn't keep quiet any longer. "Chief, why would they kill Eleanor on their own property? They'd only draw attention to themselves."

"So you say." He sniffed and wrestled himself out of his chair. "Ladies, I appreciate you coming in today. We're done here."

"Chief Wade—" I began.

"I said we're done. Now scat." He strode to the door and yanked it open, looking at Jake over his shoulder. "Officer, please escort the Nancy Drews out of the building. Then report to my office. No dilly dallying."

***

Jake looked worried as he led us down the short hallway. "I hope we haven't gotten you into trouble," I whispered.

He wouldn't meet my eyes. "Thank you for coming in," he said.

Outside, the morning's gray clouds had thickened in a way that hinted at an evening squall. I looked across the square and saw Polly Finkle standing in front of the local cafe, chatting with another woman. She wore a sunflower yellow pantsuit, quite a change from her previous mourning attire. When Polly spotted us, she cupped her hand and said something into the woman's ear. It gave me flashbacks to high school.

When the women disappeared into the cafe, I saw Carmen on the bench where Gordon had earlier been instructed to wait. Carmen sat so still she might have been a hallucination.

I moved toward the bench, intending to sit beside her,

but the writhing on her wrist stopped me in my tracks. The snake lifted his anvil-shaped head and flicked his tongue.

When I stepped back, Mrs. Finney brushed past me and settled in next to Carmen. She put out a finger and ran it across the snake's back. Carmen graced her with a smile.

"This one is Fernando," she said.

"A striking creature."

Carmen nodded. "Not everyone agrees, I'm afraid."

I cleared my throat. "Were you waiting to talk to us?"

Carmen tilted her head, then nodded. "I'm here to give you warning."

A shiver tickled up my spine. "What do you mean?"

"At the dawn of each day, I spend an hour in trance time. My mind attains a transcendent state in which visions and sensations come to me. Today's visions involved portentous omens, and they arrived cocooned in the aura of Moonglow Ranch."

She paused, her eyes glazing. "The visions didn't appear to me fully formed. They were veiled in smoke. But the sense of doom sizzling over the ranch and all who reside there blazes as brightly as anything that's ever come to me."

She stroked her snake. "I can't tell you specifically what these visions mean, but this much is certain: a storm is coming, and you need to prepare for it."

33

We were quiet on the drive back to the lodge, and I figured we were all mulling over Carmen's ominous warning. I'd pooh-poohed her psychic abilities from the get-go, but now I experienced a niggle of doubt. I mean, what did I know? Could some people truly possess the ability to commune with spirits or tap into a collective stream of consciousness? Just because I couldn't see it, touch it, taste it—or explain it—did that mean it didn't exist?

Ugh. The woman had gotten under my skin.

So much so that, as we arrived at Moonglow Ranch, the very air seemed to thicken. It felt as if the clouds might reach down with gray fingers and wrap them around my neck.

As Mrs. Finney put the car into park, my mother hurried down the lodge steps, looking frazzled. My heart raced. Had Carmen's prediction come to fruition? Had a dark force already paid its visit to the ranch?

But no. Mom's stress had to do with our late arrival. The three of us had forgotten about the scheduled spa afternoon we'd planned as part of the bridal shower week.

"Hurry it up," Mom said. "Time is money."

She wasn't just going for the cliché. This event constituted the single biggest expenditure of the entire week, and I couldn't believe it had fled my memory.

We trotted up the steps and into the banquet room, which had been transformed into a luxury retreat. The aroma of eucalyptus drifted through the room, which was lit with dim lamps and candles. A nature-sounds CD played from small speakers, invisible waves crashing against an imaginary beach. Two massage tables stood in the center of the room, with nearby racks of towels and oils at the ready. Three pedicure stations lined one wall, across from two facial chairs. Against the back wall, snacks and pitchers of sangria waited on a buffet table. Eight women dressed in white slacks and salmon colored polo shirts waited for us with towels draped over their arms. For a moment, it seemed I was boarding a cruise ship.

"This looks fantastic," I whispered to Mom. "Thank you for overseeing the setup. I'm sorry you were stuck with everything."

She waved. "We both know this is more my purview than yours. But these people are on the clock, so we need to get moving."

For the next hour, we took turns visiting the various stations. My first stop was a twenty-minute facial. An attendant wrapped my hair in a towel, then covered my face with a thick paste like a cross between mud and Silly Putty. As I listened to the soothing nature sounds—now a waterfall rushing into a river—she worked the goo into my skin, moving her fingers in small circles over my cheeks, forehead, and neck. It relaxed and soothed me, so much so that I nearly dozed beneath her touch.

Then I heard the familiar sound of a camera's shutter. I lifted a cucumber slice off one eyelid and glared at my mother. "Tell me you didn't just take a picture of me looking like this."

"We have to document the party, darling," she said, and I heard giggles. I sighed, knowing my friends would paste the photos on their social media accounts. Sam and his new friend Isabella would probably have a good laugh, but I didn't care. Nope, not one bit.

Once the attendant rinsed the creamy goop from my

skin, my face tingled. I caught sight of myself in a mirror and saw that my skin glowed, appearing more youthful than it had in years. It was as if one coating of sludge had sealed up the worry lines.

Jessica's face appeared next to mine in the mirror, and she nodded approvingly. "I'll have what she had," she said, plopping into the chair I'd just vacated.

My next stop was the pedicure station. I took a seat between Tonya and Mom, and we sipped sangria as we chatted about inconsequential topics while women rubbed and sloughed and soaked our feet. I'd always been phobic about anyone touching my feet, so when the spa owners had suggested this as a station, I'd balked. I couldn't have imagined the pure ecstasy I experienced now. This wouldn't be the last pedicure of my life. They'd made a believer of me.

As the technician painted my toenails a glittery blue way outside my comfort zone, I noticed Lydia sipping her drink near the buffet table. I leaned toward Tonya. "Things still seem chilly between you and your mother."

"Chilly? More like glacial. After the big blow-up, she came upstairs, supposedly to 'make things right.' Maggie's doing, no doubt. But she won't listen to my concerns. Just tells me she's been in charge of her own life for a long time. She said when she's ready for me to make her decisions, she'll put me on her payroll."

"Did you tell her about Colby's secret trunk?"

She nodded. "I repeated that there was no way I'd let her keep seeing that creepy cowboy. She said I'd have to handcuff her to the bed to keep her from visiting him. Then she made an inappropriate joke about how it wouldn't be the first time she'd worn handcuffs. Ugh."

I turned away so Tonya couldn't see me smile. Lydia's flirtation with Colby was inappropriate, yes, but I couldn't help but think what a firecracker Lydia was— much like her daughter. In different ways, of course. "You want my advice?"

She rolled her eyes. "I know what you're going to say. That I can't control my mother and need to stop trying."

"More or less."

"As if you'd leave it alone," she said with a wry smile. "You're the queen of butting in."

"Hey, I resent that! I never—"

The soft chime rang again, indicating it was time to move to our next station. For me, that meant the massage. My gut clenched.

It wasn't so much the massage itself I was dreading. I never declined a nice back rub. No, it was the public facet of this set up—undressing and lying on a table with only a sheet between me and a half dozen sets of eyes. I wouldn't label myself a prude, but I fell on the far side of the modesty spectrum. You'd never catch me on a beach in Isabella's bikini, even if I had her figure. Or so I told myself.

But everyone else had taken a turn and seemed to enjoy themselves. Despite my reluctance, I went behind the screen, dropped everything but my undies, wrapped a linen sheet around myself, and forced myself back into the room.

When she spotted me, Tonya lifted her glass in a mock salute to my bravery. I stared at the massage table, trying to figure out how to mount it without giving everyone a peek at parts better left unseen.

Then Mrs. Finney appeared from behind a second screen. Like me, she'd wrapped herself in a sheet. When she approached the adjacent table, she climbed onto the padded table, not caring who saw what, plopped face down, and sighed in contentment.

In light of her emboldened display—and with everyone's attention thus diverted—I felt more confident. I lay on the table, wriggled the folds of the sheet out from under me, and rested my blushing cheeks (the ones on my face) in the padded cut out. My masseuse, a sweet young thing whose body hadn't yet glimpsed the ravages of middle age, introduced herself and asked what level of touch I preferred.

"Um, I don't know. Whatever you think is best."

That turned out to be the wrong answer. My masseuse must have thought I was sanctioning my own torture. She dug powerful fingers so deeply into my muscles that, if I hadn't been half naked, I'd have reared up and slapped her hands away. I'd been expecting someone to knead the knots out of my shoulders, much as Sam did on occasion, but what I'd gotten was a ferocious pounding that bordered on abuse.

I tried everything I could think of to distract myself—deep breathing, counting backwards from a thousand, trying to remember the lyrics to *American Pie*—but nothing worked. Ten minutes into the so-called massage, I'd finally diverted my focus to Eleanor's murder, when I heard a commotion in the foyer. A man's voice, followed by Georgia yelling. Heavy footsteps pounded across the floor. I yelped as the masseuse rotated an elbow into my shoulder blade.

Then the door to the banquet room slammed open, and the torture ceased. I lifted my face from its hidey hole to get a look at the person who had caused this reprieve.

There stood Allen Simonson, and it appeared his façade of cool composure was on the verge of crumbling. He looked like he was ready to slug someone. And in my current vulnerable position, I could only hope it wasn't me.

34

I grabbed my sheet and tucked it around my body, pulling myself into a sitting position on the massage table. Allen's glance darted around the makeshift spa, settling on Lynn, who sat in the facial chair with her face covered in goop. "How dare you!" he said, his voice controlled but menacing.

What was it with townspeople crashing our parties? Something in the cosmos didn't want us having any fun or relaxation. A chill of apprehension crept through me as I remembered Carmen's warning. Or maybe the chill was the result of my skimpy attire.

Lynn removed the cucumber slices from her eyes and dropped them into a bowl on the side table. "I'm not sure what you're referring to, Mr. Simonson, but this is neither the time nor the place to discuss it."

It was hard to take her seriously, given the brown sludge dripping down her face. But Allen didn't seem to find any humor in the situation.

He turned toward me, huddled in my makeshift toga. "You're in on it, too. You people are out to destroy me. Well, better people than you have tried and failed. If you're going to come at the king, you'd best not miss."

Mrs. Finney rose from the adjoining massage table, not nearly as careful about her modesty as I'd been. Allen's mouth dropped open, and he hurriedly averted his eyes. She wrapped the sheet around herself and leaned against the table. "What seems to be the problem, Mr. Simonson?"

"As if you don't know."

"For the sake of argument, let's say we have no idea. Why don't you enlighten us?"

Allen crossed his arms. "Fine. I'll play your game. I just got off the phone with a Denver reporter who wanted a quote in response to what's been going on in Mustang."

"That's no surprise," I said. "You can't have expected your wife's murder to go unreported."

"It's not only that, as I'm sure you know. The reporter had details. Private details. Information that could only have come from someone in the know—and that means one of you."

"What details?" Lynn asked.

"Eleanor's indiscretions, for one thing," Allen said. "And Gordon's misguided decision to sell my wife his shares of the company. All our family's dirty little secrets. I'm here to find out which of you was the source."

Ryll and Fritz rushed into the room while Georgia, Valerie, and Haley gathered outside the door. Fritz approached Allen, raising his hands in a soothing gesture. "Allen, let's calm down."

Allen rolled his shoulders and straightened his tie. "I'm calm, Fritz. I'm calmly picturing Moonglow Ranch with a foreclosure sign in front of it, and the two of you driving off pulling a trailer packed with everything you can salvage." He pointed at Lynn. "I'm calmly picturing this detective's badge lying at the bottom of a trash can." It was my turn next. "And I'm very calmly picturing this so-called famous photographer standing forlorn outside her former gallery." He gestured to Mrs. Finney. "And this one…well, never mind. You see my point."

No one responded. When Allen spoke again, his voice was so low I had trouble hearing him. "I have the power to do all of those things, believe me. Before this, I was happy to leave you alone. To allow you to run your little guest ranch and even make a few bucks. But now, I intend to see every one of you crash and burn."

His fiery eyes rested on each of us one more time. Then he turned on his polished loafers and strode out of the room.

For a long moment, none of us moved. Then Mrs. Finney broke the silence. "It's cold in here. Guess I should put on some clothes."

Nervous laughter erupted, and everyone started back into motion. Georgia, Valerie, and Haley bustled off to tend to their duties. The attendant began scrubbing the paste from Lynn's face. I headed behind the screen and exchanged the sheet for my clothing.

When I returned, the group was carrying on valiantly, trying to pretend Allen had never intruded.

Then Lydia, who was sitting at a pedicure station, groaned and grabbed her stomach. She yanked her feet out of the hot water, leaned over the tub, and vomited into the bubbles.

***

Tonya, who'd been standing at the snack table nibbling on a carrot, hurried over and kneeled beside Lydia's chair. "Lydia…Mother…what's wrong?"

Lydia responded with another retching sound and threw up again. I saw the expelled waste swirling in the tank and felt myself gag.

Still holding her stomach, Lydia crumpled back against the headrest and moaned. Tonya looked up at my mother, fear in her eyes. "What should we do?"

My mother said a few words to Ryll, who rushed out of the room. Mom put the back of her hand on Lydia's forehead. I recognized the gesture from the hundred times she'd done that to me when I was a child. "No fever," Mom muttered.

Lydia hunched forward but didn't vomit again. Mom rubbed her back, another familiar gesture. "Are you in pain, Lydia?"

"Stomach cramps, but I think they're easing."

Ryll hurried back into the room. In one hand, she carried a glass filled with clear, bubbly liquid and in the other, a damp wash cloth. Mom took the glass from her and put it in Lydia's hands. "Ginger ale," she said. "It should help settle your stomach."

Fritz spoke to the attendant in charge. After placing a lined trash can close at hand, he rolled the foot spa away and carried it from the room. My stomach did a flip flop of its own as I pictured him having to rinse out the contents, but I supposed when you owned a ranch, you were accustomed to unpleasant tasks.

Lydia sipped the ginger ale and leaned back. Her eyelids drooped closed, and Mom draped the cool cloth across her forehead. "Watch the hair," Lydia mumbled. Tonya rolled her eyes, but I saw the relief on her face.

After another minute, Lydia took a few more sips. "I think it's working. The nausea is subsiding."

"That's good," Mom said. "Now, let's get you upstairs to lie down for a while."

Ryll touched Mom on the shoulder. "Should I call the doctor? I'm sure she'd make a house call."

Mom studied Lydia. "I don't think that'll be necessary. She looks better already. We'll keep an eye on her overnight, but it seems like she's going to be all right."

Tonya helped her mother to her feet and linked an arm through hers. "I'll sleep in your room tonight," she said.

Lydia looked pleased. "Why TeeTee, thank you. That's very sweet."

"If you'll get her settled in bed, Tonya, Ryll and I will rustle up some crackers and more ginger ale," Mom said. "I'll bring them upstairs."

Tonya nodded and guided Lydia away.

Ryll's face creased with worry. "What could have caused this?"

"Stress, maybe. A stomach bug. Or she might've eaten something that didn't agree with her. Could be any number of things. Vomiting is the body's way of reacting to some germ or toxin. Usually, getting it out of your system is all it takes."

"You don't think it was food poisoning, do you?"

"No, Ryll, that's doubtful. We've all been eating the same things, and the rest of us feel fine." She put an arm around our hostess, whose eyes had filled with tears. "Really, dear, I'm certain Lydia will rally quickly. She'll be good as new by morning, I bet."

Ryll swiped at her cheeks and shook her head. "This week can't get any worse."

I winced. I didn't consider myself a superstitious person, but even I knew better than to tempt fate like that.

35

The spa attendants packed up their tables and rolled up their sheets. Mom spent a half hour bustling about, caretaking Lydia. Mrs. Finney sat in a rocker on the deck to read. The rest of us, at loose ends, went for a short walk in the woods under the gloomy sky and discussed how—or if—we could rescue our vacation. Summer suggested another meditation session, but the idea was met with grumbles and groans. No one was up for chasing serenity. Renata mentioned a movie theater on the outskirts of town, and that engendered mild enthusiasm.

We returned to the lodge for a subdued dinner. Mom, Mrs. Finney, and I stayed behind as the others packed into Summer's car and headed to the movies. I wasn't in the mood, and besides, I didn't want to leave Tonya.

Tonya came downstairs and told us Lydia was sleeping and hadn't been sick again. While Haley chopped vegetables for the next day's meals, Valerie fixed Tonya a plate of dinner. I sat with her at the kitchen table to keep her company as she ate. Woody curled up at her feet, partly to offer companionship and partly, I knew, in case bits of her dinner made their way to the floor. Carl, who'd seemed agitated since I'd released him from our room after Allen's departure, paced the floor.

"At least now I don't have to worry about Lydia running off tonight," Tonya said between bites.

"I wouldn't be too sure. That woman is resilient. She might sneak past you while you're snoring away."

"Thanks. You know how to cheer a girl up."

I bit my lip. "Listen, girlfriend, I'm sorry about how this week is turning out. Things aren't going as I'd hoped."

"Yeah, remind me not to put you in charge of the wedding." When Tonya saw me cringe, she grinned. "I'm just kidding, sugarplum. There's nothing you could have done. Besides, it's been exciting. Who wants a boring old stripper dressed as a firefighter for her bachelorette party when she can have a real-life murder investigation instead?"

"Wait, was I supposed to get a stripper?" I tapped a finger against my chin. "I suppose I could ask Colby. He'd be amenable—especially if tips are involved. Would a cowboy do instead of a firefighter?"

Tonya reached over and smacked my arm. "I'd get no joy out of seeing that man in his tighty-whities. Especially knowing my mother already has. Now, let's discuss something besides Colby Trent."

A bowl clattered on the kitchen island, and we looked up at Haley, whose face was bright red as she scooped up the spilled veggies. "Clumsy of me," she muttered. "I'm so embarrassed."

I hurried over and helped Haley clean up. "It's Tonya and I who should be embarrassed," I said. "We shouldn't be so crude. Sometimes we get carried away."

"Yeah, sorry. Callie's a bad influence on me," Tonya said.

Haley gave us a grateful smile and dumped the veggies in the trash. Then she headed into the pantry for more.

Once Tonya finished her meal, the two of us wandered into the front room to join Mom and Mrs. Finney. We found a deck of cards and started a game of rummy. Outside, thunder rumbled, and between hands we watched lightning flash across the sky, like the flicker of a black-and-white TV screen. The wind blew the rocking chairs on the deck back and forth, as if they were occupied by ghosts. No rain fell, though, and Mom said it must be a "dry storm," meaning the heat gathered below the cloud cover called the aerial canopy.

"In a dry storm, rain never reaches the ground," she said. "Moisture evaporates before it nears the earth. But you have to watch out for them because they can cause wildfires. A bolt of lightning cracks to the ground, and without the rain to dampen the dry grasses, fire can spark. Then the winds whip up the flames."

I shivered, thinking of Allen's threat that we'd all crash and burn—and earlier, when Carmen said her vision was veiled in smoke. So much had gone wrong this week, from a murder to Lydia's illness. It wouldn't surprise me if Carmen's vision proved true. A sense of impending doom shrouded me, and I had trouble concentrating.

Apparently, I wasn't alone. No one's heart seemed to be in the game, and after just a few hands, we called it quits. With the emotional upheavals of the day, we were all exhausted. We climbed the stairs for some alone time before bed.

Tonya brushed her teeth and put on her pajamas before carrying her pillow to Lydia's room. I texted Sam to ask if he had time to talk, and he FaceTimed me. We chatted for a half hour about the beach, his parents, Elyse's sunburn, the gourmet dinner he'd prepared. No mention of Isabella. He reminded me that he and Elyse were heading back to Rock Creek Village tomorrow and that we'd get to see each other on Friday when the bridal shower ended and my friends and I headed home. I felt a thrill of anticipation. Despite my self-proclaimed independence, I missed him. A lot.

After we hung up, I texted back and forth with Ethan for a few minutes, checking on the gallery. I'd left him in charge, along with our employees, twins Banner and Braden Ratliff. Everything was fine, Ethan said. Steady flow of customers, but nothing they hadn't been able to handle. He said they'd even sold two of Braden's photos.

Kid will have an uncontrollable ego by the time you get back, Ethan wrote.

So pleased for him!

Banner says his bro's becoming Callie Cassidy 2.0. Told him there are worse things.

I smiled at his backward compliment, feeling lucky yet again to be surrounded by such good people in my life. A flutter of warmth blossomed in my chest at the news of Braden's success. The twins had become an integral part of Sundance Studio, which was especially fulfilling considering the rocky beginnings to our relationship— back when I'd suspected them of murder and they'd retaliated by vandalizing the gallery where they now worked.

I remembered what a good team Raul and I had made in that situation, and a couple of others. Maybe it would help to pick his brain now. I decided to give him a call. No FaceTime, just old-fashioned speaker phone.

"Well, if it isn't the lightning rod for trouble," was his opening line.

"Hello to you, too."

Raul laughed. "No offense, Callie. It is what it is. So what's up? Are you calling so I can swoop in and figure this thing out for you?"

"Hardy har har," I said, enjoying the banter. I knew there'd never be anything romantic between Raul and me, but we definitely had a spark that was fun to feed occasionally.

"Have you talked to Lynn about today's events?" I asked.

"She texted me a couple of times, but no details. Isn't she there?"

I told him the others had gone to the movies in town, then filled him in on everything that had happened. When I got to the part about Allen barging into the room, he burst into laughter. "Wait a minute," he said. "Are you saying Mrs. Finney flashed the guy?"

"Pretty much," I said. The whole day had a very bizarre cast to it. Somehow, being able to talk about it with Raul lifted the blanket of anxiety I'd been carrying and restored my confidence that we'd get this murder solved.

"Want me to come help?" I heard the hopeful lilt to his voice. "I bet Frank would okay it if Butch gave him a call."

My mouth curled up. I hadn't used my father's influence since I was a teenager. Well, not much.

"Nah, it's okay, thanks," I said. "With one of Rock Creek Village's crack detectives away, they need you there to look after things. Anyway, Mustang's illustrious police chief has everything well in hand. At least, that's what he says."

"Well, stay close to Lynn, okay? That way, I don't have to worry too much about your safety."

"I can take care of myself, thank you very much."

He snorted. "You mean like you did at the hockey rink? In your darkroom? Or—"

"All right, I get the point. But lest you forget, I solved every one of those cases."

"Helped solve. I'll give you that much."

I heard a car pull up outside and looked out the window to see the moviegoers returning. "Thanks for the pep talk, but I have to go. My protector has returned to duty."

We said our goodbyes, and I trotted downstairs in my pajamas to greet my friends. In the now vacant kitchen, we poured ourselves lemonade and chatted for a while about the movie and the dry storm and Thursday's party, meant to serve as the highlight of the bridal shower week—anything but murder and threats. Finally, we climbed the stairs and said goodnight, heading into our rooms and closing our doors.

Feeling exhausted to my bones, I brushed my teeth and snuggled between the sheets. I expected to drop off quickly, given the absence of Tonya's snoring. Instead, I tossed and turned, fighting off thoughts of Allen and Gordon, Carmen and Colby. They made up my list of most likely suspects, but I couldn't narrow it any further. It wasn't Ryll or Fritz, of that I was certain. There was no way Summer's aunt and uncle, hippies and pacifists like my friend, would have struck out with violence.

At least, that's what I told myself.

After tolerating my bedtime gymnastics for a while, Woody had had enough. He jumped off my bed and onto Tonya's, stretching out full length. A moment later, he began snoring. I smiled at the familiar noise and drifted off to sleep.

An hour later, frantic barking yanked me from my slumber. I bolted upright to find Woody pawing at the window and howling in a high-pitched squeal. The hair on his neck stood at attention. Carl bayed in harmony and raked his claws across my arm.

I scrambled out of bed and nudged Woody aside so I could see what had caused such agitation. Clouds covered the moon, but an unexpected light illuminated the far side of the lodge.

Flames.

The front deck was on fire.

36

S hoving my feet into my sneakers, I flung my door open and dashed into the hall. Lynn came out, looking worried. "I heard Woody barking. What's happening?"

I started banging on the other doors. "The front deck is on fire!" I said. "Everyone needs to get outside!"

Renata appeared then, and I repeated myself. "The fire is out front, so everyone needs to go out the back."

Summer and Jessica emerged from their room, looking alarmed. "I'll make sure Ryll and Fritz get out," Summer said.

I opened Mom's door to find her standing near the bed as Mrs. Finney descended the ladder from the top bunk. "What's going on?" Mom asked.

"Fire," I repeated. "It doesn't seem to be out of control. Not yet. But we need to be safe and get out."

Mom nodded. "We'll just grab our shoes. Did you call 9-1-1?"

"Let's get outside first," I said.

Lydia's room was on the far side of the corridor. As I ran toward her door, it swung open and Tonya stepped out. "What's happening?"

"Fire. No time to explain. Get your mother and head out the back."

Woody darted past me, woofing, and started scratching on a door at the end of the hall. I rushed over and banged on it. When no one opened it, I turned the knob and flicked on the light to find Valerie tucked beneath the covers and Haley curled on her side watching a movie on her iPad. Haley sat up and looked at me in alarm as she yanked off her headphones.

"What's going on?" she asked.

"Fire," I said. "We need leave the lodge."

Haley jumped out of bed and shook her mother awake. Groggy, Valerie slitted her eyes open. When she saw us standing over her, she bolted out of bed and pulled a pair of earplugs from her ears. "What is it? Is someone hurt?"

I repeated my warning and herded the two of them toward the stairs. As they scrambled down, I snatched up Carl and followed, with Woody on my heels. Standing near the bottom step, Lynn directed Valerie and Haley through the kitchen and out the back door. I paused to glance through the plate-glass window in the front room. The flames hadn't reached the lodge's entrance, but I was beginning to get the first whiffs of smoke.

"You're last," Lynn said. "We've accounted for everyone. Firefighters are on the way."

We bustled out the back door and around the side of the lodge. When we made it to the front, we stood in the middle of the yard and watched the fire shimmer and pop. It wasn't huge, but it was spreading. I looked around the property. The stable was far enough away that the flames wouldn't reach it. Same with Colby's quarters. I'd never even seen the cabin Carmen was renting, so I didn't figure it was in imminent danger. Still, someone should check on her.

Just then, Fritz ran to the front of the deck and hoisted a fire extinguisher, which he used to spray white foam over the flames. Ryll dragged a hose from the side of the lodge and swiveled a nozzle, shooting a stream of water across the deck.

Everyone huddled together in the center of the yard. I scanned the group to double check Lynn's head count. Mom and Mrs. Finney. Summer, Jessica, Renata. Tonya and Lydia. Valerie with her arm tight around Haley.

"Wait, where's Georgia?" I asked.

"She lives in town," Valerie said.

"The ranch hands?"

"They don't live on the property, either."

"What about Carmen? Someone needs to tell her what's going on."

Valerie shook her head. "She was booked for an event in Boulder tonight and stayed over. She won't be back until tomorrow morning."

I breathed a sigh of relief. Then I saw Colby running toward the lodge with a shovel. As he scooped up dirt and tossed it onto the flames, I had a momentary vision of a shovel crashing onto Eleanor's head.

I chewed my bottom lip, watching them work and wanting to help. But the three of them moved in sync, and I knew the rest of us just needed to stay out of their way. The fate of the lodge rested on their shoulders. Small towns like Mustang usually relied on a volunteer fire department, and getting them assembled and on site might take a while.

Still, between the extinguisher, the water, and the dirt, the fire seemed to be coming under control. Within ten minutes, my heart rate slowed. When the last flame died a few minutes later, we erupted in cheers.

"Thank goodness," Mom said, her hand on her chest.

Colby pounded the blade of the shovel into the ground and wiped a hand across his sweating brow. He was, of course, shirtless, and his belt was in its perpetual state of unbuckle. Lydia observed him appreciatively. Guess she was feeling better.

Lynn pulled me aside. "I can't help but think of Allen's threats," she whispered. "Crash and burn."

My stomach clenched. "I'd been thinking of a lightning strike," I said, "but you have a point. How would we prove it, though?"

"If he used an accelerant, it would be detectable."

"Assuming they have the resources to investigate—or

the interest," I said. "I wouldn't wager Chief Wade will go the extra mile, and who knows what the situation is with the fire department?"

From inside the stable, we could hear the horses whinnying in fear. They were safe, I knew, since the smoke wasn't drifting that direction, but they had to be agitated. They'd had a rough time over the past few days. Colby trotted off to tend to them, and I crouched to cuddle my own creatures, wondering how they were handling all this.

Sirens warbled in the distance, and we watched headlights approaching. A fire truck roared through the ranch's arch, screeching to a stop. Four men jumped out and jogged over to Fritz and Ryll.

"I think we got it," Fritz told them.

"We'll need to check," said the one in charge, whose name tag read Hai Li. "Sometimes live flames go into hiding inside walls. We'll make sure the fire didn't make a leap."

They hustled onto the charred deck and used axes to open a section of the front wall and probe the area beneath the lodge. I was impressed by their expertise and efficiency. We'd sleep easier knowing they'd covered the bases.

As they worked, another set of headlights approached. The chief of police had arrived.

He lumbered out of the passenger seat. He'd buttoned his shirt crooked, the sign of someone wrested from his bed. I glanced at my pajamas and realized I couldn't be too critical of the chief's appearance.

Officer Jake, on the other hand, appeared fresh and composed, alert and curious. Ah, youth. I remembered my days as a young investigative photojournalist. I, too, had been ready on a dime, needing very little sleep, living off coffee and sugar. Now that my adrenaline rush had drained, I felt myself yawning and understood that, for me, those days were long gone.

The chief stood apart from the group, hands in his pockets, rocking on the balls of his feet. After a few minutes, Li approached him. Jake joined them, along with Ryll and Fritz. Lynn and I edged as close as we dared, enduring a sharp look from Chief Wade, but holding our ground.

"Fire's contained," Li said. "The only damage is to the deck, along with some minor smoke damage to the awning. The rest of the structure is intact."

"So we can sleep here tonight?" Ryll asked.

Li nodded. "It's stable. You probably won't even notice the smell of smoke anywhere but the front room. You can attribute that to the fact that you caught it so early. Left to its own devices, this fire could have destroyed the lodge."

Ryll and Fritz looked at me, eyes wide above sooty cheeks. "Thank you, Callie," Fritz said.

I gestured to the creatures. "It was all their doing. Their barking and hissing woke me up."

"Well, you can bet they'll be rewarded." Ryll bent to pet them both.

"How did the fire start?" I asked Li. "Was it set on purpose?"

Li shrugged. "Could be. My guys and I smelled gasoline, and there's no gas grill nearby. We didn't find any cigarette butts or evidence of a lightning strike. Even if it is arson, though, we probably can't prove it. We don't have the resources for that kind of analysis, and with this minor damage, I doubt the county will pursue it. Insurance examiners might come by to take a look, but I expect it'll be cheaper just to pay the claim."

Chief Wade hitched up his pants. "A cigarette butt could have burned up with the flames, right? Same with a lightning strike point."

Li considered. "Sure. Coulda happened that way."

"We'll just chalk it up to an act of God, then."

I stiffened. "No! He said they smelled gas. This was no

215

accident. Someone set this fire on purpose. And it's obvious who it was. Allen Simonson."

I told him about the confrontation earlier in day. The police chief scoffed, but Jake appeared interested.

Chief Wade spat on the ground. "So you're telling me one of the most important men in the state snuck around the ranch in the dead of night with a can of lighter fluid. And you want me to hightail it over to his place and arrest him, all because of some off-handed comment he made during your little spa day. That's what you expect me to do?"

I gritted my teeth. "I expect you to do your job."

"Who do you think you are, telling me what my job is? It's you I oughta arrest."

"For what?"

"For obstructing justice. You and your Nancy Drews are interfering in my investigation. You're nothing more than—"

Lynn stepped between us. "That's enough. This isn't getting us anywhere. Let's take a breath and talk this over."

Chief Wade glared at me, and I glared back, but we both shut our mouths.

"No one is saying you should actually arrest Allen Simonson," Lynn said to the chief. "But given the threat he made, which we all witnessed, and the consequent fire, procedure dictates that you should at least question him. Don't you agree?"

He huffed, not ready to capitulate. "No, I don't agree. There's nothing here to convince me this wasn't Mother Nature in a mood."

Fritz took a step forward. "Well, Chief, there just might be."

We turned to look at him, surprised. Then Chief Wade shook his head. "Like what? Some kinda intuition? Is Crazy Carmen talking inside your head?"

"Nope. I may be able to offer visual evidence."

Ryll linked her arm through her husband's. He smiled at her, then turned back to the chief.

"With everything that's been happening around here, I figured the ranch and our guests needed extra protection. Yesterday, I finally installed those security cameras I bought. Maybe one of them caught an arsonist in action."

37

My body buzzed with anticipation as we packed into the cramped office. At first, Chief Wade had refused to include Lynn and me, but Fritz told him it was his property and his decision, and the chief relented.

Now, as Fritz booted up his computer, we formed a tight semicircle behind the desk: Ryll, Chief Wade, Jake, Li, Lynn, and myself, all of us awaiting a possible answer as to how the fire started. If it turned out to be arson, would that by extension lead us to a suspect in Eleanor's murder?

Fritz had installed four cameras around the ranch— one above the stable entrance, another at the lodge's back door, one above the deck facing the entrance to the property, and the last on the ranch's arch, turned toward the lodge itself.

He started by combing through the feed from the deck camera. He fast forwarded through the night, catching flashes of lightning across the dark sky. Eventually, we saw a pair of headlights creep into view, switching off beyond the arch. A few seconds later, a figure wearing a hood and carrying a small bag slunk across the yard toward the lodge. I leaned toward the computer, but the image was too distant to make out any relevant details. It appeared to be a male, but even that assumption could have risen from a preconceived perception on my part.

Head down, the figure skulked across the open space, then beyond the angle of the lens.

Chief Wade rubbed a hand across his chin. "Huh."

"This proves the fire was no accident," I said. "It must be Allen Simonson, making good on his threat."

The chief's response was muted. "Shouldn't jump to conclusions. I can't see the person's face, and you can't either."

"I guess not," I admitted.

"For all we know, this could be an out-of-towner. A complete stranger."

"But why would a stranger—"

"Just making a point, little lady. It could be Mayor Finkle, for crying out loud. Or Fritz here, going after insurance money." Chief Wade chortled. "For all we know, it could be you."

"Well, I can assure you it wasn't me, so that narrows your suspect pool." I took a deep breath. "Listen, Chief, sometimes the right answer is the most obvious one. Allen Simonson said we were going to crash and burn. Those were his exact words. I think that warrants a conversation."

"Wait a second," Fritz interrupted. "I'm going to try a different camera."

He pressed a couple of buttons and brought up the camera positioned on the entry arch, the one that faced the lodge. Having noted the time of the car's approach, he skimmed through the evening's footage and slowed the video as he closed in on the significant time. We waited, watched, waited some more. Then we spotted a shadow. "Ah ha!" Fritz said.

We inclined our heads toward the camera. The figure crept toward the lodge. Clad in sweatpants, sneakers, and the hoodie, the person was nondescript—could have been heavy or slender, old or young. It was impossible to discern.

The figure climbed the steps to the deck, pausing and glancing around to make sure no one was watching. We all held our breath, hoping one of the head swivels would result in a glimpse of the face. No such luck. A moment later, the person set the bag on a table, unzipped it, and rustled around inside, pulling out what looked like a small can.

Sure enough, when the figure bent, we saw liquid pouring from the can. After that, the flick of a thumb, a tiny flame, and—voilà. Fire.

The person moved back to the stairs and watched for a few moments, seemingly mesmerized as the flames took root. After one last look, the figure turned and hurried back toward the car.

A sheet of lightning lit up the sky. The figure jumped and looked upward. We held our breath. The hood fell back from the head, revealing the arsonist's face. Around me, everyone sucked in a breath.

The chief had been right—it wasn't Allen Simonson.

It was his son, Gordon, looking supremely pleased with himself.

Chief Wade shoved his hands in his pockets and sighed.

"Told you it wasn't me," I said.

***

The chief departed for the Simonson estate to arrest Gordon on an arson charge. Jake, who as usual served as chauffeur, seemed energized to be in on this particular ride.

"Keep in mind," Chief Wade told us before they pulled out, "there's still no evidence that Gordon killed Eleanor. The murder case is still open."

True. But even the chief didn't look convinced. It was just a matter of time before proof of Gordon's culpability turned up. With any luck, Allen's son would even confess.

Once the police had left, the rest of us crowded into the kitchen to debrief—and to celebrate. Mrs. Finney trotted up to her room and returned with two packages of Oreos. "Contraband," she declared. "One must never travel to a health-food resort without it."

Ryll chuckled, then went to the refrigerator and extracted two bottles of wine. "In for a penny, in for a pound," she said.

Mom and I made Valerie and Haley take a seat, insisting they were off duty. We found a stack of red Solo cups in the pantry and set about pouring wine for the group. "Hmm, white or red?" Jessica pondered. "Which goes best with Oreos?"

Once we were settled, sipping and chewing and chatting, Ryll clapped her hands to get our attention. Fritz stood next to her, his arm tight around her shoulder. We quieted.

"This has been a difficult time for Fritz and me," she began. "We never imagined that our little enterprise would become so complicated or take such a convoluted course. But your presence has made the tumultuous journey easier. Ladies, we are grateful for your unwavering support." She turned to Summer, her eyes shimmering. "My dear niece, thank you for bringing this amazing group of people into our lives."

A tear spilled down Ryll's cheek as she raised her cup. "To new friends. You will always be welcome at Moonglow Ranch."

We lifted our cups and sipped, then applauded. "Those words may come back to haunt you," Jessica said. "I'm thinking this place would make a nice monthly getaway. You're only an hour's drive from Rock Creek Village."

We laughed, and Summer jumped up to wrap her aunt and uncle in a hug. One by one, we all joined in, even Woody, who wormed his way into the middle of the group.

From the corner of the room, Carl huffed and licked his paw.

38

Because of the late-night drama and the subsequent wine-and-Oreo celebration, none of us got back to bed until after three. Ryll had insisted that Valerie and Haley take the morning off, so after only few hours of sleep, we gathered beneath the pergola—yards away from the charred deck—for a makeshift breakfast of fruit and bran muffins thawed from the freezer.

Last night's storm had drifted off to the east, and the day was crisp and bright. That, along with very strong coffee, perked us up, and the runners decided to run while the yogis decided to yoga. I told the group I was heading into town on an errand. A month ago, I'd ordered a fancy cake for tomorrow's party. It had cost me a small fortune, and I wanted to pick it up myself to ensure its safety.

"Want me to come?" Tonya asked, feigning innocence.

"Nope. Your presence is neither requested nor permitted."

Lynn wiped her fingers on a napkin. "I'll join you, if that's all right. We can stop in at the police department and see if we can wrangle any new information out of them."

Ryll poured herself another cup of coffee. "I called this morning, but no one would tell me anything. You'd think since the arson involved our property, they'd keep us in the loop."

"Chief Wade doesn't strike me as the type to be concerned with victims' rights," I said. "He's just mad that his peaceful, lazy little world has been rocked. I imagine he blames you—or us."

"Very true. Anyway, try to be back before one. After lunch, we have fly-fishing on the agenda."

Summer gasped. "Fly-fishing? Aunt Ryll, you can't! I've read that fish experience pain, both physical and emotional. Even if it's catch-and-release, those poor creatures…"

Ryll gave her niece an indulgent smile. "Oh, Summer. You should know me better than that. I was a pacifist before you were even born. I'd never hurt the fishies. This is swimming pool fly-fishing, with robotic fish."

Summer blew out a breath and laughed. "Well, in that case, I'm in."

***

Fifteen minutes later, Lynn and I were ready to go. Mrs. Finney wanted to join us, of course, and we piled into her car. In town, we parked near the bakery and walked across the street to the police station. As we approached, Allen Simonson stormed out the building, followed by Mayor Finkle and his wife Polly.

Allen was fuming, and as soon as he spotted us, he redirected his ire. "This is your fault," he said, shaking a finger at our trio. In a rare moment of courage, Mayor Finkle stepped in front of him.

"Now, Allen," he said. "Let's not create a scene." He nodded toward a small group of shop owners who had gathered to observe the drama.

At the sight of them, Allen halted abruptly. He tugged at his jacket and straightened his tie, arranging his face into an expression of nonchalance. But his eyes still blazed. Without another word, he strode to his car and drove away.

Polly wrung her hands, and she and the mayor walked away and disappeared into the Town Hall building.

"Well, that was interesting," Lynn said. "Can't wait to see what else is going on." Mrs. Finney and I followed her up the walkway to the police station.

Today, a middle-aged woman sat behind the reception counter, and she peered at us over the rim of her glasses. "Can I help you?"

Lynn pulled her badge from her pocket. "Detective Lynn Clarke. These are my associates. We'd like a moment with Chief Wade."

The woman wrinkled her nose as if she'd smelled something unpleasant. "I'm afraid the chief is indisposed. I'd be happy to pass along a message."

Lynn gave her a knowing smile. "That's all right. We'll wait."

Jake stood up from a desk in the back. "I'll take care of this, Penny." He gestured toward the front door. "Ladies, if you'll follow me…"

I started to object, but from behind the woman's back, Jake made a thumbs up gesture.

He held the door for us, then led us to a grassy space on the other side of the town square. He ducked behind a tree, and we clustered around him as he scanned for eavesdroppers. Satisfied we weren't being observed, he talked low and fast.

"Allen's hired a big-city lawyer who's inside with Gordon as we speak. The lawyer is insisting we call in the county sheriff's office to take over. Chief Wade resisted, but when Allen brought in the mayor to pressure him, he caved. The sheriff's on his way now, and the whole thing will soon be out of our hands."

"I figured that was coming," Lynn said. "The homicide case alone should probably have warranted that, and now, there's really no alternative. Have they officially charged Gordon?"

"They're holding him on arson charges," Jake said.

"There's talk of adding attempted murder since the lodge was occupied when Gordon started the fire, but I think that was just the chief's way of trying to get him to confess. His lawyer balked and instructed Gordon to keep his mouth shut. But everything is on hold until the county people arrive."

Lynn nodded. "If Gordon's arraigned only on an arson charge, his father will have him out on bail before the day is out. Is there a possibility they'll charge him with Eleanor's murder, too?"

Jake shook his head. "I don't see that happening. There's still no evidence linking Gordon to her death—not even circumstantial."

"But I told you Haley overheard Gordon threatening Eleanor," I said. "That meets the criteria for circumstantial evidence."

"Yes, but Gordon denies that ever happened."

"Well, duh," I said. "Of course he does. That's what guilty people do. Have you talked to Haley?"

"The chief isn't interviewing anyone else," Jake said. "It's up to the county people now."

The idea that Gordon would soon be out on bail rankled me. "With the Simonsons' resources, including a private plane, they should consider Gordon a flight risk," I said. "Maybe they'll at least put an ankle monitor on him."

Mrs. Finney huffed. "Doubtful. In the justice system, money talks. They'll set a high bail and assume Allen will make sure his son stays put."

"Don't they ever watch true crime shows?" I asked. "People with money are always the ones who flee."

Jake shrugged. "Anyway, please don't mention this conversation to anyone. Everything that's happened will be public record soon, of course, but Chief Wade wouldn't like me giving you an early head's up. He's…umm…not your biggest fan."

I chuckled. "Shocker. Thank you, Jake. And I promise,

we won't reveal our source, even if Chief Wade tortures us with pins beneath our fingernails."

Mrs. Finney frowned. "That's a very dark image, dear. I think it may be time for another visit to your therapist."

***

We spotted Crystal Clear and decided to pop by, hoping Carmen had returned from her overnight trip. She deserved to know about Gordon's arrest since, in all likelihood, it cleared her as a murder suspect.

As before, the bell jingled when we stepped through the door. One blink later and Carmen stood in front of us, as if she'd materialized from the spiritual world. She appeared serene and untroubled—except for the dark circles beneath her red-rimmed eyes.

"Good morning, Carmen," I said. "We're here to let you know the police have arrested Gordon Simonson."

"Yes, I'm aware of that," she said.

I cocked my head. "Did it come to you in a vision?"

She gave me an amused look. "I saw them bringing him into the station in handcuffs."

"Ah," I said. "Well, you missed a big brouhaha when you were in Boulder last night." I spent a couple of minutes summarizing the events, including the fire at Moonglow Ranch, the damage to the deck, and Fritz's cameras catching Gordon in the act.

Carmen closed her eyes. "I see. That explains it."

"Explains what?"

"Remember my vision of smoke and doom? For three nights in a row, I dreamed of Moonglow Ranch with a bright haze surrounding the lodge. I woke with a sense of foreboding. Now I understand. In this case, the brightness was literal—a fire threatening to engulf the ranch."

"You're saying you knew this was going to happen?" I asked.

She waved. "As I've told you before, that's not how this works. I'm not privy to exact images of future events. I see flashes that I interpret."

"Well, these visions don't seem especially useful if they only make sense in hindsight. What's the point?"

Lynn shot me a warning look, and I shrugged. "At any rate, Gordon is being held on arson. They haven't charged him with Eleanor Simonson's murder. Not yet. But it's just a matter of time. At least, that's what we're hoping. We wanted to let you know you're likely no longer a suspect. You're safe."

The ever-present snake slithered on her wrist. Carmen's eyes glazed over, and a shudder passed through her.

"I wouldn't be so sure of that," she murmured. "I sense this hasn't ended. None of us is safe. Not yet."

39

fter we left Crystal Clear, Lynn, Mrs. Finney, and I stopped at the bakery to pick up the cake. It had turned out even better than I'd expected, and I was excited for Tonya to see it tomorrow. Though my friend had told me not to go to too much trouble, gestures like this were part of her love language. Besides, after everything that had happened this week, Tonya deserved at least this one thing to be perfect.

On the drive home, I worked to put Carmen's words out of my head and focus on keeping the cake safe as Mrs. Finney navigated the road. But how could I stop thinking about the psychic's warning, considering that her last one had resulted in the lodge nearly burning down? I skimmed back through everything Carmen had said and done since we met: revealing Tonya and David's adoption plans; predicting Eleanor's doom hours before the woman turned up dead; the visions of a fiery Moonglow Ranch. And now: "*I sense this hasn't ended. None of us is safe. Not yet.*"

I remembered Carmen telling me she'd gotten a peek into my future. I'd dismissed her offer to reveal what she saw, but now I wondered...*did I want to know?*

Then Mrs. Finney turned on the radio to a classic rock station and began singing along to "Bohemian Rhapsody," complete with the head banging. Lynn joined in, and I realized deep thoughts had no place in this car. For the moment, anyway.

No, for now I'd just relax and focus on the fact that

Gordon was behind bars. The county sheriff was taking over the investigation, increasing the likelihood of uncovering evidence linking Gordon to Eleanor's murder. In the meantime, the damage to the lodge could be repaired. Everyone was safe, Tonya's cake was beautiful, and tomorrow's party would be a smashing success.

We got back to Moonglow Ranch just as lunch was being served in the dining room. I sneaked the cake box into the kitchen and asked Valerie to hide it in the industrial-sized refrigerator. She took a quick look inside the box and smiled appreciatively before nestling it behind a few bags of kale.

After a light meal of veggie paninis and fruit, we went to our rooms and changed into swimsuits. When we showed up at the pool shortly after, we were greeted with pint-sized fishing poles and colorful mechanical fish, their tails flopping and their fake fins spurting streams of water. The next hour was more fun than I'd expected. Fritz taught us a few basic fishing maneuvers, and we took turns casting our magnetic lures, mostly missing but occasionally snagging a robotic fish. Tonya won the day, snagging three fish in three tries. I suggested we'd only let her win because she was the bride-to-be, and she responded by pushing me into the pool.

As I plotted my revenge, she executed a dive that merited an eight, then backstroked to my side. I dunked her, and she emerged laughing. Perhaps this bridal party was a success after all.

Suddenly, we heard what could best be described as a war whoop. We spun around to see Mrs. Finney, wearing a neon purple one-piece suit with a flouncy skirt, running full speed toward the pool. When she reached the edge, she leapt into the air, wrapped her arms around her knees, and landed a cannonball.

That one merited a nine, by my estimation.

When Mrs. Finney came up for air, Tonya and I dog-paddled over to her. "You never cease to amaze me, Mrs. Finney," Tonya said. "This may be a personal question, but with all the talk of the seventies and everything—just how old are you?"

Mrs. Finney lifted a soggy eyebrow. "That information is classified, dear. I could tell you, but…well, you know the rest."

Then everyone joined us in the pool—except Lydia, who lay on a lounge chair with a portable fan blowing on her face. Woody raced around the pool's perimeter, wagging and yapping happily. As soon as Ryll gave me the thumbs up, I patted my hand on the water's surface, and my golden retriever leapt into the pool and paddled toward me.

When I looked around for Carl, I spotted him sitting in the shade beneath Lydia's lounge chair, giving us the side eye.

We got out of the pool a half hour later. Woody trotted over to the far side of the pool deck and engaged in a head-to-tail water removal dance. Drops flew from his fur, glistening as they caught the sunlight. The rest of us toweled off in a more subdued manner then stretched out on lounge chairs to let the sun's rays finish the job. I felt my skin tingle and closed my eyes, as relaxed as I'd been all week. The effects of Carmen's warning on my psyche had subsided to a mere twitch in the back of my brain, almost completely forgotten.

Valerie and Georgia brought us frothy, fruity cocktails, complete with tiny paper umbrellas, and we sipped, basking in the sunny day and each other's company. This was just the ambience I'd hoped for. The week was finally going as planned.

Then a car crackled across the gravel road, and Audra's red Jeep rolled to a stop near the corral. As she hopped out, Colby jogged over to her, a grin on his face. I saw Lydia squirm.

After a few seconds of conversation, Audra trotted

over to the pool at the same time as Haley appeared from inside the lodge. Carrying a covered plate and a glass, she walked across the yard and handed Colby the goodies. He thanked her with a little bow and a kiss on her hand.

The pool gate squeaked as Audra made her entrance. "Good afternoon, ladies."

Woody sidled up beside her, and I snapped my fingers at him. "He's wet," I warned her.

She crouched and scratched his ears. "Doesn't bother me. He's a doll. If a wet dog is the worst thing I touch today, it'll be a shock."

After a few seconds of cuddling, she rose and found a chair. "Has Ryll told you what we have in store for you tonight?"

We shook our heads, and Audra rubbed her hands together. "You'll love it. It's astronomy night! We're going stargazing!"

"It'll be a perfect night for it," Ryll said, motioning to the cloudless sky. "The moon is waning, which makes the stars appear even more brilliant. We'll have telescopes, but even with the naked eye, you should be able to make out constellations and planets. I'd expect you'll even get a few shooting stars. And I predict all the wishes you make tonight will come true."

"I can't wait," Mrs. Finney said. "I've always wanted to be a stargazer. Astronomy and astrology are so closely aligned. Perhaps we'll catch a glimpse of our destiny."

"You sound like Carmen." I didn't bother to keep the skepticism out of my voice.

"You don't believe in destiny, dear?" Mrs. Finney asked.

"Not so much. In my mind, the idea of destiny is a cop-out. A crutch that allows people to surrender responsibility for their choices."

A wise smile wreathed her face. "In *my* mind, both are possible. Destiny presents itself, and a person chooses to follow it or ignore it."

From the corner of my eye, I saw several nods, including Summer and my mom. "How do you mean?" I asked.

"Well...take you and Sam, for example. Destiny put you together in high school—"

I waved. "That was chance. We both happened to be born and raised in Rock Creek Village. It wasn't destiny that brought us together, it was proximity."

Another sage smile. "If you say so, dear. But from my perspective, you pushed destiny away back then. For twenty-five years, in fact. But destiny doesn't relent. And now the two of you have stumbled back onto the path fate laid out for you."

I considered her words. Could the universe have a destiny in mind for us while still allowing for our free choice?

I leaned back and closed my eyes. "You know what? I'll think about that another day. The sun on my face is the only philosophy worth pondering at the moment. Also, much as I hate to bail on tonight's outing, you soul seekers will have to stargaze without me. I need some alone time to finish a project."

"You're not working, are you?" Renata asked. "You made us promise to leave our jobs back in Rock Creek Village. Besides, Ethan assured me everything is under control at the gallery."

"It's not work related," I said. "I'm on a clandestine mission. I could tell you, but, well, you know the rest..."

"Yeah, yeah," Tonya said, eyeing me. "If this is about the stripper, I've already told you I don't want one."

I laughed. "All will be revealed in due time."

Tonya sat up and flipped her braids over her shoulder. "That's what I'm afraid of."

40

A s soon as the sun dropped beneath the horizon, the group gathered outside near the front deck. Too close to it for my taste. Even though the damage had been minimal, the smell of burned wood hung in the air like a sinister reminder of what could have happened.

Despite the charred deck, the mood was light and cheerful. I'd gone outside to see them off, and they made one last attempt to get me to join them.

"Come on, Callie, whatever you have to do can wait," Renata called.

Jessica pouted. "How will we have any fun if you're not with us?"

"I imagine you'll make do," I said.

"I've heard there's wine," Summer said in a last-ditch effort. "It'll be a regular Bacchanalia."

"Well, it's good that I'm not going, then. Someone needs to be here to mount a search if the reverie results in you becoming lost in the wilderness."

Ryll patted my shoulder. "No worries, Callie. Audra has an inner compass like you've never seen. And a real one as backup. Oh, and there's GPS, too. But since you insist on staying behind, I've left you a sampling of all the goodies: wine, grapes, bread, cheese. Except for the telescopes, you'll have everything we do."

I expressed my thanks and waved as the group started off on the mile-long trek to the meadow. Tonya hung back for a moment. "Keep an eye on Lydia, will you?"

Like me, Tonya's mother had opted out of the excursion, saying she wasn't yet feeling a hundred percent after yesterday's stomach bug. But we figured it was a ruse. I'd seen the jealous look on her face when Colby was talking—flirting, if we're being honest—with Audra earlier. There was no doubt in my mind that Lydia was prepping for another tête-à-tête while the gang was away.

"I will, of course. But Tonya, what do you want me to do? Tackle her if I see her heading Colby's direction? Burst into his cabin and put a stop to any illicit entanglements? They're consenting adults. My power is limited—as is yours."

She heaved a sigh. "You're right, I suppose. Though the tackling image feels right in my mind…"

I hugged her, and she trotted off to catch up. I lifted my eyes to the sky, soft as a blanket above me, stars twinkling like sequins. A pang of loneliness pierced me. Part of me wanted to run after my friends and bask in the peace and beauty of the stargazing experience.

But a bigger part of me wanted to finish my gift for my friend.

I walked up the lodge steps, glancing at the charred wood that used to be the left side of the deck. A gust of wind swept through my hair like the long fingers of a ghost. Goosebumps dimpled my skin. I turned, and my eyes darted around, looking for the unseen presence. Nothing was there. At least, not that I could see.

***

After a quick stop in the kitchen to retrieve the treats Ryll had left me, I went up to my room. Once I placed the bottle wine and the plate on the dresser, I closed the door behind me and turned the lock. I told myself I only wanted to make sure Tonya didn't make an unexpected return while I was working on her surprise, but in truth, I was a little spooked. This lodge was a big place, and tonight it felt as empty as a haunted house. Except for Haley, who was in her room watching a movie, and Lydia, curled up in her alleged sickbed, I was alone. I gazed out the window toward the stable, recalling with a pang that a murder had occurred there just a few nights ago. Was the killer really in custody? What if it wasn't Gordon after all? What if the true killer was still out there, lurking in the shadows?

A loud noise pierced the silence, and I jumped. My heart thumped in my chest. Then I laughed when I realized it was just Carl yowling from his perch on Tonya's bed. The cat had little patience for my flights of fancy, and his noisy reminder that he and Woody had my back allowed me to shake off my sense of foreboding.

Or at least, push it to the side.

I poured myself a glass of wine and took a sip—more like a gulp. My frayed nerves began to settle. Where had this foolishness come from? I was a big, brave girl—woman, that is—who had faced innumerable dangerous situations over the course of my life. Now I was skittish about being by myself in a quiet lodge?

Of course, it was a lodge that had been set on fire last night...near a stable where a woman had been murdered...

Ugh. I took another gulp of wine and bit off a hunk of gouda. Then I opened my laptop and plugged in my portable printer. Time to focus on my project and put these foolish thoughts aside.

I pulled my suitcase from its spot under the bed and dialed the numbers on its lock. Keeping Tonya's gift secured in a locked case might have seemed like overkill, but my best friend was as much of a snoop as I was, so better safe than sorry. I removed the thick leather album and laid it on the bed, then sat cross-legged and flipped through the pages.

I'd been working on this album for the past three months. It was a tribute to my best friend, a chronicle of her life. Creating it had involved a little snooping of my own—compiling pictures of Tonya's younger years meant using the key to her house that she'd given me for emergencies. David had often served as my lookout, letting me know when they'd be out on dates so I could sneak in and dig through desk drawers, rummage closet shelves, flip through boxes in the attic. It had been well worth the effort, and I knew she'd forgive my intrusion.

There were only a few blank pages at the end of the album, ones I'd been saving for pictures from this week's festivities. I'd also prepared a slide show of the album pictures, one I'd present at tomorrow's official shower. Tonight, I planned to put the finishing touches on both.

I turned on my camera and plugged it into the laptop, watching as the photos uploaded. When the images had transferred, I clicked a few buttons and started scrolling through them. I chose a photo from today of Tonya lying on a lounge chair by the pool, her eyes closed and an arm thrown above her head. In another, her brow furrowed in concentration as she tossed a lasso at a metal cow. Here was one of my friend sitting in a rocking chair on the deck, pre-fire damage, laughing at something Jessica had said. And, of course, I selected several from the luncheon, with all of us dressed up and smiling like sisters.

Now I came to the photos I'd shot in Colby's cabin. The open trunk. The ladies' clothing.

I wouldn't be using any of these photos in Tonya's album, of course. But I studied them anyway. The lacy bra in the corner. The silk scarf nestled in the folds of a soft blue sweater. The panties. So many panties. I felt a tug in the back of my brain, as if something in that trunk was calling out to be noticed. Something familiar…but I couldn't connect the image with the memory.

Another noise caught my attention—footsteps on the stairs. I peeked out the window as I counted down. Five…four…three…two…As predicted, a figure appeared beneath me, gliding down the deck stairs and across the yard. With just a sliver of moon in the sky, the light was dim, but I made out a silver satin sheath falling inches above the knee, contrasting sensuously with the dark-toned length of leg. When she turned back to glance at the lodge, the glimpse of her face confirmed what I already knew. Lydia was on another lover's quest.

So much for recovering from a stomach bug.

If I jumped off the bed now, jetted down the stairs, and raced across the yard, I could probably manage the tackle I'd jokingly sketched out for Tonya. But no. I merely watched as Lydia defied her daughter's pleas and stepped onto the cabin's tiny porch. Before she could even knock, the door opened and a single bare arm ushered her inside.

Ick. I didn't even want to imagine what came next.

41

When I'd decided which photos I wanted to add to Tonya's album, I loaded a stack of glossy photo paper into the printer and let the ink jets do their thing. It was a slow process, so as I waited, I ate a few grapes, drank the fermented grapes, and stared out the window toward Colby's cabin.

I wasn't looking at the cabin so much as I was letting my mind scuttle through the events of the last few days. For some reason, I still felt uneasy. It wasn't simply Lydia's defiance of Tonya's mandate. No, I was filled with the all-too-familiar sensation of having overlooked something. Something crucial.

Another sip of wine did little to still my restlessness. Why was I so tense? Gordon was locked up—at least, as far as I was aware. Jake would surely have let us know if the county had released Gordon on bail. And though they hadn't yet charged him with Eleanor's death, I was convinced he'd done it. Wasn't I?

A clutching sensation arose in my chest, the one I always got when I grappled with uncertainty. It warned me that, despite what I'd tried to tell myself, I wasn't a hundred percent sure Gordon had murdered Eleanor.

But why? I'd been so certain just hours ago. It wasn't as if the man presented as Mr. Innocent. He'd threatened us with a golf club. Committed arson, for heaven's sake. We had him on camera. It wasn't a leap to imagine him bashing Eleanor with a shovel. What had planted this seed of doubt?

Sighing, I poured myself more wine and nibbled at a cracker. I noticed the suspect list Lynn, Tonya, and I made the other night lying on the nightstand. Maybe if I combed through it one last time, I could tamp down my misgivings.

After retrieving a finished photo from the printer tray, I picked up the paper and scanned the list of names. Then I ran down them more slowly, considering each person's motive and opportunity.

Fritz. His motive was obvious—saving his ranch. He'd been off the property when I'd discovered Eleanor's body and as far as I knew, no one had checked his alibi for the time of death. But if he'd killed Eleanor, would he have left the premises and made Ryll handle the fallout? He appeared to be a devoted husband, and I couldn't picture him doing that.

Ryll. Same motive as Fritz, of course, and same opportunity. But I couldn't see a self-proclaimed, lifelong pacifist violently attacking someone. Of course, there was that assault charge in her past…Also, if Ryll had come across Eleanor preparing to harm a horse, her protective impulses might have kicked in. I shook my head. I didn't believe it, but I couldn't ignore it.

Carmen. I supposed her motive might be Eleanor's threats to run her out of town, though she never appeared intimidated. As far as opportunity, she resided on the property, giving her easy access to the stable. Still, my instinct told me she had little to gain by Eleanor's death.

Colby. The man's predatory nature toward rich older women so vexed me that, like Tonya, I almost wished I could pin the crime on him. After all, I rationalized, the man had lied about seeing Eleanor dead in the stable hours before my discovery of her body. But try as I might, I couldn't get past one important point. When he'd said he didn't do it, I believed him.

Allen. Motives were plentiful with this one: money,

revenge over his wife's affair, rage if he'd discovered Eleanor was in the process of securing Gordon's stocks. As far as opportunity, Allen had supposedly been out of town at the time of the murder, but so far, I'd heard no definitive evidence of that. With a private plane, he might easily have come and gone. Raul had been unable to find an alternate flight plan. Had anyone been able to confirm his whereabouts? I made a note to ask Jake.

That exhausted our written list. Was there anyone we'd missed? Who else had access to the stable that night? Those of us who were guests at the ranch, of course, but since none of us had any reason to want Eleanor dead, I dismissed us from consideration.

What about Chef Valerie? She'd been in residence that night. And her motive? I remembered the scene on the front deck, her concern over the possibility of losing her job at Moonglow Ranch. Haley had sat beside her on the swing, consoling her...

Then something clicked in my brain. The beginnings of a connection. I couldn't make sense of it. Not yet. But I felt it growing clearer. I just needed to focus...

Haley. I thought of the adoring look she'd given Colby yesterday morning in the kitchen. The blush when he'd kissed her hand. The way she was always taking him fresh cookies and muffins. The girl was, if not in love, at least deeply infatuated.

How had I missed it?

Puppy love wasn't cause enough to suspect someone of murder, but there was something else...another memory trying to worm its way into my consciousness. I replayed the first time we met Haley. It was our first night on the property, and we were sitting around the firepit as Ryll presented Chef Valerie, who then introduced her daughter. I recalled thinking how shy Haley seemed. She'd been blushing and fiddling nervously with something on her wrist.

The bracelet. She'd worn an unobtrusive leather band.

I'd barely noticed it at the time, but now that I remembered it...

I had to be sure. Pulling my computer into my lap, I scrolled through my photos. Carl climbed up my back and peered over my shoulder at the computer screen. When I found the picture I was looking for, I enlarged the image and studied it, my eyes searching.

Carl used a paw to pat at the screen, and then I spotted it: Haley's leather band, tucked among the panties and bras in Colby's trunk.

I chewed my lip as I considered the repercussions. Haley's bracelet in Colby's trunk could only mean one thing. Despite her youth and lack of financial assets, Colby had made her one of his conquests. That bracelet served as proof.

I thought of the shy young woman, so demure, so fearful of disappointing her mother. She seemed the antithesis of a violent killer.

I looked over my shoulder at the cat. "What do you think, Carl? It feels a little flimsy. Am I way off base?"

Carl meowed impatiently. "What would her motive be?" I countered, to which he replied with a chattering noise. "You think it's that simple? Basic jealousy? A scorned lover, passed over for a rich older woman?"

A squeak sounded on the stairs in the hall, and I sat bolt upright. Carl hissed, which woke up Woody, who jumped off the bed and stood at attention near the door.

More squeaks as someone descended the stairs. When Lydia had departed for Colby's cabin, that left the lodge occupied by just me and one other person. Haley.

My pulse pounded in my temples. I crawled across the bed to the window to peek outside. Woody whined. "Quiet," I whispered, though at this point noise didn't matter. I saw that Haley was out the front door and moving down the steps of the lodge.

As she reached the bottom step, she swiveled her head, searching the shadows. I ducked back, realizing that my window was likely the only one currently lit. Breathing fast, I counted to ten before risking another look.

Apparently satisfied that she wasn't being watched, Haley had resumed her journey. She crossed the yard, heading toward Colby's quarters. From the stiffness of her posture, it didn't take a stellar detective to understand she wasn't paying a friendly visit.

A couple of yards from the cabin's small porch, she abruptly stopped. Her shoulders rounded. Perhaps whatever she'd had in mind suddenly seemed to be a bad idea. I crossed my fingers and whispered a prayer that she'd give up her quest to visit Colby and return to the lodge.

Instead, she gave herself a shake. Beneath the glow of the porch light, I saw Haley's resolve return. For the first time, I noticed something in her hand. When she moved toward the door, the object shone in the light, and I gasped. It was a sleek, silver revolver. Then Haley reached out and began slowly turning the door knob.

I didn't have a choice. I had to act.

42

S crambling off the bed, I looked around frantically for something I could use as a weapon. Nothing. Not even a simple baseball bat. I supposed I could bash her with my laptop, but I'd spent a lot of money on that thing…

I picked up my phone and dialed 9-1-1. When the dispatcher answered, I told her who and where I was. Though I wasn't entirely sure it was true, I explained that a woman was holding two people at gunpoint in a cabin on the premises. The dispatcher said she'd send officers right away, and she cautioned me to stay put. "Sure thing," I said, disconnecting.

As I put on my shoes, I pressed Lynn's number on my list of favorites and listened on speaker phone as it went to voicemail. Knowing my friends were a mile away in a meadow watching shooting stars, I hadn't expected to get through to her, but I left a message, along with a text, so when she got service again, she'd know what was happening.

There was no more time to waste. I hurried to the bedroom door, where Woody and Carl had positioned themselves with their noses pressed to the crack. I nudged them aside with my foot, eliciting frantic barks and angry hisses. "No," I said firmly. "She has a gun. I can't risk having you rush in and get hurt—or worse."

As I cracked the door and wedged myself through the opening, they both threw themselves at my legs. I won the wrestling match, though, and closed them inside the room. The caterwauls I heard through the door were deafening, but I ran off without a backwards glance.

Downstairs, I spotted an iron poker near the fireplace in the living room and grabbed it. It wouldn't stop a bullet, but it was better than nothing. I raced through the front door, down the deck steps, and across the yard.

Combined with the adrenaline rush, the quick sprint left me winded. I took a second to catch my breath. Then I stepped onto Colby's porch. Tiptoeing to the window, I peered through a slit in the curtains. Chunky candles flickered on the nightstand and the coffee table, wreathing the room in soft light. Lydia sat on the couch, wearing a low-cut nightie. Her robe lay in a heap on the floor, discarded in a moment of passion. Colby sat beside her. He was shirtless, and the thought flitted through my mind that the man so rarely wore a shirt he might want to stop investing in them.

His eyes were wide with fear, and I followed the direction of his gaze. A few feet away, Haley had taken a shooter's stance. I recalled Ryll lauding Haley's skills as a markswoman. At that close range, it wouldn't even take an expert to finish the task.

Haley's lips formed a tight line, and the muscles in her jaw flexed. But when I noticed tears on her cheeks, it gave me an iota of hope. Perhaps that small display of sadness indicated an ambivalence I could use to my advantage.

I inhaled and sent a plea to the fates, to the spirits, to destiny—to whatever powers might influence the universe. Then I opened the door.

***

Haley spun to face me. Her hand didn't waver as she kept the gun trained on Colby. When she noticed my makeshift weapon, she gave me a caustic smile. "You realize a fireplace poker won't stop me. But this doesn't concern you anyway. Get out now, while you can."

"No!" Colby yelped. "You have to help me! She has a gun!"

Not even a mention of Lydia in their mutual perilous predicament. It was all I could do not to run over slap him. "I think I have the picture," I said. "No need to mansplain."

Haley barked a laugh. "Exactly. I'm done with that. This cowboy's days of mansplaining, lying, and cheating end today."

Lydia sat back and snorted, her demeanor notably calm. "Cheating? I didn't realize the two of you had tied the knot."

Haley's nostrils flared, and she shifted her aim from Colby to Lydia. Even with a gun pointed at her, Tonya's mother appeared impassive. I couldn't decide whether to be impressed by her bravery or appalled at her foolishness.

"I should have used more drugs, you old bat," Haley said. "To think I was worried I might overdose you. I showed you a kindness you didn't deserve. You should be grateful."

My mind spun as I realized Haley had been responsible for Lydia's stomach ailment. I suddenly wondered, had she also been the one injecting the horses?

Lydia shot up from her place on the couch. "You drugged me? Why, you little shrew. How dare—"

Haley roared a primal howl. Colby cowered, and Lydia's mouth snapped shut. Without another word, she resumed her seat.

After a moment had passed and Haley's demeanor seemed semi-normal, I ventured a question. "Haley, what drug did you use on Lydia? And where did you get it?"

She shrugged. "I found a vial in Eleanor's pocket that night. She'd been using it to make the horses sick. I figured it hadn't killed them, so it wouldn't kill Lydia."

"How'd you know what Eleanor had been up to?" I asked.

"I overheard her talking to Colby about it. People usually don't notice when I'm around. Sometimes, I feel like I'm invisible…"

She trailed off for a moment, then used the gun to gesture at the pair on the couch. "Anyway, when I found out Colby had replaced one sugar mama with another, I had to do something. I didn't want Lydia dead—only sidelined. Now I realize I should have used the whole vial."

My mind quickly processed the extended meaning of Haley's words. She'd just placed herself in the stall on the night of Eleanor's murder. Did that mean…?

"You say you found the vial in Eleanor's pocket?"

Haley didn't respond, and Colby jumped at the momentary pause. "Come on, baby, put down the gun," he said in a wheedling tone. "You know you're my girl. You're the one I want to end up with. This was all for us."

"For *us*?" Haley scoffed. For the first time, her laser focus faltered, and she lowered the gun a smidge. Not enough, not yet, but maybe… *Keep her talking, Colby*, I willed silently.

"How do you figure you sleeping with her is for us?" she asked.

Colby rested his elbows on his knees. "It's about the money, sweetheart. A ranch manager job doesn't pay a fortune. I wanted to give you a good life. All the things you deserve."

Haley rolled her eyes. "Well, isn't that sweet of you? And how were you planning to get your hands on Lydia's cash? Marry her? Keep me as your mistress until she croaked?"

He shook his head as if he were dealing with a child in the throes of a tantrum. "You're overreacting, baby. You're being irrational."

She narrowed her eyes, and he flinched. "First of all, *baby*, you should never refer to a woman as irrational—

246

especially one who has a gun pointed at you. Second, you didn't answer my question, did you?" She nodded toward the trunk where Colby stored his collectibles. "Let's talk about what's in that chest."

His face reddened, and he could no longer meet Haley's eyes. "What do you mean? It's just for storage."

"Oh, please," Haley said. "I've seen the contents. How do you think I got this back?"

She held up her left wrist, brandishing her leather bracelet, and Colby's face reddened. "You broke into my place?" he asked angrily. "You went through my things? I trusted you!"

Bold move, I thought. When you have no defense, might as well try going on offense. Unfortunately for Colby—for all of us—his strategy didn't work.

"*You* trusted *me*? That's rich."

With the swiftness of a summer squall, Haley's demeanor shifted. Her chin trembled, and tears filled her eyes. The barrel of the gun wavered in her hand. I gripped the poker even tighter, waiting for the right moment to act—though what that action might be, I wasn't yet sure.

"I've done everything for you," Haley said, her voice filled with sadness. "Dropped out of school. Abandoned my dreams. Lied to my mother. Given myself to you. And even…"

As a sob smothered Haley's next words, Lydia sat back and crossed her legs. "Give it a rest," she said. "Quit acting like a child."

I blanched. Maybe Lydia's approach constituted part of some master plan on her part, but I couldn't see it. I cleared my throat to warn her off this dangerous path, but she ignored me.

"You're no different from me, little girl. You did what you wanted to get what you wanted. Nothing wrong with that. But when things didn't go as you desired, you threw a fit. Well, welcome to the cold, hard world. Stop whining and suck it up."

Haley inhaled sharply and raised the gun again, aiming it at Lydia. Her finger tightened on the trigger, and I braced myself, preparing to swing the poker in a last-ditch effort to stop the inevitable.

Then Haley's expression morphed again, and she emitted a bitter laugh. "The irony of a maternal lecture from the likes of you," she said. "I've seen what kind of mother you are. Your daughter barely ever sees you, and when you do show up, you humiliate her by throwing yourself at a brainless stud half your age—"

"Hey!" Colby said. "Don't call me brainless!"

I noticed he didn't object to being labeled a stud.

"Listen," I said, lifting a hand, "let's just calm down. Colby can put on a shirt, Lydia can put on her robe, and the four of us can talk this out. No one else needs to get hurt."

Lydia jumped to her feet and pointed a finger at Haley. "How dare you question my abilities as a mother! My daughter turned out beautifully, thank you very much. If anyone's mother failed, it's yours. Poor Valerie," she said in a taunting tone. "Her daughter turned out to be a pathetic loser who had to drug an older woman in a desperate attempt to keep her man."

Haley froze. Then a calmness settled over her that frightened me more than her rage. She seemed resolute.

I took a cautious step toward her. "Haley, what Lydia said isn't true. Your mother loves you. Think of her…of what it will do to her if you pull that trigger. She'll lose you forever if you fire that gun."

"She already lost me," Haley said, her voice mournful. "The second I killed Eleanor."

43

Colby gasped and jumped up. "You killed Eleanor?"

Haley turned to him in wonder. "Oh, you silly boy. How did you not figure it out? Remember when I told you we were free to be together now? I practically confessed."

"But you told Callie Gordon did it…"

She shook her head and tsked. "And all this time, I thought you were faking the stupid act."

For a moment, everyone went quiet. I realized we'd just witnessed Haley's confession to murder. Perhaps she hadn't intended to kill me before, but now that I'd heard her confess…My heart pounded. I listened for the sound of sirens but heard only the popping of tiny flames from the candle wicks. I risked a peek over my shoulder through the open door, hoping for a sign that Lynn had listened to my message and was coming to save the day. Nothing. Colby was trembling in fear. And though Lydia had talked a good game, I saw the fear in her eyes.

If the three of us were going to get out of this mess, I'd have to think fast.

I decided to try an approach that had worked for me in the past: keep the person talking. "I have to admit, Haley, I thought Gordon was the guilty party. You completely duped me with the tale of overhearing him threaten his stepmother. Smart move on your part."

Haley chuckled. "Gordon Simonson made a good patsy. Especially after he threatened you with a golf club—why wouldn't you believe him capable of murder? And who knows, he might've gotten around to killing Eleanor, eventually. He hated her enough." She shrugged. "He wasn't the only one. The woman had her hooks into everyone."

She glared at Colby. Every time she looked at him that way, I saw her finger twitch on the trigger. I quickly pulled her attention back to me. "I didn't know the woman well, but from what I heard, she was a menace. Trying to destroy the ranch. Threatening to get Carmen run out of town. Blackmailing her own stepson. I doubt many people around here are missing her tonight. In fact, they'd probably give you a medal."

She looked at me appraisingly, as if wondering whether she could trust the sincerity of my words. "I'm not proud of what I did. It wasn't as if I planned to kill Eleanor. I…"

Her breathing quickened, and for a moment, she couldn't speak. Was she in the beginning stages of a panic attack? If so, this whole wretched scene might end peacefully.

I took a tentative step toward her, feigning concern. But when she saw me creeping closer, she rallied and swung the gun in my direction. "Stay back!" she commanded.

I stopped midstep. "No worries. I was afraid you were going to pass out. I only want to help you, Haley."

She sucked in another breath and exhaled raggedly. All the while, I could see the wheels spinning in her brain. "There's no way out of this," she said at last. "Not for me. Not for him." She returned her aim to Colby, and he shivered. "But believe it or not, I'm not a cold-blooded killer. At least, the old me wasn't. I had a plan for my life. Dreams that were stolen from me…"

For a moment, she gazed into the distance, perhaps seeing a past she regretted, a future she'd never be able to achieve. Another sigh, and she returned to the grim reality of the present. "Callie, for what it's worth, I think you're a nice person. I have no grievance with you." She turned to Lydia, and her face crinkled. "And much as you disgust me, Lydia, you're not to blame for any of this, either. Besides, I like Tonya, and I'd hate for her to be carrying her mother's death with her when she walks down the aisle. So you two can go. Get out fast and close the door behind you."

Colby emitted a high-pitched screech. "No! If you go, she'll kill me!"

Haley snorted. "I'm going to kill you one way or the other."

To my surprise, Lydia's face hardened with resolve. She rose from the couch and stepped in front of Colby. "I'm not leaving without him."

I stared at her. Lydia was displaying either incredible bravery or abject stupidity. One way or the other, she was my best friend's mother, and despite everything, Tonya loved her. I couldn't abandon the woman.

I lifted my chin toward Lydia. "And I'm not leaving without her."

Haley shrugged. "Suit yourselves."

Colby clutched at Lydia's shoulder and ducked behind her. Considering Haley's sharpshooter championship in high school, I figured hiding was futile.

Haley's face softened, and the tension left her shoulders. I realized at that moment she'd made peace with her decision. For her, there was no turning back.

Her gaze fell to a group of triple-wicked candles on the coffee table. "You know, Gordon and Allen were right." When I cocked my head, she said, "Not about destroying Moonglow Ranch. No, the ranch itself is a haven—a place that deserves to thrive. But this den of lust...it needs to be destroyed. Burned to the ground."

With the gun steadily trained on Colby, Haley picked up a candle. As she carried it to the open trunk, the soothing scent of vanilla filled the air, a strange contrast to what I realized she was preparing to do. She nestled the candle into the pile of women's underwear. The flames caught hold of a piece of cloth, and the fire began to spread—slowly for now, but it wouldn't be long before the entire trunk blazed.

Haley's eyes looked empty, as if the girl I'd met a few days ago was no longer home. She moved back to her spot in front of Colby and glanced at me. "Last chance to leave, Callie," she said. "Three, two…"

Colby collapsed onto the couch, sobbing. Lydia's eyes were wide as she dropped down beside him and clutched his arm. I tightened my stance, preparing to pounce. It was a last-ditch effort, and it would likely backfire and get me shot, but I couldn't stand here and watch Haley murder Colby.

Outside, wind chimes jangled madly, like a family of fairies in a fury. A gusty zephyr blew across the threshold of the open door. A long shadow fell across the floor. Haley and I turned our heads to face the unexpected visitor.

A silhouetted figure stood framed in the doorway. She glided into the room, and the candlelight illuminated her face.

Carmen. I should have predicted it. If only I'd had a crystal ball.

A white fringed scarf covered her head and fell around her shoulders. Her white ruffle blouse opened at the neck to display a half dozen turquoise beaded necklaces. Long silver earrings dangled from her lobes. Pietro writhed around her wrist. And he'd brought friends. Draped around her neck, Carmen wore a serpent as thick as my wrist, his scales patterned in deep red. In her hands, she cradled another snake, this one bright green and at least four feet long.

Carmen stood very still. The only movement in the room came from the snakes. Their tongues flicked and their bodies squirmed. Haley groaned, and I saw beads of perspiration break out on her forehead. I remembered the other day, talking about our mutual phobia. Had Carmen known that Haley was terrified of snakes? Of course she did.

Haley seemed paralyzed. When she spoke, her lips barely moved. "Get out of here, you old witch. Take those repulsive things with you."

Carmen began a wordless chant, her eyes glittering as they met mine, sending me a signal. I gave her a slight nod. My body tensed, preparing for whatever was about to happen.

Then, in one fluid movement, Carmen tossed the green serpent toward Haley. The snake smacked the young woman on the shoulder and slid down her body. The serpent landed on the floor and slithered across Haley's feet.

She screamed. The gun's barrel dropped, and I swung the poker, landing a hard blow on her arm. She fumbled for the gun, and just as I thought she'd regained her hold on it, the snake's head darted forward. His jaws opened, and he sank his fangs into Haley's ankle.

For a moment, Haley stood frozen, her mouth open in a silent scream. Then her eyelids drooped, and she fainted to the floor.

Colby jumped off the couch, pushed past Carmen, and disappeared through the door. Lydia watched him go, shaking her head. "And the cowboy runs away."

44

My eyes darted back and forth between the fire in the trunk and Haley lying unconscious on the floor. I tried to decide which to deal with first. But then the flames sizzled and spluttered, and the fire disappeared.

Carmen stood inches away, and for a crazy moment, I thought perhaps she'd uttered some ancient magic spell to extinguish the flames. Then I saw a plastic water bottle in her hand and realized she'd done it the old-fashioned way.

With one crisis averted, I turned to the other: Haley. I started to kneel beside her, but a flash of green near her outstretched hand stopped me in my tracks. I peered at Carmen and pointed at the snake. "Could you…?"

She scooped the creature off the floor. "Nothing to worry about. He's non-venomous. The young woman will suffer no ill effects from my friend Lorenzo's nibble."

Humph. I wasn't sure that was true. No physical effects, maybe, but emotionally…I wasn't sure *I'd* recover from the sight, and I wasn't even on the receiving end of the serpent's "nibble."

With the slithering green obstacle removed and the other snakes safely in Carmen's custody, I dropped to my knees and placed my fingers on Haley's neck. A strong pulse throbbed in her artery, and her breath came in a steady rhythm. It occurred to me that, given her reaction to Carmen's charming pet, the snake in the stable must have been a coincidence after all. No chance Haley had thrown it into the stall to spook Spirit.

As I sat back on my heels, I heard a siren and saw a red strobe pierce the darkness. A car door slammed, and a split second later, Jake hurried into the cabin. He knelt at Haley's side and felt for a pulse. I assured him I'd done due diligence and that the girl had only fainted. "She's snakebitten," I added, pointing to the angry red puncture wounds on her ankle. "Carmen says the biter is non-venomous. She should still get medical attention, though."

"I already called for paramedics," Jake said. "They should be here any second."

Then Chief Wade lumbered into the cabin. His beady eyes surveyed the room, taking in the girl on the floor, the smoldering embers in the trunk, Lydia in her nightie, and Carmen with her snakes. Finally, his gaze fell on me. "All right, little lady. Tell me what happened."

I ignored the condescending label and summarized the series of events—though I did make the passive-aggressive decision to address my words to Jake. I concluded with Carmen's role in the drama.

The chief scowled at the psychic. "Eleanor was right. Those snakes are a menace. I believe it's time for you move along. Set up your tent in someone else's town."

Jake rose. "Chief, if you ask me—"

Chief Wade shot him a glare. "I didn't. In fact, what I asked you to do was wait by the car."

A war of indecision played across Jake's face. I figured he was primed to obey his boss, but then his expression turned defiant. He widened his stance and folded his arms. "I'm not your chauffeur, Chief Wade. I'm a duly appointed officer of the law. And in my professional opinion, this woman…" He pointed at Carmen. "…performed a community service tonight. She saved lives, as well as your bacon. Instead of threatening her, you should thank her."

The chief's face went blank. I doubted the young man had ever spoken to him in that tone. I expected the older man to blow a gasket, perhaps even fire the officer on the spot, so I was astonished when a look of begrudging admiration flicked in his eyes. Apparently, what Lynn and I had told Jake earlier was true: the only way to earn the respect of someone like the chief was to stand up to him.

An old dog didn't learn new tricks overnight, though. Chief Wade's pride dictated that the officer's boldness be addressed.

"I suggest you check your attitude, Officer Williams. You're treading dangerously close to insubordination." He paused and glanced at Carmen. "But your point is taken."

We saw the ambulance pulling up. Haley's eyes fluttered open, then closed again. Two paramedics rushed through the door and, after a brief update, ordered the rest of us outside so they'd have room to work.

The five of us—Chief Wade, Jake, Lydia, Carmen, and myself, not counting the snakes—moved a few yards away from the cabin, where we caught sight of Colby hovering near the stable. The chief gave a shrill whistle. "Get over here, cowboy."

Colby slunk toward us, his eyes on his boots.

"Where you been, son?" the chief asked.

"Oh, he ran off like a yellow-bellied coward the first chance he got." Lydia's voice dripped with contempt.

Colby's eyes darted from one face to the next. "That's not true! The horses were in distress. I needed to tend to them. That's the only reason I left."

Chief Wade snorted, but before he could respond, footsteps pounded down the path behind the corral. The stargazers had returned, and they approached at a run.

Lynn reached us first. "Callie, I got your message," she said, breathless. "Is everyone all right? What happened?"

Mom was hot on Lynn's heels, moving fast for a

woman in her late sixties. She planted herself beside me and held fast to my arm, not budging as I apprised everyone of the evening's events. At the first mention of Haley, Valerie sagged, and the blood drained from her face. Mrs. Finney noticed and put an arm firmly around the woman's shoulders. When I got to the part about Haley being bitten by a snake and fainting, Valerie shrugged out of Mrs. Finney's grasp and sprinted toward the cabin, with Mrs. Finney in her wake. Chief Wade raised a finger to object but dropped it and sighed.

Tonya stood in front of Lydia, her brow furrowed. I bit my lip, awaiting the inevitable scolding, but it never came. Instead, my friend pulled her mother into a tight hug. Looking surprised but happy, Lydia returned the embrace.

In the silence that followed, I heard a scratching sound from an upstairs window in the lodge. It sounded suspiciously like claws raking across glass. I looked up to see Woody pawing at the lit window of our room. Beside him, Carl was making a point of ignoring the chaos.

"They're upset," I said, pointing upstairs. "I'm going to run up and calm them."

Again, the chief opened his mouth to object, but then he shook his head. "Go on. But I'll…" He glanced at Jake. "*We'll* need you at the station first thing tomorrow for an official statement."

I assured them I'd drop by early and ran upstairs to tend to the creatures. When I burst through the door, Carl hissed at me and darted under the bed. Woody initially gave me a look of betrayal, but he couldn't maintain it. After a few seconds, he jumped up, planted his front paws on my shoulders, and licked my face. I ruffled the fur on his back before settling him onto his four legs.

Then I went looking for Carl. I crouched on the floor and peered under the bed. Two green eyes glowed from the darkness. I reached out, and the cat swatted my arm away. The claws were out, and they left a trio of scratches on the back of my hand.

"Look, Carl, I'm sorry," I said. "But Haley had a gun. I only wanted to keep the two of you safe. If something happened to either of you, I'd never forgive myself."

He blinked. I lay on my side, trying to appear penitent. "I know you feel left out, but you did your part. You and Woody discovered the murder weapon. And it was you who drew my attention to Haley's bracelet in the photo. If it weren't for you, I'd never have figured it out."

After an ill-tempered meow, he turned away and showed me his tail. I sighed and struggled to my feet. He just needed time to pout, I told myself. He'd come around.

When I headed back downstairs, Woody trotted along behind me. I left the door to my room open, hoping Carl would follow along soon.

***

By the time I made it downstairs, everyone had gathered in the front room. We watched through the window as paramedics loaded Haley into the ambulance. Mrs. Finney stood nearby while Valerie jumped in after the stretcher.

"Poor Valerie," Ryll muttered. "She didn't deserve this."

Once the paramedics slammed the doors, the ambulance peeled away. Mrs. Finney made her way back to the lodge. Then we saw Jake accompany Colby into the cabin. When they emerged a few minutes later, Colby lugged a duffel bag. He looked longingly at the lodge before trudging off toward the stable.

"There's a cot in the loft," Ryll said. "He can sleep there tonight. Tomorrow we'll figure out what we're going to do about him."

Lydia huffed. "If you want my opinion, he should be

drawn and quartered. Isn't that what they do to thieves and cowards in the Wild West?"

Tonya smirked. "Mother, I think you're just miffed that your love nest was defeathered."

Lydia waved. "Not at all, TeeTee. There are plenty of other love nests. I'll keep flitting about until I find one that suits me."

Outside, Jake secured yellow crime scene tape across the cabin door. Then he returned to the chief, and they exchanged a few words. As his boss got back into the car, Jake trotted up the steps and entered the lodge.

"The chief and I wanted to caution you that no one should enter that cabin," he said to Ryll and Fritz. "Not sure how this is going to play out, but for the time being, please stay out of there."

Ryll and Fritz nodded. Then Jake looked past our hosts to me. "Callie, Chief Wade also asked me to pass along his thanks. He acknowledges that you prevented another murder from happening. Possibly two."

I felt my eyes widen. Chief Wade was expressing gratitude? Perhaps there was hope for the world after all. "That's very kind," I said. "But it's Carmen he ought to be thanking. If she hadn't appeared when she did, with those snakes...well, I shudder to think what might have happened."

Jake grinned at me, then at Carmen. "Well, it's been a big night for the chief. I think we'll need to leave that concession for another time."

He gave us a little salute and left. I watched as he walked away, a new confidence in his step.

After Jake and the chief drove away, Mrs. Finney cleared her throat. "Whether that antiquated chief is prepared to acknowledge it or not, Callie is right. We owe Carmen a great debt. Callie and Lydia, as well as that ridiculous boy-toy cowboy, are alive and well because of her timely arrival."

Mrs. Finney clapped, and the rest of us joined in.

Carmen smiled. Her snakes wriggled. I cringed. *Non-venomous*, I kept repeating to myself.

When the applause tapered off, Renata said, "Carmen, how did you know to show up when you did?"

"Yeah," Jessica said. "Did you have one of those visions of yours? Did you witness the scene playing out in your handy crystal ball?"

Summer nudged her wife in the ribs. "Carmen, I hope you'll ignore Jessica's snarky tone. Her spiritual side is still a work in progress."

"Never mind. I'm used to skeptics." Placidly, Carmen faced Jessica. "It is only those who doubt who cannot see."

"Oooh," Mrs. Finney said. "Let me write that down for my cups. Don't worry, Carmen, I'll be sure to credit you."

45

We talked a little longer, taking comfort in each other's company. Then Carmen left, saying it was past the snakes' bedtime. The rest of us were tired too, so we made our way upstairs. Tonya slept with her mother again, so I had the room to myself—well, along with Woody and Carl, of course, though Carl still wasn't speaking to me. Despite my wheedling, including an offering of his favorite canned tuna, I couldn't persuade the cat to forgive me. He'd emerged from his hideaway beneath the bed, but whenever I tried to approach, he turned away and engaged in some rather unsavory personal grooming.

Woody looked back and forth between the two of us with obvious concern. "What should I do?" I whispered to the dog. His liquid brown eyes gazed at me, but if he were transmitting any words of wisdom, I couldn't decipher them. Then he jumped on Tonya's bed, curled up, and began to snore. It seemed Carl and I would be forced to work things out on our own.

After I jammied up and brushed my teeth, I settled onto the bed, propping myself against the headboard as I dialed Sam for a FaceTime chat. Following his usual, "Hi, beautiful," and my subsequent shiver of delight, I gave him the whole story. As I talked, I noticed Carl shooting veiled glimpses in my direction. Was his curiosity surpassing his resentment?

During the telling of the tale, I noticed Sam's jaw tightening. When I concluded, he paused and took a deep breath. When he exhaled, he looked more relaxed. "Well, my knee-jerk reaction is fear for your safety, of course, and frustration that you put yourself in danger. Again."

"Listen, Sam—"

"Let me finish, woman. I said that was my knee-jerk reaction. My second reaction, the one I choose to follow, is respect and pride. You've proven time and again you can take care of yourself, Callie. Your instincts amaze me, and they serve you well. No question that I'm thankful for that psychic and her snakes. But even if she hadn't shown up, you'd have figured out a way to take care of business. It's what you do. "I have to be honest, though. It'd do my heart good if you'd avoid killers and criminals, for a couple of months, anyway."

I grinned at my boyfriend, grateful that our relationship continued to evolve. "Thank you, my love. That's exactly what I needed to hear. I'm glad you feel that way. I'd hate to have two of you mad at me."

I explained about Carl giving me the silent treatment, and Sam asked to talk to the cat. I turned the screen toward Carl. "Listen, friend," he began. Carl gazed at him. "I understand. She's done it to me before, too. Try to look at it as an expression of her love and loyalty. She'll protect you until her dying day. The best thing you can do is accept it and appreciate it as part of her nature— just like she accepts and appreciates the...well, unique things about your nature."

Carl meowed, then jumped off the window ledge and darted back under the bed. I sighed and turned the phone back. "Nice try."

"Just give him time. He'll come around. We all do."

"I'm not sure how to take that comment," I said. "If I didn't miss you so much, I might be offended. But a week apart just turns me into a puddle of goo."

Sam gave me that smile that melted my heart. "I miss you too. Not much longer, though."

"Two more days," I said with a pout.

"The time will fly by," he said. "Just wait and see."

***

For the first time in a long while, I fell asleep alone in a bed. Carl, who usually curled up on my pillow with his paws tangled into my hair, was still protesting my earlier abandonment. Woody, who mostly slept stretched out against my torso, remained on Tonya's bed in solidarity with the cat. He'd given me a sympathetic look when I patted the bed beside me, but stayed put.

Their boycott didn't bother my slumber, though. The events of the day, the whole week, had taken their toll. Within minutes, I fell asleep. No footsteps on the stairs interrupted me, no snoring, nothing. I woke only once in the night, and that was when the bed jiggled as Woody jumped up beside me and Carl curled around the top of my head. I smiled sleepily, realizing I'd been forgiven.

***

By eight the next morning, I'd dressed and gathered with the rest of the group for breakfast. Today was party day, and we had much preparation ahead of us. Only Tonya, the guest of honor, and her mother had avoided the duty roster, so they were sleeping in. Summer, Jessica, and Renata were on decoration assignment. Ryll, Georgia, and Fritz would be in charge of food. Much of the fare we planned to serve had been prepared in advance, thank goodness, since Valerie and Haley were currently—and likely permanently—unavailable.

Before I could focus on the party, though, my presence was required at the police station. Lynn and Mrs. Finney wanted to join me, and Mom rode along to pick up the floral arrangements in town.

We pulled into a parking space near the florist shop, just down the block from the police station. As we climbed out of the car, we noticed Valerie exiting the station. She stood on the sidewalk, blinking in the sunlight as if she were in a daze.

"Poor woman," Mom said. "She must be devastated. Let's go ask if we can be of assistance."

When she saw us, Valerie burst into tears. Mom went to her, and Valerie buried her face against Mom's shoulder. After a moment, she pulled back and snuffled. Mrs. Finney took a lace handkerchief from her handbag and pressed it into the woman's palm. Valerie wiped the tears from her cheeks, blew her nose, and offered the hanky to Mrs. Finney. "No, dear, you keep it," Mrs. Finney said.

I angled my head toward the police station. "Is Haley in there? Is she all right?"

Valerie nodded and tucked the hanky into her pocket. "They examined her at the hospital and kept her a few hours for observation. The snake bite frightened her into fainting, but she's fine. Physically, anyway. They transferred her here early this morning, but they'll be taking her into the county sheriff's custody soon."

We were silent, not knowing how to respond. Valerie said, "I can't believe my daughter did those things they're saying. I knew she'd been depressed—troubled even—but never in a million years would I have imagined her capable of such violence. I guess I didn't know my own daughter at all."

Her lamentation reminded me of similar statements I'd heard when people found out someone close to them had committed a heinous act. "She was always so nice," they'd say. Or, "He was my roommate in college and didn't have a mean bone in his body." It made me wonder how well we knew anyone. Did we just project onto people the qualities we wanted to see in them?

A sudden wail startled me from my philosophical musings. Valerie's pain was so visceral, it pierced my heart.

"This is all my fault," Valerie sobbed. "Haley's father left when she was just a little thing. He never contacted her, never even sent a birthday card. When she asked about him, I handled it miserably. I told her he didn't want us, and she'd have to be content with me. Looking back, she was starved for male attention. So when Colby came along…"

"You knew about their…relationship?" I said.

"I knew they'd been seeing each other, but not to what extent. She shut me out every time I broached the subject. I didn't want to lose her…"

Valerie started crying again, and Mrs. Finney abruptly clapped her hands. "Stop it now," she said, her tone commanding. "This is no time for self-pity. What you did or didn't do, should or shouldn't have done—it's water under the bridge. If you want to help your daughter, you must focus on the here and now. There are practicalities to attend to."

Valerie flinched, but her posture straightened, and her tears subsided. "What do you mean?"

"A lawyer, for one thing. Haley will need a good one. I have contacts, and I'd be happy to help you choose one if you'd like."

"You'd do that for Haley?"

Mrs. Finney took Valerie's hand. "I'd do it for both of you."

Valerie bit her lip and nodded, speechless.

"You say they'll be moving her to the county seat soon, so you'll want to be nearby," Mrs. Finney continued. "We'll need to find someplace…perhaps an extended-stay hotel for the time being. Why don't you and I go back to the ranch to make a few calls and start packing your things?"

"Oh, I can't go back there," Valerie said, looking terrified. "After everything that's happened, Ryll and Fritz must hate me."

"My dear, that is patently untrue, as all of us can attest.

Why, last night, Ryll expressed great compassion for your plight."

When Valerie objected again, Mrs. Finney took her by the shoulders and looked into her eyes. "Will it be uncomfortable to go back there? Yes. Will it be sad to let go of the dream you had for your daughter's life, and frightening to face the unknown? Yes. Can you do it for Haley? I'm confident of it."

Valerie squared her shoulders. She'd turned an emotional corner, at least for now, and our friend had made it happen.

Mrs. Finney turned to us. "Can you ladies handle the rest of this on your own?"

I smiled at her. "Of course. You go take care of business. We'll see you at the shower this evening."

Mrs. Finney linked her arm through Valerie's, and they walked off toward Valerie's car.

Mom leaned toward Lynn and me. "I'm not sure what we did to deserve that woman, but I'm glad she's ours."

46

Mom went to the florist shop, and Lynn and I headed into the police station. Penny, once again working the front counter, led us to the interview room, where we waited in metal folding chairs at an institutional-looking table that displayed a tape recorder no doubt left over from the seventies. After five minutes—just as my patience was wearing thin—Chief Wade and Officer Williams entered the room.

With an unceremonious thud, the chief dropped into a chair across from us and spewed a disgusting stream of tobacco juice into a Styrofoam cup. I wondered idly whether he had a stack of them in his office or if he used the same one day after day.

Jake settled in beside his boss and placed a stack of files and a legal pad on the table.

"Thank you for coming in this morning," Jake said. "Do you mind if we record this conversation?"

I shook my head as I eyed the chief. Jake appeared to be taking the lead, and I was trying to figure out if Chief Wade had miraculously transformed into a benevolent leader whose only aim was justice.

Then the man opened his mouth and shattered my illusions.

"Don't know what this one's doing here." Chief Wade gestured to Lynn, who merely rolled her eyes in response.

"Are you referring to Detective Clarke?" I asked with an edge in my voice. "If so, I requested her presence. But if you're going to be unpleasant, we'll be on our way. You can contact my lawyer to set up an appointment—though I imagine it will delay the process. I bet the county sheriff won't look too kindly on that."

It was total swagger on my part. I had no intention of leaving, but the chief's continued posturing ruffled my feathers. If he wanted to engage in a power struggle, I'd oblige.

Jake gave the chief a sidelong glance. "Detective Clarke is more than welcome to stay, right Chief?"

The chief grunted and spat. Then he set his cup on the table, folded his hands over his belly, and closed his eyes. In seconds, the man's mouth hung open, and he wheezed.

I looked back at Jake, who sighed. "Shall we proceed?"

I nodded. Like a pro, Jake went through his list of questions, leading me through a recitation of last night's events. Fifteen minutes later, he closed his notebook, pressed a button on the recorder, and stood. "I think we…" He cleared his throat after a glance at the chief, whose eyes were closed and whose hands were rising and falling with the motions of his belly. "…have everything we need. Once the statement is typed up, I'll bring it by the ranch for your signature. Does this afternoon work?"

"Sure, as long as you show up before five o'clock. Because that's when my best friend's bridal shower begins, and I'm determined to make sure nothing else interferes."

"Got it," Jake said.

As we left the interview room, the chief's head fell back. He emitted a wet snort, followed by a trickle of brown drool that seeped from the corner of his mouth. I wrinkled my nose. "Should we wake him?" I whispered.

"Not a chance," Jake said. "The county sheriff will be here before long. I wouldn't mind at all if he found him just like this."

***

As soon as Lynn and I were outside, we let loose with the laughter we'd been suppressing. "Chief Wade's not much longer for the job, I suspect," I said.

"I hope they have Jake take over," she said. "I'm convinced that young man has what it takes. Mustang would benefit from his leadership."

We caught sight of Mom standing in front of the florist shop, her arms filled with flowers. I felt a pang of concern when I realized she was talking to Allen Simonson.

We hurried toward them. I wondered if a confrontation was percolating, but Mom's easy manner as we approached reassured me. "Done with your statement?" she asked.

"Just finished," I said. "What's going on?"

"I bumped into Mr. Simonson coming out of the mayor's office."

"Allen," he said. "I asked you to call me Allen."

"Yes, of course. Allen was hoping to apprise us of a few items he's been discussing with the mayor. I told him you'd be right along, and he wanted to wait."

Allen Simonson wanted to talk. This should be interesting. "What can you possibly have to say?" I asked.

His lips tightened at my tone, but he let it go. "I met with Mayor Finkle this morning and told him I'm throwing the full weight of my support behind the Bauers' request to open Moonglow Ranch as a guest resort. If I don't see immediate progress on that front from the town council, I'll be contacting my friends at the state legislature. The mayor has assured me that won't be necessary."

Mom gave me her *wonders never cease* look. My inner skeptic wondered at the root of Allen's reversal. "That's...well, it's very helpful, Allen. I'm sure Ryll and Fritz will be grateful. But if I may ask, why the change of heart? We were under the impression you'd been spearheading the resistance in the first place."

"No, that was Eleanor's doing. I didn't even know about it, really. I've been…preoccupied, I suppose you could say. I wasn't paying attention to my family's enterprises as closely as I should have been. But I fully intend to remedy my lapse."

Preoccupied? It occurred to me that Allen might not have spent his time off the grid alone. We'd heard rumors of his infidelities. Perhaps Eleanor wasn't the only one who'd been engaging in extracurricular activities.

"That's good to hear," Lynn said. "We just have to hope it isn't too little too late. After the damage the ranch sustained—"

"At my son's hands, I'm well aware. And I'm prepared to make it right. I've instructed my lawyer and my accountant to make full restitution for the damage to the lodge and the adjacent cabin."

"But Gordon had nothing to do with the fire in the cabin," Lynn said.

Allen waved a hand. "Doesn't matter. I'll be paying for it. I will also be providing the Bauers with a settlement for the pain and suffering caused by my family's interference. They can use the money any way they see fit—an expansion of the lodge, perhaps, or more horses."

Had I misjudged Allen Simonson? Or was this, as I suspected, simply a savvy public relations move? Or perhaps he intended to preempt a potential lawsuit. Either way, I supposed his motivation didn't matter. Summer's aunt and uncle would be the beneficiaries.

Allen straightened his tie. "I'm regretful of my son's actions, as well as my late wife's. She started the dominoes falling by forcing my son into selling her his stock."

"We heard," I said. "What exactly did she have on him?"

He hesitated, seeming to weigh how much to tell us. "Well, let's just say Gordon's financial situation was more dire than he'd led me to believe. Eleanor knew Gordon didn't want me to discover the depths of his mismanagement, and she held that over his head." He sighed. "Her schemes also resulted in the mayhem at Moonglow Ranch. She didn't deserve to pay with her life, of course, but she did victimize the Bauers. I consider it my duty to undo the damage visited on them by my family." He buttoned his jacket. "I appreciate you hearing me out, but now I need to be on my way."

"Wait," I said. "I still have a couple more questions."

Allen's face clouded, but he acquiesced. "Go ahead, then."

"Did you ever figure out who leaked the story to the press?"

He paused. "I suppose there's no harm in telling you. It was Ms. Clemens, my administrative assistant. Former administrative assistant, that is. She apparently received a tidy sum for her betrayal."

I waited for him to apologize for accusing us, but it wasn't forthcoming. Instead, he glanced at his watch and said, "Is that all?"

I looked at Lynn. "Just one more thing," she said. "What's going to happen to Gordon now?"

Allen shrugged. "I'm told they'll arraign him tomorrow morning. His attorney has assured me she'll procure reasonable bail. The question I'm left with is, do I pay it?"

Huh. It hadn't occurred to me that Allen wouldn't go to whatever lengths necessary to rescue his son. I figured that's what he'd been doing since Gordon was a child.

"I know what you're thinking," Allen said, studying me. "And you're right. All his life, I've served as my son's enabler. Gordon is spoiled and petulant, and I'm to blame. So I'm left to ponder the best course of action. Perhaps Gordon needs to face the consequences. Perhaps it will make a man of him."

I cringed, hating that phrase. But now wasn't the time to quibble over the definition of manhood. I still wasn't convinced of Allen's sincerity, but it had to be painful to realize you'd made major mistakes as a parent.

"Anyway, it's likely a moot point," Allen said. "The attorney says Gordon should be able to plead to a misdemeanor charge since there was minimal damage and no one was injured. He'll probably get probation, a hefty fine, and community service."

"I think that's exactly what he needs," I said. "In my experience, acting in the service of others is what makes a man—or a woman—of someone."

On a whim, I held out my hand. Allen looked surprised, but he shook it.

"I should have said it sooner," I told him, "but I'm sorry for your loss. Grieving during all this chaos must be difficult."

"Thank you," Allen said stiffly. "My late wife wasn't perfect, and it's unlikely our marriage would have survived. Still…I can't believe she's gone."

After a moment, he lifted his chin. "Now, if there's nothing else I can help you with…"

Help us with? I knew then that Allen Simonson hadn't done a one-eighty after all. He was the same calculating businessman he'd been before all this happened. Had I really expected any different? *People like him rarely change*, I thought.

I shook my head, and he turned on his heel and walked away. When he was gone, I impulsively gave Mom a tight squeeze. "You're welcome," I whispered in her ear.

"And what is it I'm thanking you for?"

"Allen's kid turned out to be an entitled brat. Valerie's kid—well, her troubles are even worse. I'm just reminding you that, despite the screw ups I've made in my life, you're very lucky to have me."

Mom laughed. "That I am, darling. That I am."

47

After my friends had gone upstairs to get ready for Tonya's party, I stood alone in the banquet room. Hands on hips, I surveyed the place as a queen must view her queendom. I wanted one last check. One last opportunity to make sure everything was perfect.

And I was not only satisfied, I was supremely pleased.

Since Tonya was marrying a man who hailed from Tuscany, we'd decided on an Italian-themed shower. Every corner of the room—from the red-and-white checkered tablecloths to the candles dripping wax onto Chianti bottles in straw-baskets to the bouquets of sunflowers, orchids, and lilies clustered around the room—glowed like the Italian countryside. We had charcuterie boards layered with a variety of Italian cheeses, pancetta, olives, and grapes, as well as baskets of breadsticks wrapped in red cloth napkins. Twinkling lights hung from the ceiling, and colorful helium-filled balloons rose from stands on the floor. Italian music played from the speakers in the corners.

And center stage, the pièce de résistance—the cake. Green, white, and red fondant stripes circled the sides of the two-layered extravaganza. On top rested clusters of purple-icing grapes, vines, and miniature wine bottles. Creative, unique, and detailed. The baker in this small town was a genuine artist. My only concern was whether anyone would want to destroy this piece of perfection by eating it.

I circled the room once more, making sure every detail met my standards. Then I climbed the stairs to dress for the party. Mom had requested time with the creatures, and Tonya was with Lydia, so I had the room to myself. Once I'd dressed, styled my hair, and applied my makeup, I stared at my reflection in the full-length mirror on the back of the bathroom door.

I hardly recognized myself. My brown hair, typically pulled back in a ponytail, now hung in loose curls around my shoulders. Combined with the effects of yesterday's facial, the makeup gave my face a youthful glow. And the dress. Oh, my. I'd bought a clingy red frock for the occasion, with thin shoulder straps, a low neckline and little red bows down the front. Between the pool, the horseback riding, and the hiking, I'd gotten some sun this week, and my skin carried a light tan. Even I thought I looked beautiful. Too bad Sam wasn't here. *Eat my dust, Isabella.*

The door to my room squeaked open. When Tonya entered, I gasped. I thought I looked good, but my best friend was—no other word for it, drop-dead gorgeous. She'd pulled her long, tight braids into an exotic top knot, highlighting her sleek neck. Her makeup was subtle, except for her signature bright red lipstick. She wore a lemon-yellow floral print dress that set off her rich skin tone. Matching yellow high-heeled sandals adorned her feet, with straps wrapping around her ankles. I wondered, not for the first time, where my friend even found such shoes.

As I stared at her, open-mouthed, she did a spin. "What do you think? It was meant to be my target shooting outfit, but since that's been canceled…"

I laughed. "If you look this good for a shower, I can't even imagine you as a bride. You're stunning."

She looked me up and down and clucked her tongue. "You clean up pretty good yourself, girlfriend."

"Well, I'm no Isabella…"

"Ha. You're still obsessing over that woman? Careful, sugarplum. Remember what we talked about at the firepit? Jealousy is a natural emotion, but if left to fester, it can become a fungus on the soul."

I sighed. "As evidenced by the events of this week."

"Exactly. Haley's jealousy grew all-consuming. And for what? A man? I'm madly in love with David, but if you ever notice me changing like that over him, I invite you to give me a solid slap across the face."

I grinned. "Tempting as that may be, I don't see it happening. No man is going to alter your essence. And the good man you've chosen wouldn't even want to."

"That's the bottom line, don't you think? Choosing someone who loves you as you are. Someone you can trust with your soft, vulnerable parts. Then those little flames of jealousy flicker out fast, as Maggie said. I think you and I have both chosen well."

I slung an arm around my best friend, the person who'd held my soft, vulnerable parts for three decades. "You mean Sam and David, I know, but I have to say— choosing you all those years ago was one of the best decisions I ever made. I don't tell you often enough, Tonya, but you're the heart of my heart…"

"The soul of my soul," she finished.

She planted a wet kiss on my cheek. Her red lipstick had probably left its mark, but I didn't care. It was a mark of love, and we could all use more of those.

I heard the tapping of toenails on the wood floor and turned as Woody and Carl pranced into the room. In fitting with the theme, Mom had adorned them in red and white checkered bandanas with *Ciao* embroidered across them. Woody looked proud, and Carl appeared tolerant. For the cat, that was a huge capitulation.

"Come along, darling," Mom called from the hall. "Everyone is waiting."

"Let's get this party started," I said. Tonya clapped in delight and practically danced out of the room. I reached under the bed and grabbed the album I'd spent the past few months creating.

Tonya had just reached the bottom stair, and I was a few steps behind her when the front door opened. When I saw who was standing there, I literally pinched myself to be sure I wasn't hallucinating.

"*Sorpresa!*" David said. "Surprise!" Tonya's hands flew to her mouth, and she ran into his open arms.

Behind him, Dad, Raul, Ethan, and finally Sam gathered, grinning mischievously. Woody pushed past me and bounded down the queue, shoving his wet nose into each man's palm.

I put a hand on my chest. "Wh-what…?" I stammered.

"We decided to crash your party," Raul said.

"It's only an hour's drive," Dad said. "And the Bauers said they had a few extra rooms they'd just finished."

I looked at Ethan, a question in my eyes. "No worries," he said. "Banner and Braden are in charge. The gallery is in expert hands."

"Besides," David said, "how could I miss this?" He took a step back and eyed Tonya. "*Essere ancora il mio cuore.*" He smiled. "Be still my heart."

She gazed at him with affection, then turned to me. "Wait a minute, does this mean we have to cancel the firefighter stripper?"

We laughed, and David kissed her on the lips for a moment longer than the rest of us were comfortable with. Then he looked through the open door into the banquet room. "Ah, Italia! What a marvelous job you've done. I feel as if I'm home."

Tonya led the men into the party, to cheers of delight. Sam stayed behind, and as I descended the last few steps, he reached for my hand.

"You're radiant," he whispered. He took the album from me, placing it on a nearby table. Then he twirled me like a ballroom dancer, dipped me low, and kissed me hard. A rush of warmth coursed through me.

"How I've missed you," I said when we pulled apart.

"Not half as much as I missed you. Told you the time would fly."

"How long have you been planning this?"

"Since yesterday morning. We wanted to surprise you."

"That you have. I've had a lot of surprises this week, but this is by far the happiest."

He put an arm around me and picked up the album. I smiled at him, reflecting that just a couple of years ago, this mushy love talk would have made the cynic in me roll her eyes. Now I soaked it up and let it feed my soul.

Laughter erupted from the banquet room, and Sam and I headed toward it. But just as we reached the doorway, Carmen entered the foyer—snake-free, I noticed gratefully. I told Sam I'd be along in a minute.

The psychic watched him go, then took my hand in hers. She turned it over, tracing a finger across the lines in my palm.

"So, Callie, have you decided? Do you want to know what I see in your future?"

Another round of laughter drifted from the room. I turned to look at my friends and family gathered together, breaking bread, drinking wine, reveling in each other's company. Mrs. Finney twirled, showing off her flowing purple organza skirt to Summer and Jessica. Raul said something to Lynn that made her laugh. Ethan and Renata danced to the Italian music filling the room. Mom pulled Sam into a hug, and Dad smiled broadly at them. David reached a finger toward the cake, and Tonya smacked it away. All the while, Woody and Carl darted around the room, allowing themselves to be petted and adored.

I sighed, experiencing a deep sense of contentment. Then I squeezed Carmen's hand and let it go. "Thanks, but I don't believe I do. I'm in no hurry for the future. The present is the only place I want to be."

Next in Series:

Negative Reaction

Callie Cassidy Mysteries Book 5

Wedding bells are ringing in Rock Creek Village. But when a venomous villager crashes the nuptials, events take a toxic turn...

The long-awaited day has arrived—photographer Callie Cassidy's best friend is tying the knot. The wedding couldn't be more perfect—even Callie's golden retriever and her tabby cat have donned tuxes for the occasion. Callie's trainee is documenting every moment, with the help of twin brother. Then an uninvited visitor barges into the Event Center—the twins' absentee father—and an angry altercation ensues. When their father later winds up in a coma, the victim of poisoning, suspicion mounts against the twins. Callie is incensed, certain the boys aren't guilty. Besides, plenty of villagers despised the man—any of them might have slipped him the toxin. With the detectives stonewalling her, Callie turns for help to her family and friends—including the town's feisty new cub reporter. *Together, can they prove the twins' innocence—and reveal the true culprit?*

Subscribe to the newsletter for updates
www.lorirobertsherbst.com

About the Author

Silver Falchion and CIBA Murder & Mayhem award-winning author Lori Roberts Herbst writes the Callie Cassidy Mystery series. A former journalism teacher and counselor, Lori serves as Board Secretary for Sisters in Crime. She is a member of Mystery Writers of America, as well as the SinC North Dallas chapter and the Guppy chapter, where she moderates the Cozy Gup group. Lori lives in Dallas, Texas, and is a wife, mother of two, and (gasp!) grandmother of four.

Subscribe at www.lorirobertsherbst.com for updates and other fun stuff (including FREE Callie Cassidy prequel stories). Follow her on Facebook, Goodreads, Instagram, BookBub, and Amazon!

28575734R00170